Glimmer
As
You
Can

Glimmer
As
You
Can

A Novel

Danielle Martin

alcove
press

Published in the United States by Alcove Press, an imprint of The Quick Brown Fox & Company LLC.

Alcove Press and its logo are trademarks of The Quick Brown Fox & Company LLC.

Library of Congress Catalog-in-Publication data available upon request.

ISBN (hardcover): 978-1-64385-523-3
ISBN (ebook): 978-1-64385-524-0

Cover design by Nicole Lecht

Printed in the United States.

www.alcovepress.com

Alcove Press
34 West 27th St., 10th Floor
New York, NY 10001

First Edition: November 2020

10 9 8 7 6 5 4 3 2 1

*For my mom
and for the memory of my grandma—
with love, always*

PART ONE

An Invitation to Join

1

Lisa

Under her breath, Lisa counted backward from ten.

It happened once she reached seven: a sharp splintering sound, fine glassware smashed into a thousand pieces, each fragment marked with her name. Her shaky hands would have to tweeze those shards out from the stubborn plush of padded seats, later.

From the jump seat to Lisa, Jane narrowed her kohl-rimmed eyes, hissing, "Aren't you going to clean that up?"

"Yes, ma'am." Lisa gripped the underside of her jump seat, her knuckles tight with strain.

"It should be done already! We always hit the same turbulence. You know how much they pay per ticket overseas? About the amount your parents spend on rent for a year!" The plane bumped forward, a bucking bronco at thirty thousand feet. "These people have money! Do you know what that means?"

"I'm sorry."

The jumbo jet rumbled, fighting another airstream. Lisa tensed when she heard the clatter of a porcelain teacup, followed by a shriek from a passenger as it smashed to the floor.

⤖

Later, as Lisa waited on a bench in the arrivals terminal, Jane hovered in front of her.

Jane patted her flawless brown bun, taking furtive glances at anyone who might notice. "It's unbecoming for a stewardess to cry in public, Lisa. You're supposed to be a shining model of Pan Am in that uniform." She repeated herself amid the blur of people who entered and exited, flooding Idlewild Airport in tidal waves. "Are you hearing me right now?"

Lisa clasped her hands behind her neck and pushed her head down, between her knees, in a brace position.

Jane shook her head in disgust and departed the terminal without another look.

Two hours ago, Lisa had been a show of poise and composure. She had wiped the sweat from her brow and dusted off her uniform. She had brushed her hair until it shone golden, readying herself for Billy.

Sitting upright with her chest thrust forward, she had enacted an illusion of waiting for no man. Instead, she was an engaged citizen, scanning the day's headlines.

But now on the waiting bench, her fingers twisted the bottom half of her newspaper into fine shreds.

KENNEDY FORCES MORE CIA BIGWIGS TO RESIGN

Lisa glanced with glazed eyes at the remains of her paper. Someone plopped down on her bench on the other side of the raised page; she kept her eyes down.

"Can you believe these politicians?" The stranger's British accent felt like a cold cloth across her face. "It's always one problem or the next, isn't it?"

"I guess." Lisa rubbed her eyes to clear them.

"I wonder what those fellows did to get ousted like that."

"Hm."

"I can't hear you, love."

Lisa peered over the edge of her paper. The woman had jet-black hair flipped fashionably at the tips. She might have been twenty-eight or thirty years old—six or seven years Lisa's senior.

She smiled at Lisa with pity, a gentle curve of her lip. "So sorry. Didn't mean to interrupt your reading."

"I'm just waiting."

"Me too. My sister is thirty minutes late. Isn't it maddening when people are late? She only lives about ten minutes away, but she's still late. She's actually part-time here, behind the ticket counter—it's not as though she would have gotten lost on her way! Any chance you might know her? Catherine Huxley is the name." The woman eyed Lisa's Pan Am uniform with innocent inquiry.

"I usually don't spend much time in the terminal."

"Sorry then." The stranger shrugged, then brushed off her skirt. "Well, dear, it's been pleasant, but I'm off to look for a cab now, with my sister missing in action. I hope your friend shows up soon!"

She buttoned up her coat and disappeared into the crowds.

Alone on the bench, Lisa drifted into lethargy. Strands of her hair grazed the floor tile as she drooped her head near her shoes.

The woman returned soon, to hover over her. "Listen"—a pleasant smile—"I didn't catch your name. Quite rude, wasn't I?"

Lisa croaked out her name, her voice hoarse.

"I'm Elaine. Listen, Lisa, you know what? I just had this brilliant idea. Would you want to share a taxi? Depending on where you're headed."

"I'm in Bay Ridge."

"Good. I'm in Brooklyn Heights—we'll just have the cabbie drop me off first."

"I can't. Sorry."

"All right, take it as you will! Take care, darling. Ta-ta!" The woman departed in a hurry, with speedy clicks of her heels.

Lisa cast her heavy eyes downward and exhaled. With a huge effort, she hoisted up her dead weight. Her eyes remained glued to the floor as she waded through a sea of legs and feet.

She pushed through the exit doors. Frigid air blasted through her blazer as she craned her neck around a long line waiting for taxis.

She called to Elaine in a high, reedy voice. Others in the line stared at her distastefully as Elaine waved her forward with a genial smile.

Elaine's voice tinkled. "I gather you've changed your mind!"

Teeth clenched, Lisa forced her lips into a grin. "Still want to share a cab?"

"Absolutely—glad you came to your senses!" A fine layer of snow sprinkled down onto Elaine's fur collar; she brushed it off as if it were so much fairy dust. A taxi pulled to the front of the line, and her voice projected an elegant melody through the cruel winds. "We're headed to Brooklyn, if you'll take us."

The cabbie coughed and hawked a hunk of tobacco from his mouth. "The roads are pretty bad, so it's gonna take us a while. But hop in—I'll throw your bags in the back."

The two of them jumped inside, and Lisa shivered, even in the warm taxi.

As the cab pulled away from the curb, she pushed her face into the cold glass of the dirty window while Elaine thumbed through a magazine. Snow swirled outside in increasing blasts of havoc, and the two passed a dreary half hour in the back seat—a quiet punctuated only by the squeak of the taxi's windshield wipers.

Finally, breaking the silence, Elaine chirped, "I think we'll make it through this storm. What do you think?" She twisted her engagement ring, but the sizable diamond played stubborn on her delicate finger, resisting the rotation.

"Yeah, I think so." Lisa avoided her eyes.

"Sorry if I'm irritating you."

"It's okay." Lisa rubbed her eyes and removed something from her bag: an old stump of pastel pink, which she smoothed over her lips with distracted determination. Eventually she eked out enough lipstick and was ready to make an effort to talk. "Where did you go, on your flight?"

"Just over to London. I lived there till I was sixteen. My parents are still there. But I was mostly there for a wedding."

"That's nice. I love weddings." Lisa's face screwed up, on the verge of tears.

Elaine cleared her throat to start again. "So, tell me, dear—what it's like to be a stewardess?"

"I don't know—I've always wanted to see the world. It's just not easy with other people—I mean, when I'm jetting off." Suddenly a lock seemed to unlatch, and her words tumbled forth. "My boyfriend was actually supposed to pick me up from the airport today. He never showed up. He never even sent a message while I was away." Lisa gulped, hesitating. "I think he's done with me."

Fat tears rolled down her cheeks, and she kept her eyes averted from Elaine, her cheeks burning with shame.

She had lost all composure while still wearing her flight attendant uniform. A *shining model* of Pan Am indeed.

Elaine leaned over to gently pat her arm. "I'm sorry," she said. Lisa whimpered but didn't pull away. "Do you want to talk about it?" No response. "You're a gorgeous girl, you know. He's missing out." Silence again. "I'm not just saying that, you know."

Lisa straightened a bit, coughing from the mess of crying that had slid down her throat. She tried to regain herself, assuming a perky voice. "How about you? Do you have a boyfriend?"

"There's a chap I see." Elaine cleared her throat. "Listen, why don't you tell me what it's like to be a stewardess? It seems like a grand and glamorous job."

"It's usually just a lot of following orders. I had to light the cigars on a flight last week, and I hate that smell."

"Oh? I enjoy the aroma." Elaine paused. "So, are you planning on being a stewardess for some time?"

"I'll have to leave if I get married. Married women can't be flight attendants. I mean, it's nice to travel and all, but I would much rather be married."

Elaine cleared her throat, in a sudden clog. Finally, she spoke. "So, what are you going to do about your fellow? Are you going to ring him up? See where the hell he was?"

Lisa's face puckered, and she drew in a shallow breath.

≈

Billy had given her a quick kiss when he dropped her off at the airport the prior week.

"Don't turn into an expat this time, babe." He rubbed his thumb against the stiff little hairs of his stubble, eyes half-closed. "I heard those French guys don't kiss as good as the guys from Brooklyn." He pressed his warm lips to her ear, a smirk in his voice. "Watch out for any guys named Jacques."

Lisa laughed; she couldn't help herself.

Soon she was looking at her watch and dashing away from his car to the gate. She was behind schedule, but the passengers would never know. She pasted on her professional face, slipping into the veneer of the stewardess. Her expression was set in a glossy smile as she glided down the aisle, setting up to organize some plates. The pile of dinnerware nearly tumbled, but she used quick maneuvers to scramble and stack everything back in place.

In the middle of this delicate operation, she startled when she felt the pointy jab of Jane's fingernail on her shoulder.

Jane held her arm straight out, as a stalwart bridge; a gold chain dangled from her wrist. "Your beau wanted to make sure you had *this*."

She held Lisa's heart locket between her fingers as though it would turn her skin green. As though Lisa's necklace were from the five-and-dime.

With a sharp intake of surprise, Lisa snatched it back, tightening it around her neck.

Jane laughed, then tapped her lacquered fingernail on a little port window. Beyond the tip of her index finger, Lisa saw Billy, only a few dozen yards away, on the tarmac. He was shooting the breeze with a luggage cart porter, a cigarette dangling from his lips.

Jane's voice was suggestive—"I guess your beau charmed his way right past the gate!"

Lisa peered through the port window to watch the edge of Billy's sculpted jaw tilt upward in laughter. As the plane began to roll away, she peered at him through the window, waving at him, but he continued to share jokes with the porter, not even giving her plane so much as a glance.

Lisa found this unsettling. Billy had sneaked onto the Idlewild tarmac a few times before, but he'd always made a big show of waving good-bye, leaping up at just the right angle to catch her eye.

When she arrived at her hotel in Paris, she waited for his message. He always sent a wire to her hotel: *love you, babe* or *you're beautiful*. Reading his words, she would imagine his sensuous smile, his husky whisper in her ear.

The messages had always reassured her that he would be waiting.

But he hadn't sent any wires this time, and he hadn't shown up at the airport when she returned.

&

Now, in the taxicab, Lisa hid her face behind her damp blonde tresses. "Maybe he doesn't love me anymore."

The cabbie cursed under his breath as they inched ahead. Fat flakes of snow whirled around in an endless vortex, the road barely visible all of a sudden.

"Have you been having problems? Did you know something was wrong?"

"I didn't think anything was wrong. I must be oblivious, right?"

Elaine shook her head, then lightly rested her hand on Lisa's arm. "Dear, I didn't mean anything like that. I'm sorry."

"It's all right." Lisa's head stayed down.

Elaine continued, "I really understand how you feel. You know what might help? Spending time with the girls. There's this place, a social club—I mean, we drink some wine, and we read a little, discuss whatever we like." Elaine smiled, her cheeks red as roses. "Some of us even dance."

Lisa stayed in a sullen silence, face squished to the window.

After a duration, they arrived in Brooklyn Heights.

Elaine called to the driver, "How much will that be?"

Lisa drew a sharp breath. "Oh no! I don't think I have any money!" She burrowed through her purse, eyes stricken as she dug for change.

Elaine spoke again to the driver. "How much will it take for her to get to Bay Ridge?"

"Depends how long it takes in this snow."

"Here, just take this. How will that do, sir?"

The cabbie's eyes bulged with delight at the tight little wad of cash in his hands. "That's fine, ma'am! More than fine."

Lisa's cheeks glowed bright red against her blonde hair. "I don't want you to pay for me—I can't accept that!"

"You don't really have a choice, do you? You've got to get yourself home."

"Here, wait." Tear streaked, she reached into her pocket and pulled out a crumpled napkin and a pencil. "Write your number here."

"You don't have to pay me back."

"It will make me feel better. Please."

"Okay, dear," Elaine sighed and scrawled down her number. "This is my stop!" she called to the cabbie, and turned back to face Lisa. "Nice meeting you, dear. But don't bother yourself about the money."

2

Elaine

The walkways were slick, slippery, and Elaine's heels twisted on the ice, but she walked fast, in anticipation of him.

The door to the brownstone was ajar.

Elaine stepped inside the foyer with caution. Books and records were scattered without rhyme or reason across the marble floors.

"I'm home, love!" she called out, then stomped her heels on the carpet to shed the snow. She set down her valise and brushed off the grit of travel. Once tidied, she cleared her throat to make her presence known. "I'm home!" Cold air puffed from her mouth. Still in her coat, she stacked books and records and rubbed her hands together in an effort to create warmth.

At last, Tommy stumbled forth from the inner lair—his hair askew, hands empty.

Elaine cleared her throat. "I see you don't have anything for me, then?"

"When you left me alone?" Tommy's voice trailed off, and he gave a short laugh. His tall frame was swathed in his velvet bathrobe, his eyelids half-closed. His dark hair was impeccable; combed back in a smooth wave, its coiffed perfection contrasting with the bloodshot red of his eyes. "Ma'am, ring-a-ling, ting-a-ling!" He sailed into another whistle. "Why don't you come inside?"

Elaine shivered with the cold. "Why was the door wide open?"

"Gotta let in some air!" Tommy laughed to himself, then made some nostril inhalations, like a perfumer sampling a scent.

From inside came a higher-pitched laugh.

It was a woman's voice. A tinkling.

"Come join us, baby!"

Elaine didn't flinch. She set down her valise, then closed the front door. Her hands moved with intentional precision as she removed her overcoat and untied her scarf.

"Hello, Catherine."

At the kitchen table, her sister giggled, then cradled her gin and tonic. "Your fiancé is really quite the amazing man," she laughed. "You know he has all of the sonnets of Shakespeare memorized?"

"I was waiting for you at the airport, you know. I had to take a taxi home."

"By Jove, Elaine! I didn't know you were flying in today. What day is it, anyhow?"

"Thursday."

Catherine affected a high-society accent and rid herself of responsibility. "Well, I'm quite sorry, dear. But I really thought you were coming back on a *Friday*."

"You were supposed to be at work anyway."

"Well, they weren't going to keep me forever. I'm an old duck now. I'll be *thirty-one* next week. All of those other ticket girls are young things, fresh out of high school."

"You got fired?"

"I left before they could fire me. A girl's got to keep her dignity!" Catherine stood and adjusted the patent-leather belt on her pencil skirt.

Elaine was slight, yet Catherine was thinner, with her black hair arranged in a straight bob. Everything was angular with Catherine, which allowed her to assert her body like a pointed arrow in her chosen direction. Now she headed back to the bottle for another pour.

"So where are you going to stay, dear sister?" Elaine inquired. "How are you going to pay your rent?"

"Well, your fiancé here has made me an astounding offer. He said that I could sleep right in there." Catherine waved her hand at the parlor. "He informed me that I could reside on that very couch! Wasn't that grand of him? He's a generous sort."

Tommy, only a few feet away, set his record player on full volume. Beset by the music, he trilled his lips, bobbed his head up and down, and slapped his hands on the sofa while a trumpeter in the song blared a speedy yet mournful melody. "Elaine!" he yelled above the cascade. "Listen to this!"

Elaine yelled back, her voice cracking. "You're out of your bloody mind!"

She gave a tap to her grumbling stomach and searched for some provisions; the fridge was almost bare, containing only a sliver of cheese and a stick of butter.

"The music, Elaine!" Tommy sailed toward her, his eyes barely open. "Do you hear me, babe?" He tried to grab her waist. "Come and dance with me now. It's this Dizzy Gillespie album! Come on."

Elaine held her body firm, not allowing him to move her. She chewed rubbery cheese as he danced with her frozen limbs. "I'm eating."

Catherine tried to talk to her. "So how was it in the *motherland*? Oh, and Elaine—did you tell Mum and Dad that you're pregnant?"

Elaine shot her a look of death, though Tommy was oblivious as his shoulders jived in musical rapture. "I'm not pregnant," she hissed.

Catherine continued at regular volume. "I don't understand why you don't just go get a prescription from the doctor for those hormone pills. My friend Mindy goes to a doctor on Eighty-Sixth Street who gives her a regular prescription. You just take it once a day. Her life is so much simpler now. No concern of babies. Oh, and as a bonus, she's developed this *beautiful* bosom."

"Let's not talk about this right now."

"*The music of the moment. The Siren's song of now.*" Back in the parlor, Tommy hummed his own words to a song.

Elaine sighed. She couldn't bring herself to keep chewing, and the cheese sat on the back of her tongue. "How long do you plan on staying?"

"You're not trying to kick me out already? Surely you have enough space here on *easy street*."

Catherine poured more gin. It came quickly, in a splash, and she laughed.

"Please," Elaine said, but she shrugged. From the parlor, Tommy's song had switched to throaty snores as he rotated belly-up on the sofa. "I think I'll follow suit. Retire upstairs and rest for a while. It's been a long day."

"Suit yourself, dear sister."

Elaine switched off the blaring turntable, then trudged upstairs slowly. She lay on her bed, fully clothed, squinting at the outline of her face in the mirror. She and Catherine shared the same nose, delicate and upturned, but her own eyes were a different shade of gray, almost silver at certain angles.

Elaine sat back up on her bed and unearthed a sheet of paper from deep in her bedside drawer. Before she left for her vacation, she had sent some queries to newspaper editors and made a chart to track their responses. She had applied for fact-checker positions at several prestigious publications, including the *Tribune,* the *Tri-Star News,* and the *Chronicle,* hoping that her fact-checking experience at the radio station would earn her an interview.

The *Chronicle* was Elaine's top choice; she had wanted to work there as long as she could recall. As a young girl in England, she had watched her father devote significant attention to the *Chronicle.* The paper had arrived weekly at their London flat, shipped via transatlantic mail. Her father would always rip open the package with incredible focus, devouring each page, using the updates to inform his decisions for his import-export business.

The *Chronicle* was big news, and her desire to work for the publication had influenced her choice to major in journalism at Briarcliff College. Elaine hadn't applied to the *Chronicle* straight out of college—instead, she had worked for a few years at a news radio station in Manhattan, hoping that the experience would redound to her benefit later on.

There was slim chance that a *woman* could become a reporter at the big-news *Chronicle,* but she hoped to at least get in the door as a fact-checker.

Now, in the bedroom, Elaine flipped a page in her calendar to make a note of the date. Tommy never answered the phone, so there would be no way to know if an editor had rung while she was in England. She drew a line over the upcoming two weeks—if she didn't hear from one of the papers within that time frame, she could assume that interviewing at the *Chronicle* was out of the question.

Soon she heard the phone ring from downstairs, and she scurried to get it, breathless. "Hello?"

"It's Lisa, from today . . . from the cab? I'm so sorry to bother you."

"It's fine, dear."

"I'm awfully sorry. I was just calling about the money."

"Like I said, dear, consider it a gift."

"But I really feel bad. How about this: I'll slip the money under your door tonight. I have to be on an early flight tomorrow, but I would feel good knowing that we're even, that I don't owe you anything . . ."

"Don't bother yourself about it, dear. It's just a pittance."

"Please? If you would, just give me your address. Then I can fly overseas with a clear mind."

"All right, if you insist, dear. You have a pencil? The address is 890 Livingston Street. I'll give you directions."

"You really don't have to come to the door. I'll just slip the money envelope in your mail slot."

Elaine coughed and cleared her throat. Then her voice once more assumed its crisp, refined aspect.

"No; I'll see you at 890 Livingston, dear."

3

Lisa

"You're still young, dear. There's plenty of time to find someone else."

On the kitchen table, Lisa's head rested on her crossed arms. "Please, Ma. I don't want to talk about it right now."

"There now, honey." Her mother stroked her hair. "You're dripping on your flight attendant uniform, you know." She grabbed a dish towel and attempted to absorb Lisa's wet patches.

Lisa yanked away, released herself to her bedroom, and then slammed her door. Curled into a ball on her bed, she nestled against her old baby doll. It was nighttime now, and Billy hadn't even called to explain.

Though he barely needed to explain. It all added up—his lackluster good-bye on the tarmac, his failure to send her a wire in Paris—finally, the fact that he had left her stranded at the airport. She had waited for over two hours in the terminal, hiding her embarrassing tears from the crowds.

Billy's behavior made sense to her now.

He must have lost interest in her.

Lisa had heard of this happening—men suddenly *losing interest*. One of her friends from high school had been dating someone for four years. They seemed serious—a real item—but then he just disappeared from her life without warning.

Lisa hadn't observed any warning signals from Billy either. When she was in Brooklyn, they would go out on dates almost every evening, and he had always acted like he was enraptured with her.

She had been dating Billy for a little over two years. She met him at a New Year's Eve party for his labor union. Lisa was attending the party as a guest of her friend, a secretary for the labor union, and Billy approached her as she chatted with her friend near the punch bowl. He flashed her his dimpled smile, asking her to dance.

Wordlessly, Lisa nodded yes, her heart fluttering as his muscled frame guided her effortlessly to the center of the Knights of Columbus hall dance floor. He twirled her around the floor, cracking jokes about his "manly" dance moves, and she giggled in girlish hysterics as his hands loosely surrounded her waist.

When their dance was through, Billy paused in front of the labor union's photographer to sling his arm around her shoulders. Lisa felt a crackle of electricity at his casual touch as she smiled for the camera. Billy then took her out on the floor for a few more dances; when the night was over, he asked her for a date.

During the first few weeks of their courtship, they went out to the movies, out to the pizza parlor. They took long walks around Brooklyn together. She was entranced by his charm and the casual way that he laughed. Everything seemed light around him.

Everything moved so effortlessly with him.

At the end of that first month, they sat next to each other in a booth at the pizza parlor, and he pulled something out of his pocket. It was a copy of the New Year's Eve photo from his union's newsletter. Billy had drawn a heart around the two of them, and below their picture he had taped a jewelry box, which she opened to reveal a gold locket.

With a boyish grin, he squeezed her hand, asking her to go steady. They had been an item ever since.

Yet now he was ignoring her, as though none of it even mattered.

Tears started to stream down Lisa's face, and she sat up to grab a handkerchief from the dresser adjacent to her narrow bed. As she dabbed at her tears, she observed herself in the mirror—her eye makeup was smudged, her mascara had leaked to form black splotches around her lids, and her eyelids were puffy. Her blonde hair lay in knotted clumps around her face.

Lisa closed her eyes, unable to look at herself, and set her head on her pillow.

Shortly, her mother's voice shouted through her door, "Honey, I meant to ask—how did you get home from Idlewild?"

She paused to take a deep breath, then answered, "I shared a taxi with a girl from the airport. She loaned me money."

"That was nice of a stranger, to give you some money. But you know we're not beggars."

Lisa cast her eyes around her tiny room: the frayed carpet, the paint flakes on the windowsill.

The words spilled out before she could stop them. "Why were we almost evicted, then?"

The other side of the door grew silent.

Lisa closed her eyes and exhaled. She peeled herself off her damp coverlet and opened the door.

Her mother was no longer there.

⌐

A few hours later, she left her apartment. Lisa didn't usually drive around by herself at night, but here she was, steering her massive boat of a car between the pillars of the elevated train tracks, alone.

For their dates, Billy would pick her up in his red convertible. Sometimes he even borrowed his father's car, an expensive Oldsmobile designed primarily for the race track. Billy was a skilled driver, and he always operated the steering wheel as an extension of his sinuous muscles, even inside the tight boxes of the Brooklyn streets.

Next to her, he might sometimes place a bouquet of fresh flowers, along with a golden box of fine chocolates.

For my queen, he would say. Then he would kiss her, with feeling.

Now, Lisa took a sharp intake of breath as she navigated another tight bend. Night trains passed on the tracks above; their headlights bounced down through the rail gratings and shimmered on the icy streets in quickly moving lines of light.

She was lost en route to Brooklyn Heights; the directions Elaine had given her on the phone earlier were too vague. Though Lisa had crossed the Atlantic Ocean multiple times over, she struggled in this closer terrain of Atlantic Avenue. Elaine's directions had sent her toward a little strip of stores on Livingston Street, not the brownstone Elaine had skittered toward this afternoon.

Lisa started to turn back home, then looped back in a last effort to find the place. At last, a sign caught her eye: a street address in gold numbers at the corner.

The building wasn't a brownstone, but it said *890*, which Lisa had underlined in her notes.

The block was mostly desolate, but a few fancily dressed women walked briskly toward a storefront. Lisa parked and watched them enter as she clutched her little envelope of cash with numb fingertips. She looked up to see:

The Starlite Dress Shop

Elaine hadn't mentioned anything about working in a dress shop. She had exited the taxicab toward an elegant brownstone residence, not a storefront. It seemed unlikely that she would be out in the shopping district at nine o'clock at night. Yet, from a distance, there *did* appear to be some lights aglow in the Starlite Dress Shop, even as all the surrounding shops were closed.

The sidewalk in front of the dress shop shone with patches of ice, though there was a thin clearing near the door. This store's window boasted a full display of mannequins, each in a different jewel-toned ensemble, fit for an evening fete. The mannequins were backed with displays that obscured much of the store's interior. Between these displays and the tall silhouettes of some clothing racks near the windows, it was difficult to tell how many shoppers might be inside at this hour.

Lisa cautiously stepped out of her car, making her way down the icy sidewalk. She stood beneath a narrow awning, which shielded the dress shop's door but provided little protection from the winter chill. She trembled as she slowly lifted her hand, using her knuckles to rap on the door. It was solitary on this sidewalk in the silence of the night, and the wind whipped up her little stewardess skirt.

From across the street, a man sweeping snow paused to look up. "Do you need some help, lady?"

Lisa ignored him and knocked on the door more urgently. It swung open swiftly, catching her by surprise.

"Hi there!" It was a woman with a cheerful smile. "Are you Elaine's friend? She literally *just* asked me to step around the block and look for a girl who might be lost."

"I guess I'm the lost girl."

Festive sounds of laughter, music, and chatter leaked through the open door.

"Come in, dear, follow me." The woman took Lisa's hand and pulled her inside, ushering her through the crowd.

Lisa let herself be dragged like a puppy, yanked through a maze of people, racks, and tables. The shop buzzed with beautiful noise as ladies appeared and disappeared behind the A-lines and taffeta skirts. To the sides, the place was shiny and gleaming, walls lined with silvery mirrors, multiplying each reflection. Everything was resplendent.

On a table, nylons had been displaced to display tea plates of delicate pastries. Women were drinking, debating, laughing. A makeshift dance floor in front of the fitting rooms boiled with the energy of rapid-fire twists. They were actually doing the Twist, though the music was hard to hear above the laughter, and they were giddy with hilarity, collapsing into giggly heaps as their full skirts tangled on the floor.

Lisa smoothed down her airline-issued skirt. The women here seemed utterly at ease as they frolicked around the space, sashaying and shimmying to the music. She felt stiff and out of place—like a dull spot in a field of luminous joy.

Lisa heard a playful voice shout at her from somewhere within the crowd. "Hey, I see we have a new friend!" The woman gave a friendly laugh. "It looks like she's about to take us somewhere!"

From within the group, the lady was suddenly next to Lisa, patting her arm in a friendly way. She glowed, with auburn hair curled into dramatic flips. She was voluptuous in a tight-fitting black dress, and her ears glittered with chandelier earrings.

She looked like the happiest woman in the world.

"I'm Madeline, darling."

She extended her hand, which Lisa accepted through the baggy sleeves of her mother's old brown coat.

"Wow—a stewardess! I would absolutely *love* to hear about your adventures. You must have stories to tell, working for the airlines. Come over here—I'll fix you something to drink." Madeline pulled her to a table strewn with dozens of liquor bottles, which cast a glint of amber into the room.

"Oh, I don't really drink." Lisa's voice was high-pitched.

Madeline led her to the far side of the store. A group of ladies played cards between the dress racks, sprawled out on rugs. "Look, everyone! I have another player!"

"Fabulous!" someone squealed.

A petite woman in a large bouffant hat tried to deal Lisa into the game. She slid the cards into Lisa's curled-up fingers with a stream of girlish giggles.

"I'm so happy we found someone else to play!" She grabbed Lisa's chilly hand, and her warm brown eyes danced with mischief. "I'm Harriet. I'm the dealer tonight. Usually Catherine deals the cards, but she's not here yet."

"I'm sorry, but I don't know how to play. I'm actually supposed to meet someone—her name is Elaine."

"Oh, yes, Elaine! She's doing a reading on the side there." Harriet gestured casually. "But why don't you play with us for a bit? We'll teach you as you go along."

"I'm sorry, but I'm very tired. And I've been up for hours, and I have to catch a flight tomorrow."

"So, you're one of *those* ladies?"

Lisa's cheeks reddened. "What do you mean?"

"You work for the airlines?"

"Yes, Pan Am."

"Oh, I wasn't sure. We have dress-up nights here, and sometimes girls just come in costume for the fun of it."

"Like it's Halloween?"

"No—just to experience being in different roles. It's a costuming experience. We play different roles all the time, you know."

"I'm sorry; maybe we could play another time."

Lisa pushed the cards back toward Harriet, and she moved to make her way across the shop. As she waded her way through the crowd, she struggled to maintain her balance in the whirl of activity.

This was all so *different*. Lisa had been living in Brooklyn her entire life, but she had never beheld a place like this. Women streamed around the space, holding delicate cups of drink, as others sat cross-legged next to mannequins, making pastel sketches of fashion. Still others emerged from the fitting room, modeling glamorous ensembles for clusters of friends.

It all sparkled, and it was such a shock to Lisa's weary eyes that she nearly forgot to look for Elaine. Then she suddenly remembered her envelope of dollar bills, still clutched in her fingers, now coated with sweat.

She searched the store, unable to find Elaine, until she finally spotted her head of jet-black hair behind some coatracks.

Elaine was in the lead position of a circle. The other ladies were observing her with rapt attention as they held little instruments, metallic triangles and miniature drums, which they plinked and thumped as Elaine rested, with half-closed eyes, between reading the lines of a poem.

Lisa thought of Billy, who had often talked of beatniks. He used that term for people he didn't like. *Those damn beatniks.* He would gyrate his hands in a series of little snaps, and Lisa could never help but laugh.

"Drip, drop."

Lisa's cheeks reddened. Elaine's voice was husky, breathy—*sensual*.

"Heated rain on my tongue lashing besides your body. Mind open, thoughts closed, the time has come for a little—wandering."

A woman struck a metallic triangle with a little mallet.

"Elaine!" Lisa's voice quavered.

Most of the women in the circle gawked at her—this interrupter—yet Elaine didn't even lift her head. In some sort of trance, she continued. *"I'd like to know the wistful world in which you live. I'd like to eat your sugared words, and your silent dreams."*

"Elaine!" Lisa hissed.

Elaine seemed to hear her at last; her half-open eyes widened as she brightened and gave Lisa a friendly smile:

"Well! You made it here!"

Lisa clutched her sweaty little envelope. "I'm sorry to interrupt."

"That's fine! I was worried you got lost!" Elaine set her poetry book down on her chair. "Can you take over, Gloria?" She whisked herself away from the group and grabbed Lisa's arm as if they were old friends. "I'm so happy you made it here safe! I really should've been firmer about not having you come out—it's so nasty out there."

"I feel awful for letting you pay for that cab ride, but thanks so much." Lisa kept her eyes averted and pushed the envelope into Elaine's hands. Lisa scratched her own wrists, itchy from the wool of her mother's coat.

"It's perfectly all right, dear, but thank you. It's all worked out. You've gotten to experience the Starlite!"

Elaine led them over to the cashier's counter on the side of the store, which was piled high with poetry books, novels, and biographies. Behind the counter, women perched on high stools, sketching portraits of each other on long shopkeeper ledgers.

Lisa turned to Elaine, her voice tinny. "May I ask, what sort of club is this?"

"A women's social group. But, you know, it's a lot of things, really. Improvement of the mind, joining together for fun. Girls being girls, really!" Elaine's laugh had a melody like a song.

"Yeah."

To the side of them, Madeline held a tray of drinks in balance as she gyrated her shoulders in dance.

"Care to join us for another read?" Elaine asked as she flipped through a poetry book.

"I really have to get going."

"Oh?"

"I do," Lisa insisted. Her twenty-two-year-old lips were drawn, and her eyelids sagged with exhaustion. She bundled herself back up into her thin brown coat.

Lisa opened the heavy door to the sidewalk and exited the shop, entering the quiet night. The air was bitter. On the street, tiny snowflakes glinted like glitter in the beams of the streetlights, a crystalline path in the night.

She made her way around the block, trying not to slip, and hoisted herself into the driver's seat.

Alone, she rubbed her hands on the steering wheel, trying to warm them. Her breath formed a thin white cloud in front of her face, which soon faded to darkness.

Lisa sat without driving for some time, her mind pulsating in shock from what she had just seen—all of these women, so free.

4

Elaine

It was about two in the morning when Elaine made it back to the brownstone—a little tipsy, but mostly infused with other potent elements.

It was an hour of calm at the brownstone. Tommy snoozed on the sofa downstairs, his face quiet as his jazz record finished its rotation. Elaine switched off the record player and turned off the overhead light, went upstairs to the bedroom, and flopped under the cold sheets. In only a short while, a comfortable cloud of slumber had possessed her.

Tommy soon tromped upstairs with a tense energy. He scrunched on the bed next to her with lengthy puffs of a cigarette.

She groaned. "I'm trying to sleep."

Tommy's voice was rough, accusatory. "You came home late. Why did you come home so late?"

"I need to sleep." She exhaled and buried her face in the valley of the pillow.

"Guess that none of those women at that place you go have got a man in their home." She kept silent. He continued. "A man in his home . . . lonely in his home. All alone in his home." He turned on a dime suddenly, chuckling to himself. He whistled a tune.

Elaine exhaled with a roar of primal exhaustion. "Go to sleep, Thomas!"

He seemed to decelerate a moment later. He sidled up to her, rested his head on her shoulder, and fell asleep soon after.

Elaine slid the cigarette out of his still-upright hand and extinguished it on a marble coaster by their bedside.

Shortly afterward, she collapsed into a deep sleep, with scattered visions of a countryside farmhouse playing out in her head. Her as a little girl on the moors, trying to get back to London. Her parents sheltering under a kitchen table as she and Catherine ran to the city, trying to save them. Always the same dream since they evacuated the flat years ago, during the war.

At four in the morning, she woke again. This time, it was to the sound of his feet on the creaky boards.

When Tommy was in a melancholy mood, he would play blues records for her in the dark, wrapping his fingers around her waist and telling her stories about his childhood. He said he had been alone a lot in the large, empty rooms of this brownstone, and he would take things apart—cabinets and radios—just to see how they worked, then try to reassemble them. Each night, a maid would feed him dinner as his mother remained in bed. Maids never lasted too long; his mother always forgot to pay them.

Tommy couldn't stay too long in bed, he said. His mother always stayed too long in hers.

With heavy eyes now, Elaine watched him pace the bedroom with a Marlboro clutched between his fingers. He moved in little winding paths, unable to settle.

She grasped his hands for a moment. Then he stood still.

The steady pressure of her fingers, at times, could still tame him.

⁓

In the morning, Elaine woke to the bleeding part of her cycle. She sipped her tea slowly, holding her temples as her head throbbed.

Though it was late in the morning, her sister still wasn't back—she must have slept at the Starlite. Catherine had made her grand entrance at midnight, well dressed for such an hour, in an emerald-green gown, her limbs stretched languid, catlike. She was lucid, in her typical way of drinking only to the precipice of possibility and emerging unscathed, ready to go full-out. Catherine could sip gin all afternoon and go on to win game after game of cards.

Last night, Elaine had followed her to the card circle, where the ladies were engaged in a game she had never heard of, called bridge. Elaine couldn't muster enthusiasm to learn the rules, but she made herself mingle and dance with the others. Catherine started to sing to the ladies—she'd brought along some new record album—but Elaine soon said farewell to Madeline and the others.

Now Elaine's body seized in a turgid twinge as cramps squeezed her from within. She threw her gaze upstairs; Tommy was still sleeping. The phone rang—loudly, near her ear. She grabbed it.

"Hello?"

Tommy stirred in the room above. His thuds rumbled on the ceiling above her head.

"Miss Huxley?"

"Speaking."

"This is Frank Stephens, from the *Chronicle*. We received your application for fact-checker. We would like to invite you in for an interview, if you're available."

She blinked in time with the pulse of her headache. "Oh?" A flush came to her cheeks.

"Are you still interested in the job?"

"I'm very interested!" Her voice was ebullient—too childlike; she quieted herself. "When shall I come in?"

"Next week, if you're available. How's Monday at two?"

"That should be fine." She suppressed a sudden tickle in her throat as her throat seized with the unknown. The noise of Tommy opening a closet came from upstairs.

"We're on Forty-Third Street, between Seventh and Eighth."

"Yes, I know the area."

"Okay, then—we'll see you on Monday."

Elaine subdued her heavy exhalations. "Thank you."

Mr. Stevens hung up. She cleared her throat and mechanically took a sip of tea.

Tommy came bounding down the stairs. This morning he appeared full of energy—giddy. His black hair was wet, slicked back from the shower. Seeing her, he made a little satisfied sound and slid behind her, arms wrapped around her waist.

∽

Five years ago, she had worked at a news radio station with Tommy. He was an engineer, she a fact-checker. Elaine had applied for the fact-checker job after graduating college as a possible stepping-stone to a better position, yet she felt alternately lonely and bored in the role—calling sources but never permitted to hunt down a new story on her own.

Her lunch hour was spent with the other girls at the station, each talking over the other as they ate their cold-cut sandwiches on white bread. Their chatter would inevitably tilt toward wedding planning—all of these girls were engaged, which made Elaine twitch, because she'd never even had a steady boyfriend. She usually excused herself mid-lunch to hide out in the hallways of the radio station building.

It was during one of these jaunts that she first caught sight of Tommy, through a control room window. He was tall and broad, with wavy, jet-black hair set above a Roman nose. She stood for a moment to admire this handsome man as he wrote on a clipboard. Soon he noticed her looking, and he flashed her a grin.

Elaine reddened and fled to the restroom. But she couldn't help herself; on the following day, she returned to linger by the control room window again, until he noticed—giving her a wide smile that made her heart thump wildly.

He opened the door and peered into the hallway. "I saw you casting an eyeball in here. Care to take a tour of the control room?"

She began to stammer, which was quite unlike her. "That's all right. My-my-my lunch break ends in a few minutes."

Tommy smirked. "How about the abbreviated tour, then?"

"All right then," she consented.

Tommy led her on a tour of the panels, the wires, and the buttons, explaining their functions in turn. Elaine had actually never seen the control room, although she had worked at the radio station for a few months. Female employees weren't usually invited into the mechanical rooms.

"Where does the sound go from here?" she inquired.

"The tower transmits everything from a little island off the Bronx."

"An island off the Bronx?"

"Sure, a little island. Nothing fancy." Tommy's posture was casual as he held his clipboard in hand. "There's really nothing on that little island but that tower."

"I didn't even know there was an island in the Bronx."

A grin spread across his face. "Yeah."

"It's all quite interesting." Elaine didn't want to interrupt him any longer, but she couldn't bring herself to leave. "I've only been to the Bronx a few times."

Tommy looked down at his clipboard for some time, seeming to take notes about the functions of the control panel. Then he looked up, locking eyes with her.

"You seem interested the workings of the station. How would you like to take a trip to see the island?"

"Right now?" Her kitten heels felt glued to the linoleum.

"I have to go do some maintenance on the tower. You can come check it out with me, if you'd like."

Elaine tried to swallow the nervous knot in her throat. "Go with you to the island?"

"Sure. We'll have to take the boat. The station owns a little boat; we use it for inspections."

"I don't know if I can do that."

"Why not?" He was matter-of-fact, confident. "You're a station employee, aren't you? You should learn about the operations of your employer."

"I'm just a fact-checker. And I've only been working here for a few months."

"Hey, well, I've been here for three years, and I know the rules around here. There's no rule saying you can't assist me off-hours."

He grinned at her again, and her heart thumped fast. She would have to be bold in order to be given more responsibility at the station.

She *did* want hands-on involvement with the workings of the news. She also sensed that there could be another kind of opportunity with this man.

Tommy smiled at her, and his blue eyes danced across hers playfully. "So, what do you say? How about tomorrow, after your shift? I get off at four. We could take the bus together."

"Well—"

"Well?"

"All right." She took a deep breath. "I'm Elaine, just so you know."

"And I'm Tommy." His eyes twinkled as he gave her a firm, businesslike handshake.

☞

After work the next day, they waited for the bus together. Tommy was smoking, and he gave her a light for her own cigarette. Elaine smoked only when she was nervous; her fingers trembled as she brought the cigarette to her lips.

After they boarded the bus, Elaine took the window seat and Tommy sat next to her, his legs crossed in the opposite direction, slung all the way over in the aisle. They were quiet for a bit, and then on impulse she offered him a biscuit from her purse. He accepted the snack, and they sat eating crumbly bits of the biscuit and talking about food, which led to a conversation about the portrayal of food in books. Just like her, Tommy liked to read—and just like her, he spoke French. As they chatted, he swung his legs from the aisle closer to her own, though not touching.

Elaine had never been that close to a man's legs, having barely even *seen* a man at Briarcliff College.

Tommy struck up a dialogue about nineteenth-century French literature, and they discussed their favorites as their bus crossed the bridge onto City Island. The quiet main road was flanked by narrow residential streets lined with picturesque homes. Every one of these side streets terminated in the choppy, blue-gray expanse of the Long Island Sound. Elaine gazed at the water in the distance, feeling the leg of Tommy's trousers graze against her own, ever so slightly.

At the last stop on City Island, they got off the bus. She dawdled behind Tommy's long strides as he led her down to the radio station's boat, a little dinghy docked in the sound. As he helped her into the boat; Elaine took his arm, her face growing warm. He set up some paddles and pushed them offshore, down toward the radio tower, which was perched on a little mound of land.

Tommy's dark eyes were alert and focused as he paddled—then he paused, looked at Elaine, and leaned forward. At once, his lips were touching hers. It was firm and quick, of a piece with their encounter—something else that moved ahead unexpectedly.

Her first kiss.

They continued to see each other, maintaining a professional distance at the radio station but spending hours together each weekend at cafés in Greenwich Village, sipping tea and espresso, talking in French and reading poetry. He would kiss her in alleyways, long and slow—then they would head out for the evening to literary readings or plays or sumptuous afternoons under the oaks in Central Park.

He was intense, and he captivated her.

⌒

Now behind her, in the brownstone, Tommy nestled his chin, heated from the shower, straight into the soft spot above her shoulder. It was an exquisitely sensitive place—the same spot where a gossamer scarf had rested on her neck the other night at the Starlite. A beautiful melody had drifted over to the literary circle that night. She had sailed into song as the ladies around her clapped, and she had danced in a way like never before, with her arms wide open.

Elaine closed her eyes. There were so many demands on her attention.

Yet there were also so many things for which she wanted to be present.

"You look ravishing right now, with your cheeks flushed like that," Tommy laughed. His lips were hot on her neck.

He didn't enjoy it when she left for the Starlite—and he certainly wouldn't want her to leave him alone for most of the day if she got a job at the *Chronicle*.

There was no way she could tell him about her interview—not just yet, anyway.

5

Lisa

Lisa's mother was up at six, pressing a shirt for her husband to wear to his factory job while he shaved.

Last night, when Lisa arrived home from the Starlite, past midnight, her mother had been upright on the living room chair, hair in curlers but face in full makeup, writing in the crossword pages. She didn't acknowledge Lisa's return but simply swished her slippers down the worn carpet and settled in near the snores of Lisa's father.

Lisa couldn't sleep. Her covers twisted up in knots as she ran from hot to cold. A faint perfume lingered on her skin from the night, a scent that curled its thin tendrils into her nose.

At the crack of dawn, at the kitchen table, she ate farina with a melted pool of butter and sugar. Her head hung over the bowl, eyelids swollen.

Her schedule showed an international flight this morning.

"How are you?"

Her mother ironed in quick bursts. Lisa stared at the scene and started to gag on a lump in her throat—a congealed mass stuck down low. Steam from the iron puffed up into quick clouds, and Lisa watched it billow as she swallowed the lumpen bit.

"I'm fine, Ma."

The steam recalled to mind the condensation escaping from the vent pipes of a diner, an idle sight from a darkened parking lot in Brooklyn. The other week Billy had lain with her in the back seat of his car, his warm lips close to her ear. His cologne was musky. *I'll never leave you, babe.* His arms had wrapped tight around her waist, as though he'd caught her. He was the only boy who knew the warm, close curve of her breasts.

For nearly two years, she'd had *him* to look forward to upon her rearrival in Brooklyn. When he picked her up from Idlewild, he would grab her electric-blue valise, ushering her through the crowds and outside to his red car with the soft leather seats. As he drove them from Queens to Brooklyn, he would sing to the radio, turning to kiss her at traffic lights.

Yesterday was the first time he hadn't shown up.

He still hadn't even called to explain himself.

He just lost interest.

Lisa struggled to take another bite, to shake herself awake.

Her mother spoke through another cloud of iron steam. "How long will you be gone on this trip, Lisa?"

"A week and a half, Ma."

She forced her voice to come out brisk and informative. She would jet out in the usual way, her legs shiny in her pharmacy nylons.

"Where are you headed?" her mother asked warily.

"Paris, then Rome the next day, then Beirut."

"Bay rot?"

"Beirut."

"Where is that?" The iron blew out a loud burst of steam.

"Lebanon."

"Are there any Catholics there?"

"I don't know."

"Well, I think it would be nice for you to be able to go to church. You haven't gone to Mass one time since you've had this job."

"I'll see what's there." She held her forehead.

Her father called out from the bathroom as he rinsed soap from his face. He always took his time, trying not to use too much, trying not to waste it. "Don't get in trouble walking around by yourself!"

"I won't be walking around by myself."

"Well, how do you get places, then?"

"I don't know. Usually the airline hires cabs," Lisa answered, though they never did.

She was thankful that her father had slept through her early-morning return from the Starlite. He would have asked her where she had gone—she would have found it difficult to make up a story at that hour. He would have been shocked to find out about those women laughing and dancing, as free as they were.

Lisa shot a glimpse now at the clock in the kitchen. It was eight o'clock, time to leave. She scraped the last pearls of farina from her bowl and rushed to her room. She had a schedule to keep. She packed swiftly, scouring her closet as usual. Her clothing rack was nearly bare, flanked by peeling fibers of wallpaper. Only one decent dress hung from a wire hanger: a dark-violet piece with a pleated skirt. She placed it in a plastic garment sleeve in her suitcase.

Effort completed, she climbed into her hard bed and closed her eyes to rest for a moment; the scent of the prior night played on her pillow.

"Where is Lebanon, anyway?" her mother shouted through the door.

"It's in the Middle East."

Come evening, her parents would still be in this small apartment— her mother making dinner, her father watching TV.

I'll never leave you, babe.

Lisa opened her lids halfway, blinking through the sudden moisture in her eyes. A note Billy had once written stuck out from a stack of papers on her shelf. He had given it to her with a single rose. His smile was wide and earnest as he grabbed her hand to slide an invisible ring on her finger, resting his lips on that very spot.

⚭

Lisa's flight was delayed because of ice on the runway, so the crew went to dine together in the staff cafeteria before departure.

As they took their seats at their customary table, the copilot smiled at Lisa, taking the seat adjacent to her. He was in his late twenties, golden haired and clean-cut, with a gleam in his eye.

When Jane saw his choice of seat, she narrowed her eyes at Lisa, sitting herself on his other side. She batted her eyelashes at the copilot and primped her bun, engaging him in conversation about Beirut.

Lisa sat quietly, even as Betsy, her friend on crew, joined them at the table. She gave Betsy a weak hello, but she didn't say anything else. Too many people were around to talk about what had happened with Billy.

The air at the crew table crackled with predeparture energy, especially once their energetic pilot joined them. As the rest of the crew engaged in high-velocity chatter about the nightlife, beaches, and watersports in Beirut, Lisa remained quiet, picking idly at her food.

The copilot took observation of her silence. "How about you, Lisa? Will you join us for some water-skiing in Beirut?" He was straight-backed in his airline cap, masculine.

"I don't know how to swim, actually." Lisa's cheeks grew red. "I never went to summer camp."

"You don't know how to swim?" Jane giggled.

"Nope, never learned." Lisa mixed together her mushroom sauce and chicken fragments.

The copilot flashed her a smile, his teeth a shade of blinding white. "Oh well, they have life jackets anyway. I think you'll do great!"

From across the table, Lisa felt Jane burrow her eyes into her skull, planting hatred like a seed. Lisa looked over to Betsy, who gave her a sympathetic look.

Once onboard the jet, Jane wasted no time putting Lisa to work on drink service—cups in a line, *just so*. Napkins—perfectly flat. A pour with only subtle wrist action—no ungainly movement of the arms. As the purser, Jane was in control.

Lisa set the fine glassware down in careful rows as the plane's motors roared to life. The engines were deafening, with heavy blasts, but Jane's hisses were louder. "You need to offer everyone blankets right after they board, remember? Quick. It's chilly."

"Yes, ma'am." Lisa scurried to grab a stack of blankets, trying to maintain their crisp folds. "Care for a lap blanket?"

She pushed the edges of her lips upward as she glided down the aisle, smiling at each passenger. Betsy took the back of the plane, keeping up the tempo. It was a full plane today for this leg of the trip, and the passengers were subdued, in anticipation of transatlantic travel.

Soon, a passenger in row two broke the quiet with a series of barking coughs. Lisa searched the cabinets to find him a handkerchief as Jane delivered the preflight announcements over the loudspeaker. The passengers stared to the front of the cabin, their eyes glued to Jane; she soaked up their attentions with a cutesy voice and perky smile. The passengers clapped when she finished, and she gave them a little curtsy.

Lisa scanned their faces. Couples and families, business travelers. Her eyes fluttered to the middle rows to estimate how much she would need to bring out for service.

She drew in a breath.

It was the light-brown hair. Strands of gray slicked in a V shape. The cleft in the chin. His horn-rimmed glasses. His smirk.

Billy's father was on her plane.

His arm was around a woman who wasn't his wife. She was a young thing with platinum-blonde hair and bright-red lips, gazing up at him like a smitten puppy.

They were seated in Lisa's section, and she would need to serve them drinks.

Lisa buckled herself into the jump seat, hand over her chest.

With ascent at a full ten minutes long, she turned away from the passengers. The chicken and mushrooms from her lunch reconstituted in her throat.

The woman's laughs traveled down the aisle, high-pitched scratches in her ear. The plane reached cruising altitude. Drink service would commence.

Lisa raised herself with effort and grabbed her beverage cart. Her hands shook like an aged woman's as she poured the beverages into the little Pan Am cups.

"Water?" she asked everyone in turn.

She ambled slowly, but eventually she was one row in front of him. He had his mouth to the ear of the woman; giggles bubbled up from under her plump pink lips.

Lisa's legs swayed on her unsteady feet. She tilted her head to make eye contact with Billy's father as she would any other passenger.

"Water?"

He didn't meet her eye as he wordlessly accepted the cup. His arm was slung over the woman's shoulder. His hand grazed the woman's breast.

Lisa had met Billy's father at least ten times over the past two years. Just a few weeks ago, at meat loaf night at Billy's apartment, his father had embarked on a long, steady monologue about his "important" job in politics. Lisa had listened politely.

Now, from down the aisle, Jane watched Lisa's every move with the intensity of a panther.

Lisa stumbled toward her as she finished drink service, and her heel tipped sideways in an ungainly way.

Jane communicated silently, pointing to her legs.

You're representing Pan Am.

Lisa contorted her lips into straight folds and averted her gaze.

"Get it together, Lisa! Remember who you represent." Jane sprung forward in a sudden blast of sour breath.

Lisa's mutter was barely audible over the whir of the jet engine. "You don't even know."

Jane turned, fire in her eyes. "Did you say something?"

Lisa cleared her throat, unable to speak at first. Then she pointed to a patch of exposed white skin on the back of Jane's leg, below the hemline. "You have a rip in your nylons."

Jane reddened. "You should have told me sooner!" She scurried to the restroom.

Lisa smiled faintly—but her smile soon faded.

In her peripheral vision, she could see Billy's father, nestling his head into the crook of that woman's neck.

6

Madeline

The Starlite's first Valentine's Day Bash had been a last-minute affair. The ladies had listened to the radio and nibbled on Madeline's homemade cupcakes, in decorous avoidance of the burned parts.

But now they were at the Fifth Annual Bash—a startlingly different affair. It was a big and beautiful hoopla, with three kinds of strawberry cakes, four varieties of cocktails. Thousands of pieces of pink confetti fluttered through the air like rosebuds.

This night was alive with dazzling music. Catherine Huxley worked at full strength, belting out her gorgeous songs for hours on end. A clear and powerful jazz singer, she concluded her sets with flourishes of her delicate wrists. Between these sets, Madeline set Elvis on the turntable. Then at eleven o'clock, it was rhyme-and-rhythm time. Elaine Huxley read her poetry, and the rest of the literary circle presented the audience with works about love, lost and gained.

After midnight, the three sisters from Italy put on a play near the fitting rooms. They opened and closed the fitting room doors, and each assumed the part of a different character in a performance about looking for love in Brooklyn. The sisters took turns playing the roles of failed suitors. Graciela was a long, limber brunette who usually had a heavy Italian accent, but in this performance she put on the voice of a Brooklyn guy and postured with her legs spread wide, mocking.

"Why don't we just go and eat a *hot dog* at Nathan's?" She slouched forward, laughing, everyone in on the joke. "Hey, I have an auto dealership on Eighty-Sixth. I'll take you for a *ride* after."

Danielle Martin

Everyone was giddy at midnight. They laughed until salty tears flowed from their eyes into their drinks. They giggled into their cocktails and nearly snorted them backward, in chokes and sputters—it didn't matter. Someone put Elvis back on, and Madeline took out the roses she had bought for a couple of dollars on the avenue and stored in the back room all day. She passed the roses to the women, who began to toss them on one of her mannequins, and then someone made a sign for the mannequin's neck: *Aphrodite*. More and more women joined in; soon Aphrodite was transformed into a goddess in full bloom, strewn in an array of crimson petals.

Madeline posed next to the mannequin, beckoning everyone onward, and the ladies took the cue to decorate *her* too. She became their own goddess in full bloom as the ladies sprinkled rose petals on her hair, gathering the petals back up from the ground in a chorus of laughter, then showering her in a floral cloud.

Petals fell from her auburn locks, and Madeline twisted to the music with a beatific smile on her face.

Everyone danced, danced, *danced* and she cranked up the record player. She had made a little red mark on the dial, as she knew just how loud they could get before the music leaked through the door. She maintained the volume at this careful threshold, enough to fill their ears without drawing attention from the outside.

Men weren't supposed to know about the Starlite's social club, after hours.

Madeline's high-backed mannequin displays stood in front of the windows, along with her tallest dress racks. Everything was positioned strategically to obscure the bustling activity within the shop.

Now, it was time to eat. Madeline brought out the chocolate cake, along with some champagne, and the confetti flew everywhere—landing on bouffant hairstyles and ballerina buns. It even adhered to the cake. Everyone squealed when the little pink squares stuck to the cocoa frosting on their plates and lips.

Madeline was everywhere at once, and she mingled with all. But when it neared two in the morning, she was almost asleep. The dress shop had been open since midmorning; she had been going for hours.

Yet most of the women remained in the store. Madeline gave them a hint with some big-band music—slow-tempo swing, a wind-down. At three in the morning, the shop was almost empty. All that remained were those few who always stayed later to help clean up.

They started to do what they usually did when they cleaned: argue about the movies. Tonight, it was *Breakfast at Tiffany's*. Madeline declared that Holly Golightly was a misunderstood fashion plate, but the other girls called the character "weak" and "irritating."

"She has no real backbone!" Harriet was adamant, her brown eyes blazing. "She's living life for a dream!"

"Well, what is anyone doing? We're all trying to live our dreams!" Madeline bit her lip, her eyes stuck on the piles of trash strewn about.

Together, the women plucked little pieces of confetti from the carpet.

Harriet shook her head. "You know, Madeline—Holly Golightly doesn't even come close to living her dreams. I mean, don't you get that she's a hooker?"

Gloria chimed in, her hazel eyes flashing with earnest indignation. "And what about her desperation? She was selling herself to these bastards!"

Cynthia shook her blonde curls in laughing disbelief. "I mean, Audrey Hepburn is beautiful, but let's not confuse a beautiful woman with a crazy character!"

"I guess." Madeline's voice went low. She picked at the confetti, which clung to everything. "Listen, why don't you girls just bunk in the back room for the night? I got a few extra bedrolls, you know, and a space heater."

The women smiled at her, thin lipped. They made excuses, reasons why they had to leave. Everyone was on borrowed time. Gloria lived with her parents—they believed she was babysitting. Harriet's husband was coming back home from a business trip, and she had left her phone off the hook. Cynthia had to be in Canarsie in a few hours for her shift at a convenience store; she was able to change her hours only with well-timed references to an "ailing sister."

The women soon pulled on their muffs and hats to leave. Madeline trudged around and switched off the small red lamps she had placed out for atmosphere. They said good-night to her, and she locked the door.

Only the clothing racks and bags of garbage remained. She turned off the overhead lights and raced into her little bathroom. She always sprinted to the back rooms, in a flush of heat, to outrun any rodents or shadows that might slink in the desolate space. Once she had seen something move, a shape like a rat beneath the clothing racks. She had screamed so hard that her voice didn't work quite right the next day.

In the bathroom now, she gave herself a sponge bath to wash away the sweat of the evening. She pulled her nightdress over her head and dabbed some cold cream in the corners of her eyes, and then she headed to her back room to set out a blanket on the fold-out sofa. It was chilly, but cheaper to bundle up than to keep the heat on.

She slipped on her sateen eye mask and tossed in discomfort on the lumpy mattress of the pull-out sofa. The Valentine's soiree had been a smashing success, and there had been no disagreements except for that *Breakfast at Tiffany's* incident.

It had been a time of laughing, crying, and being free.

It was almost enough to make Madeline forget that she had been living at the shop for four years, since '57.

None of the girls even knew that Madeline didn't have her own apartment. She still didn't have enough to pay rent on a place of her own, since any extra money from her dress shop went straight back into the social club.

She was choosing to support something even bigger than herself.

⚭

The social club had started off small, as just a fun activity—finger foods and chats in the evenings. Madeline still had her apartment at the time, but she needed something to distract herself in the evenings so she wouldn't think about Fred.

From the outset, she tried to make it special. Fresh flowers. The latest records.

It wasn't too long before she had started to draw a little crowd. It was a small group of women during those early months—invitation only, a select group of customers from the dress shop to join her after hours.

Back in '57, as she readied herself for the fifth meeting of the club, she decided to get a strawberry shortcake from a place on Henry Street to share with the girls. But she wasn't quite fit for the outside world; sweat dripped down her neck from unpacking boxes of nylons all day, so she dashed to her apartment first so she could freshen up and fix her makeup.

She climbed the stairs in her building, puffing with exertion. For a moment, she stopped to rest and leaned on the banister. From upstairs piped two voices: a baritone and a tinny squeak. She shook her head back and forth, trying to clear her ears.

At the final flight of stairs, a pressing pain punched through her rib cage.

She knew the baritone, and soon she observed the source of the tinny voice.

Fred—in her very own kitchen. He was sitting next to his mistress.

Fred's unsightly girth was parked on one of Madeline's kitchen stools—and he was wearing a shirt he often wore to city council meetings, a shirt that *she* had sewn for him once, by hand.

It had been a month since Fred paid Madeline a surprise visit. When she came home from work that last time, she'd found him at her kitchen table with a bouquet of flowers, red in the face. His big drops of sweat dripped down on her tile.

"I want to start over with you," he panted.

"Did Rachel kick you out?" She gave him a short laugh.

"No, babe. I just keep thinking of you. I made a mistake. You're the one for me. You've always been." He moved to touch and kiss her. His great tire of belly fat leaned into her as he caressed her neck.

"Get off me!" She tried to shove him away, but he persisted, hands on her waist, moving them downward, whispering in her ear like when they were new.

With a final force, she pushed him away, and he smirked. He cleared his throat with his signature cough. "We have an event tomorrow, Maddy. A soiree at the Bridge Club. The theme is black and white. I'm sure you can find something to wear." His moustache flexed upward in a grin.

Fred held Madeline by the reins of his money—cash he gave her toward rent on the apartment, even after he started living with his mistress.

He always arrived unannounced. He would slide an envelope of cash across her countertop and ask her to play the role of wife for another society event.

When Madeline had first caught him in the act, she kicked him out of their apartment. He pleaded desperately to prevent an annulment, not wanting his Brooklyn city councilman's name tarnished.

She didn't fight Fred too hard. He could spread lies, after all. She knew he would sully her name and discourage the other councilmen's wives from visiting her store. Those society ladies bought a lot of dresses, a substantial part of Madeline's earnings.

She had kept her lips drawn, yet she was in no position to deny him.

But this was the first time Fred had brought *her* to the apartment. Madeline had never seen the girl up close. At barely twenty years of age, Rachel was a skinny mouse, with stick-figure legs. Sitting with Fred at Madeline's pink counter, she kicked her patent-leather heels in rhythm as she licked brown sauce off her knobby fingertips. She dug heartily into a bag of food, smearing the grease on Madeline's baby-soft leather swivel stool.

Fred chomped down on the gristles of animal fat like the most relaxed man in the world. His voice caramelized into burnt honey even as he gnawed at his greasy meat. "Rachel's telling me I should divorce you."

Madeline stared wide-eyed, a deer in headlights. Her silence was interrupted only by the cuckoo clock, which chirped the hour.

Fred threw back his head and chuckled: a scratchy, raspy laugh.

Madeline's eyes locked on her shoes. She studied her neatly polished heels. She shut out the sight of their poultry bones on their paper napkins. She closed her nose to the smell of rendered grease and department store cologne.

She started to walk out.

The two of them continued to eat, their lips smacking.

"She must be in shock."

A low giggle passed through the kitchen door as Madeline closed it. She trembled, like a leaf in the wind.

Her hand rested on her doorknob at the exit to her own apartment. The cuckoo clock rang out with the final ding of the hour, and her body froze. A piece of pink caught her eye. It was a receipt on her coffee table; she had prepaid for the shortcake when she ordered it.

The bakery on Henry Street would close at five thirty.

Her new social club was set to convene at six o'clock. She picked up her RSVP list—over thirty women had signed up in the affirmative.

With a deep breath, she burst back into her kitchen with newfound energy.

"This is a ridiculous game we're playing. I'm tired of it."

"C'mon, Maddy, I want you to tell her. Isn't it true that you don't want a divorce?" His eye twitched and he jawed his gums, his greasy moustache moving up and down.

"Well . . ." She caught a glimpse of some errant, pointy hair in his moustache. He never groomed himself to look flawless—only to look powerful.

Fred represented a swing district in the council. He usually gave her a third of the rent and maintained the annual lease of her shop in his name; initially, her landlord wouldn't assign leases to women.

"I think I *do* want a divorce, Fred." Her knees shook as she clutched the doorframe.

Fred began to cough on a chunk in his throat, and Rachel patted him on the back, showing no effort to hide her glee. He gazed at her with one half-closed eye, over his hacking cough.

Madeline's entire body continued to tremble. An invitation sat on her counter, addressed to *Mr. and Mrs. Abbott*. Its glossy stationary announced a banquet, yet another function that would begin with a cocktail hour in which councilmen slapped each other on the back and talked in code about resolution numbers, ballots, and other things they made no effort to explain.

She suddenly removed her hands from the doorframe, her posture erect. "Yes. I *do* want a divorce." More of her words poured out, crystal clear over the havoc of Fred's coughing fit. "I'll pay my own way. You give me back your key to this apartment, and you and your girlfriend could leave right now."

It would be the fifth meeting of the social club. She looked at her watch.

"Maddy, let's talk about this a little bit more." He tried to plead and grabbed her arm as Rachel shot him daggers with her eyes.

"Give me the key." Madeline held out her hand, fingers trembling.

Fred stood motionless, but his mistress thrust her hands into his coat pocket. She removed the key and slapped it down on the counter.

"We need to talk about this, Maddy." Snapped out of his paralysis, Fred assumed a saccharine tone, trying to submerge his sins under a wash of sugar.

"I can't talk about it. I have to be somewhere. And I have to pick up a cake." A new kind of earthquake rumbled in Madeline's core. "My lawyer will be in touch about the divorce."

There was no lawyer yet.

Fred wiped the grease from his chin, sputtering about the financial help he had given her, and his mistress yanked his sleeve with her skeletal arms, dragging him out the door.

Madeline stood slack-jawed in the middle of her living room.

She looked at herself in her ornamental mirror. Fantasies flickered in her eyes.

A new thrill in her blood coursed through her veins, deepening the color in her cheeks. Like a dress design gone astray, she would toss her marriage in the trash, and start anew.

⁓

Fred told the other councilmen in due course.

It wasn't too long before the society ladies stopped patronizing her store, and she entered a deep debt—a darkness she couldn't admit.

She had to sell her things. She couldn't take care of herself. She cried as her neighbors rifled through her treasures for sale. These were people she used to greet in the lobby, exchanging niceties as they brought up the mail. She had laid out her best china and all her dearest possessions. They scrounged through her belongings as though she were dead and gone. The neighbors paid pennies for her most beautiful hats, and her dresses—the ones she had fashioned with her own two hands.

The net of the sale was enough to pay for one month's rent on the apartment.

After the month was through, she left before she could be evicted, moving into the back room of the Starlite with only a small suitcase, two pairs of shoes, and a coat.

After Fred was out of the picture, she had to beg the landlord of her dress shop to reassign the lease in her name. Over the years, there were times when she could barely make rent for the storefront alone. But she was finally starting to put away a bit of money. There had been a recent uptick in sales from a larger, more loyal customer base—girls from the social club.

Madeline tossed and turned on the fold-out mattress in the back room. Through the open doorway, she eyed the vagabond Aphrodite mannequin, now in the shadows. Cleared of her flowers, the mannequin was bare, open to any possibility.

The sun would rise in a couple of hours, yet Madeline still couldn't sleep.

PART TWO

The Opportunity

7

Lisa

A few hours' sleep, a croissant, and a coffee, and Lisa was on her hotel shuttle to the departure terminal, where she would serve the plane to Rome.

Sometimes there were opportunities for sight-seeing, but today she had time only for sights from the shuttle—*rue* after *rue* of elegant boutiques, each displaying windows of avant-garde fashion for the well-heeled.

If one of these boutiques hosted a nighttime social club, like the Starlite, Lisa imagined that a line would form around the block each night. Parisian women would shed their trench coats to display elegant silhouettes, their fashion as an art form, full skirts atop stiletto heels. They would dance and sip champagne, carefree.

It was snowing in Paris today. Lisa's shuttle dropped her off at Orly Airport and she entered the public plaza, heading through the Pan Am terminal to the boarding bridge. Flakes fluttered and melted on the airplane's windows as it idled on the runway. Passengers filed in quickly, and the comfort of the large crowd enveloped her. The world was a big place with a lot of people, and she was only one of them.

"Bring the woman in row four a pillow!" Jane barked.

"Yes, ma'am." Lisa brought out the pillow. She cradled it like a baby to keep it warm. Full service. But the passenger already had a pillow tucked behind her head, and the woman was nearly asleep.

"Another pillow, ma'am?" Lisa asked anyway, to fulfill orders.

The woman startled from her sleep. "*Hrmph.*" The woman made a throaty sound and tilted her neck.

The pointed red peaks of Jane's lips turned upward.

Blood rushed up Lisa's face as she turned down the aisle and dropped her upright posture.

It had been a setup.

"She has a pillow already."

"So? You're trying to show me up?" Jane snarled.

Lisa kept her head down; Jane's words fell to her feet.

⌒

It was early afternoon when they landed in Rome. The smell of Jane's breath lingered in Lisa's nostrils. Her demands had only increased as the flight went on, especially after the copilot spent a few minutes during his break making small talk with Lisa.

Jane had watched the two of them, narrowing her kohl-rimmed eyes at Lisa, then pulled her aside afterward to admonish her for wasting time.

"You shouldn't be talking to him anyway, during a flight." Jane's red lips were tight with apparent jealousy.

Lisa had to bite her tongue to stifle a little giggle. Jane couldn't stand that the handsome copilot usually preferred to talk to *Lisa*, of all people.

When it was finally time for the passengers to leave the plane, Lisa's chest flooded with a surge of relief. Once they disembarked, she shuttled through the airport quickly. A feeling of forward thrust surged in her veins, a sensation that she was in unstoppable motion. The other crew members were dispersing to their hotel on the outskirts of Rome, but she wasn't ready.

On impulse, she hopped in a cab, which was more cramped than an American taxi, with a tiny back seat. She asked the driver to take her to the tourist district; he rattled off questions she couldn't understand, except for the word *Pantheon*.

"*Sí,*" she responded.

He sped away from the curb, tires squealing as she searched for a seat belt. They wove in and out of traffic, and the motor gunned on and off. Lisa made the sign of the cross, and they motored faster and faster, through scrubby brushlands. Soon enough, the streets grew close together—crowded. Edifices of antiquity rose from the sidewalks, light-brown buildings that had stood through countless births, deaths, battles, and reconciliations.

A tear dropped from Lisa's eye as she drew a breath. The taxi pulled into a gorgeous, stone-laid plaza, and she beheld the gargantuan stone columns of the Pantheon. She entered the building behind a few British tourists who chatted in reassuring words of English.

Inside the great rotunda, a perfect window brought forth the pale-gray sky. All colors blended in harmony, as though Nature had coordinated its hues with the timeless structure. Next to her was a small statue of a saint; Lisa squinted at the Italian words, and her ears flooded with a quick stream of Latin. A chant echoed through the chamber. She turned on her heel to see a small wedding party. A pale bride in a simple white shift stood next to her nervous groom. He tapped his foot as a priest raised his arms.

Lisa turned away.

She had her own bridal shoes—flawless white satin heels. She had skipped some meals on the week she purchased them in order to pay for them. She had often stood in the window of the bridal store, torn between two gossamer veils.

Billy had never popped the question, but it had felt like only a matter of time. They were always seeing each other and had seemed fated to be together.

Back in Lisa's little Brooklyn room, the white shoes remained in their box, hidden under her twin-sized bed, beneath clumps of dust and a broken music box. In the Pantheon now: the first kiss of man and wife. The bride was radiant, with an ethereal glow.

Lisa hid her face. She bent down to gaze at a centuries-old figurine as tears smarted in her eyes. Even amid the beauty of Rome, she couldn't escape the fact that he didn't care.

8

Elaine

On interview morning, Elaine woke with a start.

Tommy had remembered to sleep in the bed. She pulled her leg from beneath the covers, and he rolled over with a little moan.

The day before, he had been in a glorious mood. She'd distracted him from booze, cooking him three-course meals as he tinkered with his gadgets. They made love several times, read some French philosophy books, and lounged around in a warm mist of bodily satisfaction.

She had the power to draw his attentions where she intended, at times.

It had been a luxurious, heavy day. Tommy was still naked beneath the covers, and she watched his eyelids flutter slightly as his chest rose up and down in his sleep.

Elaine managed to get out of bed without waking him and scurried downstairs to the washroom. His musky scent still clung to her. She quietly cleaned herself with a washcloth, bleeding still, on her cycle.

Her head dropped with heaviness as she painted on her makeup. She made her lipstick lines more crisp than usual.

Professional.

Her eyeliner curved at demure angles. She used a gentle coating of mascara.

Next, the finishing notes: creams and powders. Tommy didn't see any of it, dead to the world in wheezes of sleep.

Bang-bang-bang—she jolted.

Catherine was at the bathroom door.

In the few days since she quit her job, Catherine had been gone most of the time, staying at the Starlite long after Elaine left, going back to the brownstone only in the early morning for a few hours' sleep in the parlor.

Catherine wanted to be a singer now, and at the Starlite she would wail into song, serenading the ladies with her clear, silvery tremolos. Conversation would hush as everyone stopped and stared at the source of this lovely voice; they showered Catherine with spare change and adoration. She always beamed at the whole bunch of them, glittering with self-possessed flair.

Elaine peered in the mirror to set her powder; it wouldn't quite stick.

Catherine's voice was husky and hoarse as she shouted behind the bathroom door. "Elaine, I need to use the loo!"

As Catherine banged on the door loudly, Elaine listened for Tommy's footsteps.

She exhaled in a tight puff and opened the door in a rush of products. Her eyeshadow applicator was tight between her fingers; lipstick tubes tumbled from the vanity.

"You look like you're off to court." Catherine appraised her.

Elaine was suited up in her gray woolen dress, which she hadn't worn in two years. It was made of brushed felt, and Madeline had once tailored it to fit her perfectly. When she worked at the radio station, it had cost her half a paycheck.

"I'm going to Midtown."

"What's in Midtown?"

"I'm going to walk around, take in the sights. You know I like to walk around Manhattan."

"But it's freezing outside."

"Maybe if you got more sleep, you'd have more energy to withstand the cold. I thought you had to use the loo—go ahead already." A sisterly snipe—weapon for distraction.

"I *do* have to use the loo," Catherine retorted.

Elaine stepped out of her way and set her nose powder in a rush. She dashed to the kitchen and grabbed her résumé from the typewriter she stowed beneath the sink, behind the cleaning supplies.

She pulled out a piece of blank paper and scribbled a note for Tommy: *Going for a walk in the city.*

She arrived at the *Chronicle* building too early, with an hour's time to do nothing but pace in her heels outside the double doors.

After a half hour of huddling beneath her coat, Elaine shook herself and strode into the building. Her heels clacked on the tile, precise and controlled, even as her teeth chattered together uncontrollably.

The lobby was warm and smelled of newsprint. A man at the front desk directed her up to the fifth floor.

Women clustered in the elevator, though women's names didn't usually appear in the credits of the paper.

Elaine attempted to smile at a woman she was squished against. But the woman avoided her eyes. Elaine's cheeks colored pink; she drew her gaze downward.

As the buzzer sounded for the fifth floor, every woman in the elevator, including Elaine, exited.

The office was crammed with noise and clatter—phone conversations, the *click-clack* of typewriters, scurries of heels on the tiles. She tried to crane her neck to find where to go. Someone stood behind her; she stepped back on his foot, unaware.

"Oh!" she shrieked.

The man pardoned her with a wave of his hand. "Are you Miss Huxley? I'm Mr. Stephens. Frank Stephens. Pleased to meet your acquaintance." He was of slighter stature than his voice on the phone had indicated. He had graying hair and a tic in his eye.

"I'm really early, I know. It's fine if I have to wait."

"Coming in before the deadline suits us just fine. The other girl is late, as it turns out. So, how's about I bring you in and we can chat for a while."

Elaine took a breath and followed him into the interview room. An unknown man and woman waited at a long table, with unreadable facial expressions and fancy fountain pens. Behind them, a large picture window provided a panorama of the busy street below.

"Pleased to meet you."

They shook hands. The woman introduced herself as the head fact-checker; the man was a news editor.

"I brought my résumé." Elaine's hand trembled as she gave them her extra copy, but she raised her lips into a smile.

The head fact-checker kept a serious expression. She was one of the few women in a senior position at the *Chronicle*. She had little wisps of gray on her forehead. "So, it looks like you spent three years at the radio station. What made you leave?"

"A personal obligation." Elaine paused. "I had to look after someone."

The head fact-checker nodded and exchanged looks with the other staff members before continuing. "Tell us about your college and professional experiences."

Elaine described the research and journalism classes she had taken at Briarcliff College along with her day-to-day duties at the news radio station a couple of years back. Her face shone bright and friendly in the sunny meeting room even as her shoulders shook beneath her woolen suit jacket.

"Describe a difficult scenario you had to overcome at your past job."

She froze, staring out the wide picture window. Then she recalled for them an incident where she took a subway to the end of the line at Rockaway Parkway and was forced to walk a couple of miles to interview someone about a house fire. It had been her first time in that neighborhood, and she got lost a few times, but she kept on walking, even after the heel of her shoe had separated from its sole.

The news editor smiled. "Well, it sure sounds like you're willing to do what needs to be done."

Mr. Stephens cleared his throat. "But what about children?"

Elaine folded her lips as her mouth went dry. "What about them?"

"Do you have any?"

"No."

"Do you want any?"

"I don't believe that I do."

"Oh, but every lady wants children, doesn't she? I don't think you could do this job with little ones to take care of."

"I'm not going to be having children," she repeated, as her cheeks flushed red.

"Well, I guess we'll see what happens," he chortled. "We have a blunt newsroom here, Ms. Huxley," he explained.

Elaine made herself chortle, like she was one of them. "Well, I guess you have to be blunt—there's no time to waste in the news!" Her chest filled with a rush of sudden boldness: she winked her eye at them and cocked them all a sideways smile.

Everyone chuckled.

The mood in the room relaxed, and the staff took sips from their coffee cups.

The news editor had another question. "So, tell us, dear, what would be your main professional aspiration?"

"To work my hardest."

The lot of them nodded and scribbled things on their pads.

They soon gave her a parting handshake.

Mr. Stephens ushered her out with a quick pat on the back. An unreadable expression set his lips tight. "We'll ring you by next Tuesday."

Elaine boarded the elevator to the lobby, upright in a sea of fedora hats, as men discussed the latest pre-season move from the Yankees.

In the lobby, she took another whiff of newsprint to carry her home.

On the bus ride back to Brooklyn, she scribbled some lines—the beginning of a poem:

I'd make a confession for your perceptions
I'm sorry to report that I can't.

She returned to the brownstone to find Tommy at their kitchen table, his mouth aflame with drink, mumbling that she had taken too long in the city.

9

Lisa

The copilot dared Lisa again to go water-skiing in Beirut, but she sat on the beach with her knees to her chest as Jane cruised the shore in showy sprays of water.

The day was sunny but chilly, and the salty water of the Mediterranean splashed Lisa's lips as Jane whirred past.

Everyone clapped as Jane rounded the bend in an Olympic-style performance.

Lisa averted her eyes to the snow-white sand. The blue-green waves lulled her, and she allowed herself to feel the breeze, chilly but refreshing. The surroundings nearly enclosed her, like the women at the Starlite—who twisted and turned for nobody but themselves and the music.

Jane coasted back, on a slow ride to the shore. Everyone gave her another round of applause as she swam from the boat dock to the land, impossibly slender in a clinging wetsuit.

Lisa looked down at her own stomach, pinching a roll of fat.

The number was always 130. She couldn't weigh more than 130, or she would be fired. Then she would be without a job, and without a man.

It was near lunchtime now. Lisa's belly rumbled, but she ignored the snack in her purse.

⁓

Back at the hotel, she weighed herself. One twenty-six. She was cutting it close, but she had enough wiggle room for some dinner this evening.

Someone knocked at the door to her hotel room. Lisa startled and glanced through the peephole.

It was Jane. Her hair fell in tousled waves, casual and windblown. With her hair down, she was barely recognizable.

Lisa slowly opened the door partway.

Jane pushed the door open fully, allowing herself into Lisa's room. "So, what's going on with your *beau* these days?" She sat down in a corner chair, her long legs crossing over each other as she twisted her damp hair back up into her bun.

"Who—*Billy?*" Lisa said his name with a light, airy quality. "I have no idea."

"You sure seemed upset about it last week!" Jane wrapped her hair tie around her bun—*one, two, three.* "You were a mess when he didn't come get you at the airport!"

Lisa crossed her arms in front of her chest; she should have ignored the knock at her door. "Well, I couldn't care less about him now. In fact, I'm all done with men, for now at least. I'm on to other things. I'm thinking of joining a club, a woman's club. It's a whole different set of girls. They're thinking about things that matter."

Jane's voice lilted. "What do you mean, things that *matter?*"

There had been no signs or markings on that door at night. The social club must be underground—a secret. But she had already started.

"It's like no place you've ever been. Women talking about all different things. Poetry, dancing, stuff like that. I was scared at first—I mean, it's late and it's at night, and you have to go out in the dark to get there. But now I can't wait. The more I think about it, it's a place that's *real.*"

Jane sat upright suddenly, then adjusted the straps of her padded bra. "That sounds strange, if you ask me. And it's at night? It sounds dangerous, with women out by themselves." She tilted her head with suspicion and narrowed her kohl-rimmed eyes.

"It might be dangerous. I don't know."

After Jane left, Lisa called down to reception. No new messages. Billy wouldn't know where she was staying. Meanwhile, Billy's father was in Paris, in another hotel, coupling with a strange woman.

She couldn't tell Billy about his father's affair. Especially now that he was ignoring her; he wouldn't pay attention to what she had to say.

Lisa trembled in the chilly air as she changed into her old nightgown and buried her head beneath the pillows.

The bed was creaky as she tried to fall asleep. Tomorrow would be another long-haul flight.

She heard the sounds of laughter from the room below. It was the camaraderie of friends—the sound of happiness, in no particular language.

The last time she laughed had been when Billy tickled her so hard that she could barely breathe. It had all mixed together in fierce attempts to get enough air, her lungs exploding, the dimples of his sensuous smile warming next to her.

Something so golden—gone.

10

Elaine

The overhead lights were white-hot, and the women's winter scarves and skirts floated and fluttered in the air as they danced at the Starlite, laughing and twirling the night away.

Elaine danced herself into a dizzy frenzy, her own private celebration in the crowd. Only two days after her interview at the *Chronicle*, she had received a call from Mr. Stephens. She'd gotten the job.

Everything could change. Elaine could have her own money again, and something to do. Something important.

"I need to stop." She gasped for air. She was covered in sweat, though her mouth was suddenly dry, as Catherine spun her around. Elaine released her hand and stumbled toward one of the garment tables. She snatched a cup of water from the edge and put effort into taking breaths and sips.

Cynthia came to her, a grin spread across her face. "My goodness, lady, I didn't know you could dance like that! You have to teach me the steps!"

"Okay, darling, let's go!"

Elaine didn't usually allow her body to release itself on the dance floor, but tonight she grabbed Cynthia's hands and they swung around each other, switching arms in waterfalls of laughter.

❧

The mood was less celebratory on the other side of the room as the women waved around newspapers, sparring in a high-energy debate.

Harriet and Gloria were locked in disagreement about President Kennedy's expanded embargo against Cuba, and the other women were taking sides.

Harriet shouted above them all, in a fury: "You just think he's cute! Let's see how you'd feel if you were the wife of a Cuban cigar maker and suddenly had no money."

Gloria's arms twisted around in the air like corkscrews. "What are you saying, that we should just support the Communists? If they're so self-contained, they should do just fine supporting themselves, right?"

"It's not about Communism. It's about free trade. And guess what— we're not a free-trade country if we don't endorse free trade."

"You think we should support every damn country no matter what? Do you even *know* what's going on?"

"I only know what I've been told. And what exactly *are* we being told?"

The women were loud—sharp and clear over the music that was already boosted to a high volume. Elaine shuddered in this agitated blaring of opinions: the American way. No physical violence here at least—only a lot of shouts, flails of the arms.

"Ladies, let's consider both sides . . ." Madeline seemed bemused; she lit the ladies' cigarettes and smirked, aglow in a tangerine-orange dress.

Catherine hissed in Elaine's ear. "Come out with me for a smoke!" She yanked on Elaine's arm and threw their coats over their shoulders.

The sisters emerged from the heated, pulsating storefront onto the chilly sidewalk. With the icy bite of the outside air, Elaine drew inward, snapped back into a cold reality.

Catherine was oblivious, as she puffed her cigarette and formed smoke rings with wide circles of her lips, nudging Elaine to do the same.

"Not in the mood, thanks."

"C'mon, give it a stab!"

"Nope."

"What's wrong?"

"Nothing."

"I beg to differ."

"I'm dandy."

"You're doing that thing you do with the left side of your mouth when you're worried. You're touching it too much or something."

Elaine blushed. Her words came out thickly: "I got a job."

"You don't say! Congratulations!"

Catherine gave her a sisterly slap on the back, though the edges of her mouth curled down soon after. Catherine didn't have a man to support her. She was hanging on the coattails of Elaine and Tommy. The story about quitting her airport job was fake; she had been fired. Elaine had discovered her crumpled dismissal letter beneath the velvet couch in the brownstone, citing her sister's chronic problem with lateness.

Elaine forced herself to smile for a moment. "Thanks for the congratulations, dear sister. It *is* nerve-racking, though, honestly. You know how Tommy is. He may start getting into more trouble, going out with his worst friends. He'll be alone the whole day if I'm at work."

"All men have problems, Elaine."

"Tommy's different, though."

Catherine laughed and puffed out another cloud of smoke. "All people have problems, dear sister. All women have problems. Some people *are* problems."

Elaine's head spun around; she snapped, "Can you please stop trying to make light of this?"

Catherine puffed smoke directly in her face. "So why did you go for that job interview if you need to play chaperone to your man?"

Elaine gulped, and her lips seized shut.

During her vacation in England, her parents had asked about Tommy. Of course, she had skipped over his drinking and his madcap reveries. *Just taking a little vacation with his father's inheritance money,* she claimed.

She also didn't bring up the other things: his poetry reading, his talking about the meaning of time and life. Assembling some complicated gadget that he'd drawn up from a scribble. No matter how many bad days he had, there was always a good day with him—some demonstration of his fiery brilliance.

There were those electric shivers she would get from his other side as he tapped his feet to his jazz—the two of them nestled together in the plush pocket of the parlor sofa. He might do something with his nimble, genius hands—run his strong fingers down the outline of her body.

"He's just drinking more since his father died. Everyone goes through a spot of something in their lives." Elaine shivered and extinguished her cigarette. "I'm going home now; are you ready?"

Catherine laughed. "I'm gonna stay for a while. The ladies are just getting warmed up. I want to learn what politics is all about."

"Suit yourself." Elaine wrapped her scarf around her throat and headed to her car.

She always blasted AM radio late at night, fueling her trips with late-night news from overseas. Her parents would be sipping their morning *cuppa* at their flat in London. Her father would be quiet, as usual, as he had never recovered from wartime and his body quaked every time a door was slammed or a plate was shattered.

"Shell-shocked." Her mother would shake her head. "What if you had been in the war? You didn't even go to war, George."

Wartime made her mother prone to talking. Her parents' relationship was a duality of the loud and quiet, as her father always retreated. But Tommy was different from her dad; he rarely read the papers in distant silence. Instead, he would listen to the news as he poured himself a whiskey. The news hour would pass and he would get heated and loud, growing more and more certain of his beliefs.

Elaine pulled up to the brownstone just as an ad for the *Chronicle* blasted from the radio.

Her new job would start soon.

The ladies of the Starlite would celebrate her victory. *Three Cheers for Elaine; she's got herself a gig!* Madeline would be sure to get a special cake for the occasion.

There would be a new dynamic in the atmosphere—something extra after she started work as a newspaper lady. She would join the fun and blow off some steam of the day.

It would be a different variety of pressure to release.

11

Madeline

Madeline wore a sapphire-blue ball gown, and her elbow-length white gloves pointed the way inside.

"We have a special theme tonight!"

With gleams in their eyes, they all protested. "But I didn't come dressed for the occasion!"

Madeline laughed, using her heel to kick down a thin velvet strip of rug, creating a skinny catwalk. She unrolled it to the door with her dainty shoe; a display of auburn curls bounced atop her head.

"You've rolled out the red carpet for us!" The ladies tilted their heads high in the air and sashayed up and down as Madeline set the needle on a record. Proper old regal chamber music, with pomp and circumstance.

"Tea with the royals!" Madeline sang out.

Catherine Huxley squealed. "Oh! A night made just for me!" She twirled and grabbed a cup of tea from the counter. She took a sip, then puckered her lips. "Bloody me, what have you got in here?" A smile flickered across her face. "Never mind—I *know* what you've got in there!"

The ladies keeled over in hysterics as Madeline brandished a bottle of pure-proof whiskey from behind the counter. "My darlings—the 'regular' teas are over there, by the stockings."

"This one will do just fine for me!" Catherine poured the liquid down her throat. "Now, Madeline, do you have another proper ball gown for me to try on?"

"I do, my dear, as a matter of fact. And I have white gloves for everyone!" Madeline scuttled into the back room and emerged with a box of the long, stretchy gloves. "Do tell me, dear, why is your sister not in attendance this evening?"

Catherine shrugged. "Some issue with that bloke of hers." She was getting a little fogged over with the spiked tea; despite the early hour, her eyes were turning red.

Madeline patted Catherine's arm and sauntered over to the front door. "Welcome, ladies!"

More women dashed inside the Starlite. Their hats glittered with freshly fallen snow. The room turned abuzz with a crescendo of conversation: the purging of the personal before the party could begin.

"Wow, look at that!"

A group was convening around Gloria; she had been slinking unnoticed along the edges of the room until someone caught sight of a new mammoth rock on her finger. Gloria was compelled to the middle of the floor as they gaped at the thing: an impossibly flawless diamond which rose upward from a platinum band.

"I've never seen something that big!"

Gloria blushed and crossed her arms above her gray pencil skirt. "I don't know—I guess it's pretty big! It almost feels strange, though. I feel a little . . . *exposed* . . . wearing it."

"Do you think you'll still be able to come to us after you're married? I mean, will he make you stop coming?" the ladies asked.

"Oh, no, I don't think so." She spoke a little too quietly. "He's a modern man, my Joey. I'll just tell him that I'm spending some time with my best girlfriends. He knows that I like to have fun with the girls."

Madeline broke away from the group and went to her hot plate to boil water for more tea. Soon Harriet sidled up alongside her, squeezing a cigarette holder between her fingers and tracing the trail of smoke, on the path to sharing some secrets. "Hey, you see Jackie over there? Did you know that she actually sneaks out of the house to come here?"

"Yeah?"

"After her husband is asleep, she runs over here as quick as she can. She knows she has a few hours before he has to get up and use the bathroom."

"What would her husband do if he found out she was here?"

"I would think he would ask for a divorce, wouldn't you? It's not exactly in good form to sneak out of the house at night. Or he might even do something worse. I think he hits her, you know."

"Really? She never mentioned anything."

Madeline looked in Jackie's direction and saw her dainty arms covered up by her elbow-length white gloves. Jackie wore a polite half smile as she chatted with a girl next to her.

"Is he violent?"

"I don't know."

"I hope he never follows her here."

Madeline's white enamel teapot whistled savagely on her burner. The teapot was one of the few things she had salvaged from the apartment, before she sold off her possessions to pay her final month's rent.

Four years prior, when Madeline cleaned out her apartment, she had unearthed a small cache of things Fred had left behind: a moustache trimmer, a box of cigars, an expensive fountain pen. Various items he'd used to mark himself as special—even one of those pinstripe suits he'd had tailored in Manhattan. Fred had never allowed her to hem his pants, even though her customers told her she was the best seamstress this side of the East River. He would only wear the shirts she had sewn for him if she claimed to have picked them up from an expensive male tailor in Manhattan.

You go and make things for women, *Madeline. I don't want you making clothes for me.*

Now, she shook herself awake and sipped more tea. On rotation, she moved to make quick contact with everyone. She would arrive for the pivotal moments in everyone's conversation—such was her special privilege to flit in and out, privy to any and all.

A small group was gathering near the fitting rooms around a girl who talked a million miles a minute, in verbal puffs of smoke. The girl's boyfriend was in Vietnam; she had just received a letter from him, written in code. "It's going to get worse. I don't think he's going to be there for just six months. They told him six months, but it seems like it's going to be more. What am I even going to do? Should I even stay with him? We were dating for two months before he went off."

"Do you love him?"

"I don't know! How am I supposed to tell if I'm in love? It's been two months! There's no way I could tell in two months."

"Well, if something happens to him, would you be sad?"

She was irate. "Of course I'd be sad! What kind of ridiculous question is that?"

"That's not what I meant. I meant—well—would you have wished that he could have married you?"

Her voice quivered over the chamber tones of the classical music. "Why are we even talking about this?" She sputtered and slammed her teacup down.

The sharp clink drew Madeline from her post—she ran to intervene with an elegant flourish of her wrists. "Hello, ladies! Care for any more tea?" She would always fly into conversations, cut off conflicts before they got too heated. With lots of ladies in a small space, tempers would flare, the wrong thing might be said, and bonds could be broken. At the sight of Madeline soaring in, the women would cast their eyes down in guilt; then she would whisper to them, "Only a feeling of bonhomie."

Now she procured an enamel flask, and a few of the women allowed her to pour a little liquor in their tea. Just a splash of booze—enough to make them feel like they were having something.

"Can I interest you in a little game?" Madeline said, and the women eyed her, seeming to warm up. "I created this amazing little conversational game that I wanted to share with you tonight. Come, gather around."

Under pressure, she could pull out something verbal and elaborate, with a great scheme of rules to keep everyone talking and laughing. Her games would start small and evolve—folding chairs would come out from the back room, and everyone would sit around the tables as she played ringleader.

"Come now, everyone!" Madeline tapped her teacup with a spoon and called for order. The din lowered, and she closed the lid of the record player. "Bring out the chairs!"

The women knew what to do; they got the chairs, laughing, and threw off their heels.

With everyone settled in their stocking feet, she passed around the slivers of tea cake. A satisfied air of eating underscored her announcements. "Now, you sit over there, Marcia, and you put your chair across from her. See, it's a talking game; everyone needs to be facing one other person, and you need to do it in less than a minute's time."

She proclaimed the rules to the crowd with confident waves of her hand. Improvisation was a challenge that she usually embraced with a devious smile.

But today she faltered—and her smile wavered.

Something was out of place. Something unnatural for this hour, when all the ladies had already settled in for the evening.

She squinted.

There was a spot of motion behind the gauzy curtain on the front door, the flash of a person who moved in the way of being unfamiliar with the social club yet prepared to enter anyway.

Madeline's heels ground into the floor; she flashed a glance at Jackie, who took delicate nibbles of tea cake, unaware.

She headed toward the door with assertive steps.

Brave.

Bold.

Then her lips turned once more to a wide smile.

It was only Lisa, the sweetheart who had once come looking for Elaine. Madeline opened the door and pulled her inside the store.

"So happy to see you here again, darling! No need to lurk around!" Madeline patted Lisa on her back, a wash of relief softening both sets of brows. "We're just about to start a game! Why don't you join in?"

Lisa hesitated a bit as she stood amid a bustle of ladies moving around their portable chairs. With a shy smile, she accepted an empty folding seat. She was decked out in her blue airline blazer as though she had just stepped off a flight.

Lisa darted her head from side to side with the anxious awareness of a little bird; Elaine was nowhere to be found.

Madeline had moved to the center of the room, where she egged on the crowd. "Now, the first thing you do is say your name. Loudly, so everyone hears you. No shrinking violets here!"

The women went up and down the line and shouted out their names. Some yelled made-up monikers, like "Mozzie" or "Cup-cup."

Madeline tapped Lisa on the shoulder. "You're up next, my love!"

"Stewardess," Lisa said feebly. She laughed along with everyone else, though her cheeks burned red.

"Okay, now say ten words that begin with the first letter of your neighbor's name, in one minute or less. I'm timing you, ladies. Go!"

Madeline pounded her wristwatch, and they all raced the clock. As women were eliminated, one by one, those removed from the game looked on from the perimeter as the competition dwindled down to the final few.

"Um, Rebecca . . . let's see. Raspberry. Running. Run. Raisin. Risk. Rice. Roof. Rough, r . . ."

"Five seconds!" Madeline trilled.

Harriet's cheeks glowed a fiery crimson even as her mouth curled up in a wide grin. "Rope . . . um, I'm stuck! Too many of you staring at me!" She took a deep drag of her cigarette to blow a smoky O into the center of the circle.

"Time's up!" Madeline sang out.

Lisa was up next. She turned even more scarlet than Harriet as she began. "Okay, um . . . Harriet. Handsome, handles, hot, harmony . . . hills . . . healing . . . hurt . . . hawk . . . hen, and—"

"Five seconds!"

"Hat!" Lisa finished.

Everyone howled and cheered, Lisa grinned from ear to ear, and Madeline brought forth her prize: a pair of sparkly, elbow-length gloves.

The tips of Lisa's ears grew pink as she slipped the gloves over her arms, admiring them from all angles.

The ladies gathered around to offer congratulations. "Wow, you are a quick thinker!"

"Well, I guess I perform well under pressure. I have to be on my toes on the plane all the time . . ."

"Oh, tell us all about it!"

"I would love to travel!"

"Well—I just came back from Beirut, where people were water-skiing. The Mediterranean is so beautiful. It's even nicer than Sheepshead Bay!" Lisa's face was slowly returning to its normal color.

Their discussion turned to water, and vacation, and culture, and Lisa seemed to fit with them as if the club were a jigsaw puzzle and she a missing piece, talking up a storm. A woman from Greece entered her in conversation about her home country; Lisa wanted to be assigned to fly there one day. The conversation flowed to men: Lisa revealed that her boyfriend had just left her, and everyone began their own confessions of heartbreak.

Madeline excused herself from the group—she had talked about her own heartbreak too many times already. She switched the music back to the top forty and the women started to dance, making up steps, twirling around, going with it. Harriet literally kicked off her heels, which sailed across the room, flying upside down into a rack of brassieres. Cynthia created outlandish hairstyles on anyone who would sit still, and Catherine Huxley crooned at the top of her lungs. Lisa seemed to be enjoying herself too—wreathed in smiles at their antics. The ladies welcomed her, pulling her into their dances. Now there was someone else to have a good time with.

❧

Madeline remembered the first time she had met Catherine Huxley, when her sister brought her to the social club back in '57. Catherine had been spunky from the beginning, ready to dance and grab a drink as soon as she burst through the door.

Madeline was thrilled that Elaine had brought her sister to the social club as a guest. Elaine had first entered the dress shop earlier in the week. After she had browsed the shop for some time, Madeline had taken the initiative to bring something out from the back room. It was a burgundy-colored ensemble, to do Elaine's delicate coloring justice.

While she was trying her outfit on in the fitting room, Madeline busied herself with unpacking a new shipment of hats, straight from Italy. When Elaine emerged from the dressing room, Madeline knew she had made the right selection for her, with a fitted bodice that showed off her dainty figure.

"My goodness!" Madeline squealed, unable to help herself. "You look gorgeous!"

"Thank you."

Elaine didn't look too pleased, though, as she scurried back into the fitting room, then returned with the dress slung over her arm. "My apologies. I'm actually not going to be able to get this."

"What's that, dear?"

"I don't have enough money."

"Twelve dollars, then." Madeline had resigned herself to taking a few losses each day at that point. Better to have customer loyalty than a quick sale.

"Twelve?"

"Twelve." She smiled knowingly. "A lucky man is gonna love this dress."

"Well, it'll be our third date." Elaine blushed.

As Madeline brought the dress over to the cash register, Elaine fumbled in her purse, digging for her wallet, and a little book tumbled out onto the counter.

"You like to read poetry, dear?"

"Oh, I love to read poetry! And sometimes I write it." Elaine's eyes sparkled.

"Do you ever try reading it out loud?"

"I memorized a few Shakespeare sonnets back in school and recited them to the class."

"That's not what I mean. I meant, have you ever read with feeling? Out loud?"

Elaine laughed—a musical sound. "I can't say I've read it aloud with *feeling*."

"Well, if you get interested, let me know. I've recently started a social club for women. Some poetry readings would really bring things together. We're meeting later, if you want to join us."

"Thank you, but tonight is my date. Perhaps next week?"

"Keep us in mind! We've been trying to meet regularly." Madeline had tucked the shop's phone number under the knotted twine atop the box. "Enjoy the dress, darling."

∽

Now, with the Starlite in full swing, Madeline was thrilled to see that it was still growing nearly five years later. The new girl Lisa seemed to be enjoying herself too, and it was all a mess of clothes and tea, laughter and music. And they were loud, with the thumping music and their shouts and their laughter. Madeline eyed the door. The cops could come and see them, but Madeline didn't have a license to sell alcohol—not that she was selling it, as everything was gratis. She sold enough extra dresses on social club evenings to provide refreshments for the girls—but the cops could get her on anything, if they wanted to.

But they had been loud on other nights, to no consequence. So she had taken to sliding in her stocking feet with the rest of them—donning a tiara; letting the movement, mood, and music take her where it would.

"Madeline!" Down near the front door, Catherine waved a pair of long white gloves to grab her attention.

Breathlessly she responded. "Yes, darling?"

"Who's that outside?" Catherine might have been a tad too tipsy, hovering near the front mannequin displays in full sight of Livingston Street. Maybe she'd drunk too much spiked tea—but she was insistent, pointing outside, her voice elevated.

Madeline followed Catherine's gesture—squinting across her mannequin displays, peering out through the storefront windows.

Behind the glass: a flash of wide, pale forehead.

Madeline inhaled sharply.

The person disappeared.

She drew closer to the window. There was only emptiness—the dark of the night.

A cop would have banged on the door. It wasn't a policeman out there.

It had looked like Fred's forehead instead—with that vulgar, distinct tilt of his brow.

Fred.

Or just her imagination.

Madeline poured the rest of her spiked tea down the drain.

12

Elaine

Elaine paced her bedroom early in the morning.

She always had to be careful with Tommy.

She waited as she made half loops around their bed.

One wrong move might cut the spindle-thin fibers that held him in check.

Her breath came quickly as she stared at him, asleep—the rhythmic rise and fall of his chest as he slumbered into the morning, his eyelids fluttering gently. In the light of day, as he snoozed, Tommy's intensity was hidden. He made soft murmuring sounds as he mumbled in his sleep.

She paced still more, and the minutes trudged by; she trod heavily, but Tommy didn't stir. He needed to be fresh for her news. Receptive. She would get him before he was clogged with the cobwebs of the day.

She would reveal the news about her job at the very moment he woke.

Now she perched on their bed, bouncing a little, creating some motion. Tommy turned over in his sleep.

After thirty minutes, she tired of this and went downstairs.

The waiting was endless—maybe she could leave the house for a diversion.

She picked up the phone. She needed a breath of fresh air—someone different, disconnected from all of this . . .

"Lisa? Good morning, my dear! It's Elaine!"

"Oh, hi!" Lisa sounded flustered but pleased. "It's great to hear from you."

"Yes, I wanted to call! I would love to get together! Are you free this morning? I was thinking Benny's Ice Cream Parlor?"

Lisa hesitated for a moment. "Oh, Benny's? Ice cream on a winter morning?" But then her voice lifted. "Oh, well, sure! Why not? That sounds like fun! How about eleven? A prelunch?"

"Absolutely. See you then."

Elaine hung up and pulled on her shoes and coat. She would escape the brownstone quickly, before she had a chance to change her mind.

⁓

Elaine paced more, this time outside the door to Benny's Ice Cream Parlor.

She startled back as a tot burst through the door, pushing it open with a surprising amount of energy as he wailed, his face covered with chocolate. His mother chased after him, and the two of them bumped into Elaine.

"Sorry!" the mother apologized as she ran to grab his hand.

Elaine pardoned them with a wave of her hand. "It's fine."

She had arrived extremely early, and as she waited on the chilly sidewalk, she took to planning, bringing out a small notebook:

Today

1. Buy him something nice.
2. Make an amazing dinner.
3. Tell him casually.

She stared at the third item on her list, then crossed it out, replacing it with:

3. Inform him with conviction.

She nodded at her own writing, though her lip furled inward, and she hesitated.

She was startled, all at once, by a cheery voice—"Elaine! Great to see you!"—as Lisa grabbed her for a quick hug and a smile.

The two stepped inside the warmth of the ice cream parlor, and Elaine suddenly salivated for a scoop of strawberry, topped with a cloud of whipped cream. They sat at the counter in their coats and settled in.

Elaine laughed. "We're a bunch of silly ducks, I suppose, getting ice cream in winter!"

Lisa laughed uproariously; Elaine's accent was entertaining. "Sorry— the way you said 'silly ducks'—too hilarious!" she squealed. She sput- tered into another fit of chuckles as she attempted to order. "A scoop of pistachio, please!" she snorted to the worker.

Once their desserts were scooped, Elaine reached for her own, and for a brief moment it captured her: the tart taste of frozen berries on her tongue. But the ice remained, her throat numbed, and she struggled to spit out her words: "How have you been these days? It seems like you've been enjoying the Starlite."

"Yes, I'm having a ball! I'm finally getting to use the dance steps I love on *American Bandstand*!" Lisa took a bite of pistachio with her spoon as a guilty smile played across her lips. "I'm trying to get more into the writing, you know—the literary circle and all that. I mean, I do like poetry—I just don't have a knack for it like you, I guess."

"Well, dear, it's not that I have a knack for it so much as the *need* for it." Elaine coughed. "It's a way I couldn't express myself otherwise."

"So, it's almost like another way of talking for you?"

"That sounds about right."

"You make it sound so easy!" Lisa laughed. "Is your fiancé a poet too?"

"He doesn't write, but he likes to read it from time to time. He's really more of an engineer." Elaine cleared her throat. "Well, he used to be an engineer. That's not what he's doing right now."

"What's he doing right now?"

The words froze on Elaine's tongue: "On break . . . *he's* on break." She glanced at the question in Lisa's face and hesitated, then decided to keep going. "*I'm* actually going to start a job soon, though."

"Oh? You are? Where?"

"The *Chronicle*." There was some embarrassment in her voice, almost as though it were too big for her. "I'll be a fact-checker."

"Wow! That's so exciting!" Lisa grinned and held up her ice cream spoon. "Cheers!" She clinked Elaine's dish with her spoon; the two of them laughed. "So, your fiancé must be excited for you too! What did he say?"

Elaine gave a weak smile and fiddled with her dish. "To be honest— it probably sounds absurd, but I haven't told him yet."

"Oh? Is he one of those men who doesn't like for a woman to work?"

"At this point, I gather that he doesn't."

"Oh." Lisa studied Elaine's face, which bore little expression. "Well, that sounds hard! Are you sure you want to do it?"

Elaine took a deep breath and pushed her spoon into a bit of whipped cream, letting it melt on her tongue. "I think so."

Lisa nodded. "I guess you'll have to tell him soon, though, right? And see what he says? It's the *Chronicle*, after all . . ."

"Right." Elaine nodded, her lips set in a straight line. She would be opening Pandora's box if she told him. Tommy might feel abandoned. Alone in the echoing brownstone, his drinking could escalate.

Yet there was a small chance that he could be inspired by her ambition. He might even feel motivated enough to find a job of his own.

At the ice cream counter now, Lisa searched her eyes. "So, you think you'll tell him about it?"

Elaine gulped. She had wanted to join the *Chronicle* for years, even before she worked at the radio station.

"I think so."

"Good." Lisa smiled in encouragement.

Elaine gave her a weak smile in return. It would be *embarrassing* to deny such an opportunity, at one of the world's leading newspapers. She couldn't very well scorn her chances at success.

❧

Elaine had decided: she would need to set the scene for him.

He would need to be coaxed into the idea of her return to work. She would need to distract him—transport him to his happy place.

After saying good-bye to Lisa, Elaine traipsed all over Brooklyn, searching for things that would fit the bill.

She came to a used bookstore and hovered in the back, where she made a nice find: poems by Théodore Aubanel in the original French. A rare book, from the turn of the century. She paid and inscribed the front cover—*Elaine amour*—in her most beautiful handwriting.

On her way home, she made a stop at Woolworth's to buy some tissue paper and ribbon so she could make a nice little package for him.

She would go home, and she would cook him his favorite meal: beef tenderloin with roasted carrot puree. They would share a nice sparkling wine, something lower in proof than his usual. Catherine would be out at the Starlite, so it would be just the two of them.

Elaine rubbed her palms; it was difficult to hold so many packages with her palms coated in sweat. But it would be easier to reveal her truth when Tommy was relaxed.

⟡

When she returned, it was still daytime, yet the blinds were drawn down low. In the guest bedroom, Tommy was hunched over on the old red velvet couch. He was mumbling to himself as he pieced together wires with a pair of electrical pliers.

"How can you see anything in here?" Elaine squinted uncomfortably.

He held a little light to his contraption. "I have an eye for these things, Elaine."

"What are you making?"

Old ideas lay in piles around the room. "A transistor," he said briefly. His hands worked deftly, resetting small parts. His eyes were deep pools, and he peered into the device with a single-minded focus.

Elaine held her breath. "Do you want more light?"

He didn't answer.

"More light?"

"I'm fine," he finally answered.

She left the room—she would give him the time alone before she dropped her news.

In the kitchen, she unwrapped the tenderloins. Meat juices on wax paper dripped down to her hands. She had visited the best butcher in Brooklyn Heights—Marty on Remsen Street. It had been a long walk on the icy sidewalk to watch Marty pound the meat, and Elaine's stomach had churned with each smash of the bloody hunks.

At the produce store, the carrots were ancient, so she hiked another three avenue blocks to a different store. A blister was developing on her heel, but she still had to trek down to the wine shop, which was surprisingly crowded for that time of the afternoon.

Now, back at the brownstone, she was making scalloped potatoes—a new recipe that Harriet had passed along to her at the Starlite.

She stirred things in pots and heated up the oven, and the scent of cooking food wafted through the house. Tommy was quiet in the other room, except for intermittent bursts of expletives when the wires didn't twist to his expectations.

"Dinner's ready!"

No response. She shouted again, to no avail. Tommy would be gritting his teeth, trying to wrap a piece of wire around something. She put on a low, alluring voice; she would sound more interesting than the wire.

"I made you your favorite . . ." She held her breath, waiting.

"That's nice." He answered in a monotone.

Elaine swallowed the lump in her throat and retreated to the kitchen to sit alone at a wooden table Tommy's father had made years ago, back when his mother was still alive. After Tommy's mother died when he was in grade school, he was raised mostly by his aunt Mary, a sweet but sad woman prone to bouts of drinking and crying. *I never cry. I'm not like my silly aunt, just bawling away*—he'd once said during a particularly sour bout of drunkenness.

Elaine ate by herself; the food turned to a mess on her plate. When she had finished, Tommy finally emerged from the other room.

It was some time before they spoke.

"I was reading something you would adore, Elaine. A French piece on existence—what are we made of, what will continue?"

Elaine drew in a sharp breath. "Perhaps only that which is started will continue. Everything else . . . who can say?"

Tommy's dark brown eyes flickered over hers; then he finished his food with a satisfied smile. "You really take care of me, you know."

He looked her in the eye, and she gulped.

"I . . . I got you a little gift," she stammered, and handed over the little package she had made.

He ripped open the tissue paper. "Fantastic, babe. Really fantastic! The original French, too! A great find. Let's go check it out. And I see you got us a bottle too!" His demeanor turned to excitement as he cracked the book open and poured himself a glass.

He read aloud in French and stroked her leg. Heat crept up Elaine's body as she sipped from her own glass of sparkling.

It was getting late; then the moment faded as he drank more and more; then it was too late, as the entire bottle disappeared.

Tommy grew sullen again, with dull eyes, and laid himself in the corner of the guest room, as if the sharp corners of the walls were a napping nook. He was talking about his childhood.

"She was never happy, my mother. Never, never happy. Never happy!" His eyes were inebriated squints.

"What makes you say that?" She usually didn't ask him to explain.

"She drank a lot, for one!" He found it amusing in spite of himself, and chortled with a low, throaty sound. "And apparently I was too difficult to take care of, because she ended her life. We found her right here."

"You what?"

He didn't elaborate, and she didn't ask him to explain. His eyes were fully closed as he hummed softly, ready to fall asleep on the floor.

He would be alone in this house when she went to her job each day. Alone for hours.

As he fell asleep, she went up to the bedroom and laid a damp cloth on her forehead, which also covered her eyes. She kept herself encased in the void behind her lids—awake in the darkness, her breathing short.

Her thoughts twisted in circles, around and around in the darkness.

I wouldn't be the first to give up on a dream.

Yet she couldn't play second fiddle to his problems forever.

13

Lisa

Lisa giggled until she was crying, clinking teacups with the ladies at the Starlite.

As she wore the sparkly, elbow-length gloves she had won the prior night, she could breathe better. She walked around like a ballerina on tiptoe, with the fancy chamber music in the background, and others did the same. They pirouetted like dancers all over the store.

She had smashed down some wall with these invisible pointe shoes. She joined the others in an improvised ballet class near the nylons, using the table as the barre. It was perfection, them in their vibrant dresses, prancing about the place. They acted like little girls, although Lisa looked more like an adult than ever before in the light of the golden lamps.

She hadn't met friends like this in a while. And it was all fun and free—until she noticed Madeline.

Madeline's face—previously lit a sociable glow—had turned pale, her pupils darting.

Something must have happened in the blink of an eye.

Madeline was talking quickly. "He came again; then he ran away."

She rushed everyone out the door, urging them to be careful. Her beautifully made-up eyelids twitched with the unknown.

As they streamed out the door, a woman named Jackie spoke in a panicked whisper. "I hope my husband isn't tailing me!"

Jackie's makeup was melting in her sweat, and Lisa caught sight of deep purple on her cheeks.

They headed out in shifts, clustered together in tight packs to navigate the dark streets.

Power in numbers.

They each found their cars and headed home.

⌒

Back at her apartment, Lisa's mother was still awake, doing needlepoint. Bent over, her mother looked older than her years.

"I'm sorry, Ma." In the shadows of the night, Lisa turned away from the lines on her mother's face, the creases of age.

"Oh no, it's my own issue, dear. When you're traveling and I don't know what's going on, I just go to sleep. You know what they say—ignorance is bliss! But when you're out and about in Brooklyn and I don't know what's going on, it's a little different."

Her mother was ready to nod off. Lisa wrapped her arms around her mother's thin shoulders. Her bones were fragile, knobby.

It was cold in their apartment. The radiator knob was turned all the way to the left—her mother's technique for saving money.

"Ma—you should come with me to this place. There're all these women there. There's some closer to your age too."

She could give her mother something else. Something beyond grocery money.

"That's quite all right, darling. I really have no desire to be out and about. My only desire is to see you home safe. Good night, dear. I'm going to bed." With her robe dragging behind her, her mother shuffled into the bedroom, where Lisa's father snored.

Lisa pulled her skirt over her knees, alone in their shabby little living room. She had a few days before she had to jet out of town, and she wasn't ready for sleep.

But she forced herself to her bedroom, and once in bed, she fell asleep quicker than she'd thought—straight into her Technicolor dreams of the Mediterranean Sea and the Starlite, where they all danced on aqua-blue waves, like ballerinas.

⌒

It was almost noon when she woke the next day. She stumbled out of her room feeling hungover, though she hadn't drunk too much the previous night.

She poured herself some cereal, trying to feel normal.

Bzzzzz. The buzzer rang, and she jumped.

Her mother wasn't home. Sometimes she went shopping and forgot her key. Lisa peeked out the window, parting the curtains so she could see down to the sidewalk.

It was Billy, on the stoop.

He was rubbing his hands together in the cold, stomping in place in his work boots. The sound was familiar: a quick two-step on the sidewalk that Billy always said made him a "winter Fred Astaire." He would grab her hand and twirl her around, right on the street. His eyes would twinkle. *A Brooklyn Ginger Rogers.*

Now the top of his head disappeared under the awning to her building and the buzzer rang again.

Lisa struggled to inhale. She darted her head around the room. Then she crawled beneath the table, where she crouched for ten minutes on the linoleum, next to the stained legs of the kitchen chairs.

Once the buzzing stopped, she scooted over to the edge of the window frame on her hands and knees.

Billy was stepping down the icy sidewalk, away from her apartment.

Lisa exhaled and stood upright, pacing in the narrow aisle between her dresser and bed. An animal energy pulsated in her legs as she circuited the messy space in leaps.

Elaine.

Elaine probably hadn't started her new job yet—she should be home.

Lisa located the crumpled airline napkin with Elaine's phone number on her dresser, and she bounded to the phone on the kitchen wall. The line rang a dozen times; there was no answer.

She slammed the phone in its receiver and paced in little loops around the furniture. On the corner of the table, she made a misstep and slammed her leg too hard. Rare expletives erupted from her mouth. She pressed the injured area, pushing her muscles inward.

A slam of a door downstairs meant that her mother had returned home from food shopping.

Lisa held in her shakes as she jumped to help. She sprinted down the steps to get the bags, one by one.

Then her mother handed her a piece of mail retrieved from the mailbox, without comment.

It was a white envelope addressed with her name. She ripped it open. *DEAR LISA.*

Billy liked to write in capital letters.

I'M SORRY. I HOPE YOU CAN FORGIVE ME. Next to this pitiful apology was a small, blurry sketch of a face, maybe his own face, with a juvenile drawing of a mouth tilted in a sideways line of guilt.

Lisa smuggled the note into her room as her mother put away cans in the cabinets.

Her mother shouted to her bedroom, "You slept late! You must have been tired."

"Yeah."

She slipped the envelope into her underwear drawer, in the back— underneath the lingerie she'd purchased for a fantasy of a honeymoon. She slammed the drawer shut and turned on the radio. It was a Western, some irritating show with twangs and blasts.

She raised the volume to produce a protective cloak of sound and threw herself on her bed. She grabbed a photo album from a shelf, something she had once made, from when she and Billy had first starting dating.

She flipped through photos of them together at Coney Island, on the Jersey shore, and on their day trip to Philadelphia, with a silly shot of his smirk next to the Liberty Bell.

They had gone out to Philly that day in his red convertible. Her thighs were warm and solid next to his. The leather seat compressed with each movement of her body. Billy related that the car was a high school graduation gift from his father. He said that he had almost failed

English. The words blurred together whenever he tried to read and write, but he had found a way to pass by paying the honors students to proof-read his essays. Sometimes they wrote entire essays for him, from their own goodwill. Billy could charm almost anyone.

His car was his pride and joy, an example of what his charm could win. It had chrome wheels and a massive hood ornament. It was a smooth ride, and it spoke of more money than Lisa could imagine.

Lisa had shuddered a little when he told her where it came from, but it was easy enough to move on to new things as her long hair whipped around in the wind on a leisurely, breezy ride with the convertible's top down. The air changed as they drove over the state line to New Jersey. The trees were tall, and she had never seen so many at once. Her own car would have broken down at the speeds Billy traveled. It always smelled like a leak, and the motor made a clunking sound at forty miles per hour.

Billy talked more about himself on that trip than he ever had on their dates in Brooklyn. Let loose from his usual stomping grounds, he held his identity less tight.

He admitted that he was always restless and that his feet itched to move when he'd been sitting still for too long. His parents used to pun-ish him as a child until they realized that buying things worked better. As he got older, the toys got bigger.

Lisa didn't tell him that she had received a grand total of *three toys* throughout her childhood. She didn't tell him that her parents used to save all year for her annual gift at Christmastime, and that usually it was just a new coat. Her old baby doll remained in her room as a trea-sured memory.

She didn't take anything for granted—yet Billy was used to having so much.

⟶

She could barely even look at her clothes closet anymore, it was so empty.

Her standard-issue Pan Am uniforms and a few well-worn skirts and blouses weren't enough.

She wanted to buy something special at the Starlite Dress Shop—a nice number that could impress Billy, or anyone else.

She decided to leave a few less dollars on the counter that morning for her mother's grocery shopping.

Her mother noticed as she organized her pocketbook for the week. "Honey, are they paying you less money all of a sudden?"

"Pan Am started making the flight attendants pay for their food at the hotels, Ma," she lied.

There were only so many ways she could break free.

14

Madeline

Madeline had last seen Fred face-to-face four years ago—a few months after he came to her apartment with Rachel.

It was at the divorce proceedings. One of his crony friends served as his lawyer. He denied adultery and got to keep all the money. He rolled out of the courtroom in his dark-gray suit, shaking hands with his representative and talking loudly about sports, as though a divorce from Madeline was yet another easy deal.

Madeline bit her lip when she saw him smoking his cigarette in the lobby. She slumped past him like a used tire.

Deflated. Useless.

He pulled her aside. "Listen, Madeline—" He hissed and exhaled a puff of smoke, which went straight into her eyes. "You'd better not start trying to spread any of your nonsense around about me. Nobody will believe you or give a damn about what you say."

Fred towered over her, enormous in his elevated shoes.

She used to spit shine those same shoes.

"You must think you're a big shot, Fred. A really big, fat shot."

He shrugged and extinguished his cigarette. "At least I'm not a nothing, *Maddy*." He smiled, sweeping his eyes to the floor as though he was referring to a mat—a *doormat*. He knew she hated that nickname. Fred's greasy moustache was at her eye level, and the scent of his tar rushed into her nostrils. "Make sure you watch where you step, now."

He grinned, and his icy blue eyes looked straight through her.

Soon his crony emerged from the bathroom, and they left the courthouse.

It was a hot, humid day. Madeline's heels stuck to the sidewalk, which reeked like rotten garbage.

Her own lawyer caught up with her and patted her on the back. "The first installment of my bill will be due in two weeks, dear."

The lawyer left; Madeline stood alone, crying.

It took a long eighteen months to get down to a zero balance on the lawyer bill.

She entered a routine after the divorce; she sewed, ordered, and sold her dresses during the daytime hours. At night, she held the twice-weekly, or sometimes thrice-weekly, sessions of the social club. She kept her food simple: corn flakes in the morning, canned foods for lunch, sandwiches from a local deli. Pastries for dinner, leftovers from the club. She bunked like a castaway, on the fold-out sofa in the back room.

Although she had her busy times, there were always the slow hours.

Like three in the afternoon, presently. A lone customer browsed the store, a little old lady who was taking her time to pick through the woolen hats on clearance.

The doorway bells rang, and Madeline emerged from behind the counter to greet someone who was entering.

It was Mrs. Hanover.

She was the wife of one of Fred's cronies; Madeline hadn't seen her in about four years, since sometime before the divorce—but still she beamed, as if it had been no time at all.

"Mrs. Hanover! It's been so long!"

"I've been trying to stay away, dear! For my pocketbook, you know!" She smiled genially as she ran her eyes up and down Madeline's A-line dress. "Darling, I just couldn't stay away any longer. My daughter's getting married in June, and I just *knew* you'd have something special for the mother of the bride. I'm looking for something classic, you know? Something that doesn't make me look *too* ancient," she laughed.

The two of them combed through the racks for an hour, to no avail. Madeline even dove into the back room and brought out a few pieces that had just arrived in shipment, but nothing fit Mrs. Hanover quite right, so Madeline agreed to make a custom design.

Mrs. Hanover marked a few things she liked in Madeline's fashion magazines, and Madeline sketched out a plan: a vision of a long sapphire-blue gown with silver edging.

"I really appreciate this. You know, I just trust your judgment, your style. You have all of it, darling. And you *know* what an important day this is to me, I'm sure. It's my only daughter getting married." Mrs. Hanover gazed into the distance, misty eyed with maternal feeling.

Madeline cleared the lump in her throat. "Of course. It will be something you remember forever."

Then she ran to retrieve her measuring tape in a well-timed bid for supplies.

⁓

She worked harder on that gown than on anything she had ever made. The society ladies would behold her spectacular creation. They would mourn the years they had ignored her. Even after her long nights with the social club, Madeline woke at five AM and revved up the sewing machine. As the sun rose over Brooklyn Heights, she toiled in the back room, ripping out thousands of stitches in her effort to make a perfectly contoured bodice and the most fabulous flowing skirt to ever exist.

When it was complete, it was a vision.

She handed it over to Mrs. Hanover, whose whole face glowed like an angel. She spun herself around to look at it from every angle. "Making an old lady like me look so gorgeous—you're a genius, my dear! I don't know how you pulled this off!"

Madeline did a little wiggle of her hips. "Youth is all about attitude!"

After Mrs. Hanover changed back into her housedress, she paid what she owed, along with a hefty tip. "I can't tell you how much I appreciate this. Especially since . . . well, I know that none of us have been here in a while, really. But seeing you in person, darling . . . I know that none of those nasty things Fred said about you could be true. You're a doll, a true doll."

"Oh?" Madeline's face turned white.

"I'm going to tell the girls to start coming back, Madeline!" Mrs. Hanover whisked herself out the door, and the bells jangled as she left the dress shop.

～

After a few days, they *did* start coming back. One by one, her formerly frequent customers—the society ladies—ran in to grab a scarf or a pair of knickers. At first, they purchased only small accessories, but after a very prominent lady of the group purchased a dress, more of them streamed in and Madeline got busy soon after, filling out overseas orders for the latest fashions from Paris and Milan and creating her own custom designs.

She was getting a glimpse of what her business could have been like without Fred's interference.

Without his lies, she could have had something much bigger, this whole time.

These ladies had a little extra money to spend. She was finally making a nice profit. She even had to ask Harriet to come in part-time and take over the alteration requests because she no longer had the time to do them herself.

But although some of these society ladies had returned, they were wary.

They would glance over their shoulders constantly, as if checking to see if anyone noticed their whereabouts. And none ever joined Madeline in the evenings at the social club.

She would invite them; they all made excuses about their "prior commitments."

She stopped asking them after a while.

"I was probably playing it a little too fast and loose anyway, inviting them for the nights," she confided in Harriet. "I wouldn't want them telling those men."

But after a few weeks at least, as February turned to March, they seemed to glance over their shoulders less often.

～

Madeline's feverish pains took on a life of their own, bound up in something bigger. She trimmed and sheared, sized and prepared the fabric. Her hands stirred in constant motion to construct tight ensembles from loosely wrapped reams of cloth.

Harriet worked to collect the measurements, and Madeline coached her in the art of speed: the quick flick to wrap a measuring tape around a waist, to extend it the height of a thigh.

"You're getting faster, darling," she told Harriet as she flew her own needle over the crisp edge of a skirt.

"Thanks. I needed this job, Madeline. My husband stopped giving me money to buy clothes! He said I'm a clotheshorse." Harriet stood up to inspect her handiwork, shaking out her own full skirt. "Darn it!" she yelped, and bit her lip. "Nature has decided to bless me early this month." She took off her cardigan and wrapped it around her waist. "And now it looks like this stool has been through a battle scene. Disgusting."

"We'll take care of it. Not like that hasn't happened to me! Although there's something wrong with me, darling; I only get visits from my Friend a few times a year. But it's always a surprise!" She opened a small cabinet and pulled out sanitary pads and belts, tossing them over to Harriet.

Madeline's cycle hadn't been regular for years. Two decades prior, back in high school, a boy had taken her into a closet after school. She didn't really know what had happened until her best friend told her she might be pregnant. Her mother found her on the floor of her bedroom—writhing, coughing—on the cusp of death after she tried to clean herself out with bleach. She was revived at the hospital shortly after, and the doctor proclaimed her scarred for life.

During her courtship with Fred, she told him this story. She told him directly that she could never have his children.

A few weeks later, he proposed to her.

She was a streamlined wife for him; he was able to cheat on her without the hassle of little ones to complicate his life.

It had been so easy for him.

⌒

Now that the society ladies were shopping during the day, her dress shop was buzzing, and she could barely keep up. Madeline complained to Harriet that she was slacking on the social club, forgetting even to get food some nights.

But now she was at that bakery on Henry Street to try to make it up to her regular ladies.

She was eying something fancy: a layer cake with chocolate crème.

She purchased it and watched the busy attendant tie up the cake box with red-and-white twine. She was entranced by the nimble motions of his fingers—a talent that she also prided herself on, the ability to prepare something beautiful for a customer in quick time.

"Thanks so much." She handed her money over and turned to leave. Then her throat seized up suddenly.

She couldn't swallow.

It was *him*.

Fred was perched behind a little table, sipping an espresso.

She hadn't seen him since the divorce. Except for possibly the other week, two nights in a row, at the window of her shop.

It was like déjà vu from outside the courtroom; she had no choice but to walk right past him. Of course, she was wearing heels. And they clicked too loudly.

Fred turned to face her.

He gave a wide sneer of his yellowed teeth, and with a twinkle in his eye, he gestured to her cake box.

"Hosting a party tonight, Maddy?" His eyebrows rose, and he exchanged looks with his crony.

Madeline didn't answer. She scurried away and tucked the cake box under her arm.

Fred guffawed as she left; he chortled so hard that he sputtered on his espresso.

Madeline hid her face from him, turning only to catch a final glimpse of Fred's wide, pale forehead.

15

Elaine

It was all so tiring. When Tommy started to drift off on the floor, Elaine brought a woolen blanket and a toss pillow down to the carpet. He twisted around in a fitful languor before reaching to put the pillow beneath his head.

Elaine stayed on the couch near him and his unfinished transistor. She nodded off too.

He always got in his own way—she would get worked up—they both would get exhausted.

Now it was morning. They were thirsty as they sat on tall stools in the kitchen; they sipped down glasses of water and nibbled on slices of orange. The fruity acid was on their tongues—they didn't exchange a word, and the volume of French poetry was between them, the one she had carefully selected.

She broke the silence. "What do you want to do today?"

He glanced at her with a devastating look—hair slicked back, hand on his stubbled cheek. Dark eyes intent. "I'd really like to stay at home, babe. Get some stuff done. I'm trying to finish that damn transistor. Just one more piece I need to get right."

"What are you trying to do?" She gulped.

It was always just one more piece—one last stubborn piece. He always claimed to be close to complete, yet he never finished what he started.

"I just need to get the wires in the right place. It's an amazing design."

He was always so fixated on his projects—his gadgets, his music. His booze.

During their first years together, he had focused his intensity on her. He knew how to romance her, buying her extravagant bouquets or rare editions of literature. Yet during the early years of their relationship, she caught glimpses of his broken pieces. He would talk about his youth—his mother distant with melancholy, his father unable to help. But he never shaded in the details—he would always shift the conversation to something beyond himself, something about philosophy or art.

She had spent three years in courtship with Tommy before he surprised her with a magnificent diamond, a proposal on one knee, next to the Hudson River.

Without a question in her mind, Elaine had said yes. She couldn't imagine being with anyone but him.

Then, shortly after their engagement, Tommy's father took ill. He hadn't been well for some time, but his condition deteriorated, and he was in and out of wards for months with a slow-moving cancer.

Tommy had always enjoyed his drink, but after his father's illness it became routine for him to add cognac to his espresso and a splash of whiskey to everything else. It took a full year for his father to succumb to the cancer; by then, it had become an established habit for Tommy—a splash here, a splash there, and a binge more often than not.

It had been three years since Tommy proposed to her; they still didn't have a wedding date, and now she couldn't compete with his other obsessions.

Though he seemed to observe, sometimes, that she was restless. There were moments when Tommy noticed after all.

Now, he was being especially attentive: "Or how about we take in a show today instead? Or maybe a play? I heard there's a great new show downtown, in Manhattan."

A rush of excitement bloomed in her cheeks; she couldn't help it. "That sounds great! I'll check the listings."

She headed outside and grabbed the *Chronicle* from their stoop to check the times.

The *Chronicle*.

Elaine paused in the doorway, taking in the long list of editors and reporters on the second page. Her gaze lingered on the names of those who had interviewed her. She rubbed the newsprint; its ink bled gray onto her fingers. Her breathing quickened.

At once, Tommy came up behind her, arms around her waist. "Anything look good?" He pushed his stubbled chin inside her neck crevice.

Her cheeks grew hot, and she almost stammered. "What section would the theater schedule be in? I keep forgetting."

"The listings? They're usually towards the back of the paper, aren't they?" He twirled her around and pulled her close to his chest. "You should know, right, babe? I mean, I never read this paper."

He gave her tight, quick kisses up her neck, which sent chills down her spine.

"I'm not sure," she mumbled, her head down.

"Do you want to go out, Elaine? Or do you just want to stay home and save your energy for whatever that place is called? The Moonlight . . . or whatever."

She blushed. "It's the Starlite."

They were still in the doorway when Catherine sauntered in, still decked out in the previous night's outfit.

Catherine threw down her purse and flailed her hands up and down. "Look at what that damn cat dragged in! Here I am!" She giggled at Tommy's arms wrapped around her sister's waist, and Elaine sidled away from him, embarrassed. "You don't have to stop on account of me! I guess I'm just ruining the moment again, aren't I?"

"Not at all, dear sister. In fact, we were just on our way out. We're going to a show downtown. We'll see you later."

Elaine grabbed her coat and Tommy followed, close on her tail.

He chased her down the icy steps, and she couldn't help but laugh. On the sidewalk, they doubled over with laughter and dashed to the bus stop in the cold, breathless.

"You're loads of fun, babe!" His voice was husky behind her.

People swirled around them at the bus stop, the ones with regular jobs and schedules. Tommy came to life, talking up a storm. He could be like a different person sometimes, out and about. He pontificated about the meaning of modern theater and lighting—electricity as symbolism; the self-centered nature of the spotlight; the feeling of watching a character on stage leap into hubris. "You don't have any hubris in you, Elaine. You're all on the face of things—no willful pride. The theater is probably an entirely different experience for you."

He slung his arm around her, and they gazed out over the Brooklyn Bridge and the East River as their bus moved toward the skyscrapers of Manhattan.

Somewhere in that concrete jungle, the *Chronicle* staff was busy at work. Elaine still hadn't told him about her job, even as the copy of the paper rested under her arm. But after they arrived in Manhattan, more distractions awaited. They got off the bus a few blocks away from Sheridan Square, walked to a theater, and purchased tickets for a performance, a show called *Call Me by My Rightful Name*. Although the show was sparsely attended, the actors played their parts with palpable emotion.

"They're good at pretending, aren't they?" Tommy whispered to her.

Elaine nodded as she held her breath, almost forgetting to exhale.

Once the show was over, he led her in the direction of a pub.

"Let's get a bite to eat."

"All right, but we're not drinking anything, dear. Just a nice early dinner."

The pub was a warm tangle of beer steins and polka hits. Tommy ordered the large bratwurst platter and dug in, and the waitress filled his stein with more and more. His eyelids squinted as he got louder and louder with emotion.

Elaine darted glances around the pub as her face grew hot. She claimed that she had to go to the ladies' room; instead, she went on the sneak, telling their waitress to cut off his drink. She gave the waitress a little extra to ensure it—some larger coins from her wallet.

Back at the table, Tommy was waving an empty stein in the air. "Some great service over here, huh? It's like we're not even here!" His cheeks flushed as he slurred and pounded the table with his fist.

The waitress played the part, ignoring him as she served the next table over. As he turned away, raging, Elaine slipped more money into the apron of the waitress.

The waitress turned around, startled, but Elaine gave her the eye and the waitress closed her mouth.

Somehow Elaine managed to drag Tommy out soon after.

"Damn poor service, that place!" he shouted, directly outside the door, and she put her hand over his mouth.

Outside, on the Manhattan streets, the sun was rapidly descending. Peddlers and beggars loitered at every street corner. Although Tommy was plastered, he was still imposing in height. Elaine took his arm and put it around her shoulders as he stumbled down the street. This created a barrier around her person, though he actually lacked the where-withal to protect them from anything.

On the bus back to Brooklyn, he fell asleep on her shoulder. And back at the brownstone, he started round two—pouring shots and pacing, talking to himself. Catherine, sharing space with them again that evening, started in herself, and the two of them ascended in volume, voices escalating over the tinny laughs of *Father Knows Best*.

"How long are you planning on boarding with us rent-free, Catherine?" He had reached the point where his drunkenness turned into random snipes, as angry barbs that he pitched like daggers.

Catherine wasn't yet drunk but haughty, ready for his volley. "How long are you planning to live—I mean *drink*—off your father's money, Tommy?"

"Just as long as *you're* planning on living and drinking on his money, sister-in-law."

Catherine flicked her cigarette and dared him to dig further. "You want me out on the streets?"

The two of them were shrill. Elaine watched them, holding her head. She could leave and head out to the Starlite. But Catherine would try to tag along—and there would be the issue of Tommy, alone in this state. He might meet up with a bad-news buddy and drink to delirium at a pub. He might black out entirely, for hours, and she wouldn't be there to help revive him.

Elaine looked at her watch as it neared nine o'clock.

Tommy was sneering. "What do you want me to do, huh, Catherine? Go be a slob for that radio station again? I'm better than that. They were treating me like a dunce. I could have been promoted to head engineer."

The television blared a commercial for toothpaste—guaranteed to make your smile the *center of attention*.

"Well, maybe you should go back to school and actually get your engineering degree, if you're so damn smart, Tommy."

"Why don't you just have some more to drink, Catherine? It seems like it's fueling all your sensational ideas." Tommy laughed, then stumbled over to yank Catherine's shot glass, but she pulled back.

The glass dropped, and it shattered on the sharp edge of the coffee table. The liquor sank down into the red plush carpet, and the scent of pungent proof rose up to Elaine's nostrils. She would be the one to clean it up, of course.

She plucked the shards from the alcohol-soaked carpet fibers, one by one.

She gritted her teeth.

There was a pencil in her purse. She would write a poem about this experience when she went to the Starlite.

She could be trapped in the brownstone for most of her days, cleaning up his messes.

Or she could allow him to clean up his own messes.

She had things that the world was inviting her to do—beyond the parlor of the brownstone.

Something was welling in Elaine's chest, something too powerful not to release.

Before she could second-guess herself again, she spoke.

"I got a job, Tommy."

It came out of her all at once.

He seemed to wince; she noticed him pulling a fragment of glass out of his hand. Some of his blood dripped down to the floor, red blood on red plush carpet.

"A bandage, please, Elaine."

She went and found a piece of gauze. Catherine adjourned to the kitchen.

He took the gauze. "Thank you," he said, and wrapped his hand. He had turned formal all of a sudden, papering over his inebriation with stolid, practiced speech. He reclined with his feet on the ottoman as she picked up each sharp sliver of glass, forming a pile on the table as the final credits for *Father Knows Best* rolled across the screen.

Elaine moved carelessly, getting the last of the shards, almost cutting herself, too—her physical movements suddenly wide and unthinking now that she had revealed her news.

Tommy talked in a strange, rehearsed tone as he switched off the telly. "Are you ready to retire for the evening, Elaine? I feel rather tired tonight." Then his eyes seemed to sink down low all at once, like a forlorn beagle's.

"All right." Through the lump in her throat, Elaine could barely speak.

Tommy's steps on the wooden floors seemed to have more mass behind them than usual as the two of them went upstairs and he undressed in the dark.

She remained fully clothed, perched on a small wooden stool in the corner. "I'm going to the Starlite tomorrow night, Tommy. I told the girls I was coming."

"*Yeah*. You know something, Elaine? I think that I should start going out, too. Now that you won't be here during the days. Oh, and I wanted to let you know—Mr. Stephens called from the *Chronicle* a few days ago with your reporting instructions. He said that you're to be there two Thursdays from now at nine AM sharp."

In bed, he pinched his cigarette, not looking at her. A cloud of smoke loomed above his head.

"I'm sorry, Tommy."

"I'm sorry as well." He laughed, and she shivered.

He smashed the butt of his cigarette into an ashtray next to their bed, and its orange tip turned to the blackness of night.

16

Lisa

"It's me." Billy's voice sounded boyish. Apologetic, even.

Lisa dragged the phone cord into her room. "Hello," she answered quietly.

"Did you get my note? I left it in your mailbox. I wasn't sure if your mom would throw it away. I know she doesn't like me."

"I got the note."

"So, whaddya say? Wanna meet me for a soda this evening?"

"I can't."

"Why not, babe? I can't tell you how much I've missed you. I can't stop thinking about you. I'm so sorry. I really understand if you don't want to meet me. I never should have stood you up like that. But listen, babe, things at work got really busy, and I could have been fired if I left early that day. I don't want to go into the full thing right now. But maybe we could just meet for a little bit, grab a soda. I really, really want to see you again."

Just a soda.

One soda.

"All right. But I can only stay for a little while."

"Great. I'll meet you at Woolworth's tonight. Is seven all right?"

"Okay." She went to her closet, found her deep-red skirt. The one that made her legs look long and pretty.

She slipped it on and admired herself in the mirror. She puckered her lips and put on a little rouge. She played a little music and danced around.

"Lisa!" her mother yelled from the other room. "I need you to run to the dry grocery. I have a doctor appointment."

It was five o'clock, so she had a little time before Woolworth's.

"Fine, Ma."

"Bring enough to last the week," her mother warned. "Last time, you were away on another one of your trips, and your father and I ran out! No money left, either."

"Yes, Ma."

⌇

At the dry-goods store, stacks of cans shone in colorful assembly. Lisa reached for the corn, green beans, spinach, and tuna and added some extras to her basket for the slowly building stockpile at home. With the tension with the Soviets always in the news, everyone had been warned to maintain a stash. It cost extra money, but her mother always reminded Lisa that the threat was real, and that just because they were poor didn't mean they should have to starve after a nuclear attack. Bay Ridge was far enough from Manhattan to spare them certain annihilation but not distant enough to save them from starvation.

"Put those cans down."

Lisa flared her ears at the command of a man's voice, coming from behind the shelves in the next aisle.

"Donovan, please," a woman pleaded with him; she was low toned, as if she was used to keeping herself that way.

"I told you, I don't like it when you cook that shit. Last time you cooked me that shit, it tasted like dog food!"

The woman's voice lilted. "Would you calm down?"

Lisa leaned over to peek through a gap in the shelves.

"You're going to have to learn how to cook, Jackie!" The man slammed the cans down on the shelf.

A corner of the woman's face was visible between the shelves. She had a delicately sloped nose and a petite incline to her shoulders. She held her body at an angle from his; one side seemed permanently tilted, as if stooped from daily battle. The man roughly grabbed her arm, and she pulled away with a quick tug of her sleeve. In the garish light of day, the woman hadn't looked like herself. She was Jackie, the woman from the Starlite who had run with Lisa when Madeline told everyone to leave—the woman whose makeup had melted in a show of purple bruises.

The dry grocer busied himself behind his counter, pouring quantities of beans onto a sizable scale. He faced away from the ruckus, conveniently escalating his own noise as he emptied bags of dry beans.

Jackie gripped the handles of her hand basket with white knuckles, her load full of heavy cans.

"If I see you put that slop on my plate one more time," her husband bullied, his stout chin set in fury. "One more time . . ." His face drew near Jackie's and he stepped forward, placing the tips of his soles on the rounded toes of her shoe.

He stomped down on Jackie's foot, hard. With a small yelp, Jackie lost her grip on the basket.

Cans rolled across the linoleum, across the aisle.

At that moment, she caught Lisa's eye in a deadened flash of recognition, but she quickly looked away. With a small gasp, she ran to catch the cans as they spread across the floor.

Lisa went around the aisle with a wan smile. "Here, let me help."

"Thank you." Jackie returned a sad smile.

Then their communication was cut off.

"You're as clumsy as hell," Jackie's husband announced as he stood bolt upright, inspecting a can from all sides.

Soon after, the two of them approached the checkout counter to pay for their groceries. Jackie avoided Lisa's eyes.

⌒

At Woolworth's later, Lisa inhaled the familiar scents of talcum powder and wooden music boxes. Near the soda fountain she got whiffs of frankfurters and sugar syrup.

Lisa waited for Billy on one of the high stools at the counter. Her legs dangled from the tall stool as the soda jerk made small talk about the weather. He was busy mixing ice cream sodas. "Haven't seen you in a while!"

"I've been out of town a lot."

"One of Brooklyn's finest, overseas! Representing our borough well, I'm sure."

A kind man—warm, with graying hair. Always up for a chat. Though she wasn't up for a chat. She looked at her shoes as her heels went *tap-tap-tap* on the bars of her stool.

The clock behind the counter read 7:20. She got up, brushed off her coat, and left a dime on the counter for her soft pretzel. She put her arms through her coat sleeves and buttoned up, wending her way out through the aisles.

She would be gone this time.

Forget him.

"Lisa!"

Billy's head popped over a huge arrangement of flowers—roses, baby's breath, pink carnations. He was a walking garden above his construction overalls and heavy brown boots.

He smiled at her brightly beneath sparkling blue eyes. "I'm sorry I'm late." He paused. "I understand if you can't forgive me. It was a little tricky walking down the avenue with my hands full like this." He set the flowers down on the floor. The floral arrangement likely cost the same price as a month's worth of groceries. "What do you say, care for a soda?" he asked.

"Well . . . I am thirsty." Her throat was dry from the salt of her pretzel.

They sat toward the edge of the counter on the high stools. He ordered them cream sodas—their usual.

Lisa's coat was still zipped up, but her legs were sticking out from beneath her skirt.

"Relax, babe, and stay a while." He smiled, with perfect dimples. She took off her coat and watched as his eyes moved to her legs. "Nice gams," he said.

She blushed. "I'll have a water too," she piped up to the soda jerk.

"I really appreciate you coming out tonight." Billy grabbed her hand, and warmth radiated into her body. Then he whispered into her ear, "I'll do anything to make this right."

"Anything?"

"You want me to dance up on this damn counter? I'll do it. You want me to shout your name through the aisles of Woolworth's? I'll do it, babe. Whatever I need to do to prove that I still care." He looked her in the eye, earnest.

"Okay," she said. She looked into the mirrored wall behind the counter, which reflected the two of them. It was almost as though she were watching a television program.

A couple—getting back together.

"You could ask me how I've been doing," she heard herself saying.

"Sure, babe. What *have* you been doing?" He gave her a glorious grin. "I know what I've been doing. Thinking about you—nonstop."

Now she had his full attention. "Well, I just went to Beirut, where I saw the Mediterranean."

"Wow! That's really something, babe. You're really going all over." He was stroking her hand, over and over.

"I fly out again in two days. We're going to Spain. My first time."

"Aw, shucks." He made a *tsk-tsk* with his tongue. "I was hoping we'd be able to go out in two days. I got us tickets to that big band you've been wanting to see. Remember, the one with the thirty-piece orchestra?"

"Johnny and the Trebles?" She kept her eagerness low.

Billy had frequently expressed how much he hated that band—he had always winced when they came on the radio.

"Absolutely. They're playing at this club by Times Square. I got the tickets today. I know you always wanted to see them, right?" A faint smile played on his lips as his blue eyes danced over her face.

She turned away from him. "Yeah, I guess so."

Those tickets would have cost her about a week's paycheck, if she ever bought them.

"I want to take you to see them. If you're still my girlfriend, I mean." He waited for a response, no longer stroking her hand.

She didn't answer for a little while.

Eventually—"Well, I guess I'll go."

As if it was nothing.

Lisa would have to call in sick to the airline to make this show, and her supervisor wouldn't take it so kindly. Yet she had always imagined what it might be like for Billy to spin her around the aisles of the concert hall, and the prospect of fulfilling this fantasy was too tempting to skip.

Billy stroked her hand again, twirling his finger around her thumb. "That's great, babe. I can't wait." The soda jerk set their cream sodas in front of them, fizzy and brown in tall glasses, and they both took sips. "Gesundheit!" he yelled, right before she sneezed—their usual joke.

Then everything was the same as it had been again.

Comfortable.

Billy's calloused hands came to her face, and he stroked the side of her cheek, under her hair, and moved to the warm nape of her neck. The strong roughness of his hands shot an electric current into her body.

Billy's father had been on his way to Paris with another woman. His father had stroked the woman's face like that too.

His father, in a tailored suit, working some job in politics. Slick and sly. Lisa's mother never trusted politicians.

But Billy was sincere, in his construction overalls; although his family had money, he had chosen honest work, with his hands. He was a different man from his father.

⌒

"I knew you would go back to him."

"Ma, please." Lisa turned away.

"You don't seem to realize that looks are temporary. He may be a gorgeous young man, but you also want to make sure that he's a nice guy. And don't be distracted by those things he buys you. You think just because he comes from a well-off family that he will take care of you, Lisa?"

"He has his own job, Ma. Please. I really don't want to hear this right now."

Lisa sought shelter in her room. She felt bloated, her skirt tight around the waist. The stewardesses had regular weigh-ins, and if she gained more than a few pounds, she would go on probation.

Yet another reason to call in sick. She would take a couple of days to try to get her weight back down; it would be a bonus to see Johnny and the Trebles with Billy.

❧

She dialed her supervisor. "I'm so sorry. I'm feeling so queasy right now. I really shouldn't fly out today."

It wasn't so hard to sound sick.

❧

Billy arrived at her apartment the next day, right on time.

"I don't want to be late for you again, babe."

The stubble on his chin rubbed into her neck. He gave her roses, slipped his hand into hers, and said things that made her blush and giggle.

At the Johnny and the Trebles concert, the band played her favorite song. Billy swung her around to dance, his hands reassuringly strong. All the girls stared, as if Lisa was the luckiest among them. The moment felt like a daydream sequence come alive, and the thrilling wail of the lead singer pulsed through her veins as Billy held her tight.

She *was* alive, in the thrilling glow of his presence. She could lose herself in him.

But there was a reminder before they drove home. He came back from the restroom smelling like that cologne of his father's.

He wore a chipper smile—the grin of someone enjoying the evening.

She started to lead into her secret knowledge, in a rush of air, like she couldn't stop it: "Hey, I was wondering—what's been going on with your father? What's he been up to lately?"

Billy adjusted his jacket and smirked. "Politics. The usual. You know my pops."

"Yeah, I do—" Then her throat seized up, and she couldn't say more.

⌒

She spent the next few days in a glorious haze with Billy, on her sick leave. They darted in and out of luncheonettes, went to the movies, and went to third base in the back seat of his car. She had fun, although she was dizzy from skipping meals and drinking too much coffee.

Her skirt felt looser around her waist; her hands skittered downward, feeling the give of the fabric as she drew inward.

There were so many golden moments with Billy, but there were the other ones, too. He wasn't always nice; sometimes he commented about people he didn't even know: that "fat hag" or the "wrinkled raisin." He would laugh in the midst of his jokes, and he sometimes made her laugh in spite of herself. Then he would grab her with his strong arms, muscled from his heavy work at the construction site, and she would tilt her body away for a moment but then let it release.

⌒

Lisa weighed herself before leaving the apartment at six AM. Done with "sick leave"—time to fly out again.

She had lost four pounds. Her supervisor would still give her a stern look, but now she was in the *acceptable* zone, and her job was safe.

On the train and bus, some of the passengers glanced up from their papers to look at her flight uniform. Their outfits were mostly plain compared to her azure-blue Pan Am ensemble. They would take quick glances at her luggage tags; she would hold her upright stance solid. The girls at the Starlite would have asked about the countries on her tags, and she would have shared news of her journeys. Lisa was the new girl, so they would notice her even more. But she hadn't been to the Starlite for a week, and now she would be going away for another week.

When she arrived at the airport, she passed the bench where she had cried about Billy.

The copilot would have called it "a blip on the radar."

"Hey, Lisa!" Her friend Betsy dashed over to her. "We missed you the other day! There was this girl, a substitute. I brought some man the wrong cocktail, and she told Jane on me! Can you believe it?"

"Oh, no!" Lisa had played sick—now here was the consequence.

They headed into the Pan Am room, which bustled with girls getting their weigh-ins before the day's briefing.

Betsy moaned. "I shouldn't have had that doughnut. I forgot about weigh-in today!"

The acid of Lisa's empty stomach licked her throat with fire. Her last three meals had been cups of coffee, taken black.

"Good morning." Mrs. Osbourne, with a neutral expression, instructed them to step on the scales. "Lisa—one twenty-five. Passing moderately. Betsy—one twenty-nine, passing just barely."

Betsy gave a horrified tug at her waistband. Lisa, meanwhile, sighed with relief. She looked down with a little smile at the gold locket around her neck. She was under the weight limit for now, and she would hopefully be married in the next couple of years.

Stewardesses were forced to retire at age thirty-two, or when they got married. Lisa didn't want to be kicked out for her weight or for her age. She wanted to be kicked out because she had a man.

17

Elaine

Elaine would start her new job at the *Chronicle* in three days. She spent the afternoon on Nostrand Avenue, shopping for work ensembles with Gloria, her friend from the poetry circle at the Starlite.

Gloria was bowled over by the fact that she was now associated with someone who worked at the *Chronicle*. She couldn't stop talking about Elaine's luck. "It's funny, Elaine. I thought it was a big deal for me to get a secretary job at Dr. McAllister's office. But—*my God*—you'll be working at the *Chronicle*. I don't even think I can get over it." Gloria grabbed a burgundy leather purse from a shelf; then she turned, wide-eyed, after a glance at the purse's price tag. "Oy. This purse is certainly *not* made with the salary of a doctor's secretary in mind."

Elaine picked up the purse and set it back down. "Nor is this purse designed for the salary of a fact-checker at the *Chronicle*."

"Really? I thought anyone at the *Chronicle* would be doing really well. I mean, it's one of the biggest papers in the country!" Gloria furrowed her brow, seeming dubious. "You know, Elaine, I really won't think you're bragging if you tell me you'll be doing well."

"There's nothing to brag about, dear. I'll just be contributing some money to the house—that's all."

Gloria was baffled. "Who would have thought?" Then she laughed. "I thought you would be rolling in the dough soon enough. Oh well, no matter—I still want to work for the *Chronicle* one day."

Elaine grabbed a high-waisted skirt from a rack. "Maybe you can. If you really want it, maybe you can make it happen." She held up the skirt to her body. "So, what do you think about this one here? What does this skirt say to you?"

"I think it says *schoolmarm*. Is that the look you're going for?"

Elaine stared at the skirt for a long minute, considering; then she broke into giggles. "I knew I could trust you to be honest with me."

☙

After a few hours of shopping, Elaine found a couple of nice outfits and a new purse in patent leather. A professional style.

Everything looked sharp—assured.

Once she arrived home, she donned her new outfits and looked at herself in the mirror. She pretended to be the same as the clothes. Polished. Ready.

She was home, but Tommy was nowhere to be found. He hadn't left a note either.

She walked up and down the hallway in her new shoes, breaking them in. Her feet ached, squeezed into unnatural angles.

But the echoing emptiness of the brownstone was more painful.

Tommy hadn't talked much during the past couple of weeks, since it had come out into the open about her job.

He had worked more on his gadgets at home and stayed out more often.

And at nine tonight, he still hadn't returned to the brownstone. But Catherine was back at the house, so Elaine straightened her brow and joined her in the kitchen for a late supper.

"How are you, dear sis?" Distracted, she peered out the window, as though Tommy might be there.

"Just dandy! But you look a little . . . off. Where's the man?"

"We're not married. I don't keep track of him."

The absurdity of her comment fell short of Catherine, who—absorbed with herself—switched the topic to a singing gig she'd gotten at a wedding. "Even the greats had to start somewhere!" she chirped.

"That's great, Cat." Elaine stabbed her food with her fork.

Catherine looks at her sideways. "You don't seem happy for me!"

"I'm very happy for you!"

"Well, thanks—" But she appeared suspicious. "Hey, but really— you don't know what Tommy's up to this evening?"

"I haven't a clue."

"He didn't tell you where he was going?"

"No." He would be in any one of innumerable pubs, slapping the table, foaming at the mouth.

His absence was his form of revenge.

She'd gone behind his back to get a job. And she went to the Starlite quite often.

Elaine cupped her chin in her hands, moving her weary eyes to the door that wouldn't open—no matter how much she willed Tommy to come home. She could almost fall asleep at the table as Catherine droned on and on about her dream to be the biggest jazz singer in New York.

Then Catherine went back to talking about Tommy, playing the part of an adult. "You know—I really don't think he should be going out drinking, Elaine. Tommy gets so crazed when he's plastered."

"You get crazy when you drink too, Catherine."

"I know how to rein it in."

Elaine cleared her throat and shrugged. "Well, I guess I get pretty crazy too when I go out. So, he's just doing the same thing."

"You've never had more than two drinks in a row. Please. And you never get crazy."

"I had two and a half once." Elaine was on the defensive. "Please, dear sister, put our leftovers in the fridge for Tommy, so he'll have something to eat when he comes home."

She had been trying for a prework routine of early bedtimes—not late nights at the social club, especially with some strange man lurking about. But as her sister chattered on and on, Elaine bit her fingernails, waiting.

Finally, her hand moving automatically, Elaine dialed the Starlite.

"Madeline speaking!"

Madeline's voice was startlingly high-pitched with uproarious laughter; it was as though she had been caught in the middle of some grand fun.

"It's Elaine. Just wanted to see if you're hosting tonight."

"Absolutely! It's comedy night. Come on down and join us! It's been a while since we've seen you."

"I'll be there in a little bit."

It would set a precedent, when Tommy came home, to find her gone. It was like a game: who could stay out the longest, who could live it up the most. Maybe it was the end. No bickering or nasty arguments. Instead, disappearances, as they flickered out of each other's lives.

In front of the mirror above her bureau, Elaine freshened her makeup, her cheeks naturally flushed.

She yelled downstairs to Catherine. "Are you coming tonight?"

"I'm watching the telly. I need to take it easy—rest my singing voice." Catherine made pretentious little hums with her throat, scales and *la-ti-da*s.

"Fine," Elaine said, then dashed out the door before anything could stop her.

⌒

She drove to the Starlite; she wouldn't cross paths with Tommy out in the world, coming off the bus.

Once she arrived at the shop, she pounded the door, and a stray cat circled her ankles.

Madeline surprised her and yanked the door open with a whoosh of air.

Elaine was breathless. "My key wasn't working." All the regulars had a key.

"That's because we changed the locks, my dear." She ushered her inside, though they remained near the door, observing a performance from the back of the room. Others in the audience were already seated in folding chairs, facing a makeshift stage of garment boxes. Sandra was a mime—in an invisible box, its walls defined by the palms of her hands. Her box shattered and dropped her into an invisible boat, where she rowed with comic exaggeration against wind and waves. The whole room was in hysterics as Sandra built up an evident sweat, paddling on a river to nowhere.

For a brief moment, Elaine joined them in laughter, but she was out for a reason, and her hand clutched a key that didn't work.

"Why did you change the locks?"

"Well—" Madeline moved them to a corner, behind a display of hats. "I'm almost positive that Fred has been trying to get a look in here. I bet he wants to see what's going on in my dress shop at night. It *had* to be Fred—I saw him real quick, but I know that ugly forehead of his. I don't know what he's up to. I just want to keep safe." Madeline brushed invisible crumbs off her skirt and smiled, then shifted Elaine back to the audience. "Here, have a seat," she urged.

Someone else on stage was telling knock-knock jokes. The jokes were so outlandishly childish that the laughter built up as a prickly mockery of itself. The women on the ramshackle stage got more and more slaphappy as the night wore on, and even Elaine started to roll into hysterics along with them.

After the show, Harriet initiated a scavenger hunt. She asked Elaine to write little clues for the hidden objects, a task that served as a welcome focus for her attention.

Elaine set herself up in a corner, surrounding herself in bits of folded paper on the floor as she dreamed up two-liners to lead people on the right track in the hunt. These small acts of creation soothed her.

Just a few minutes into her solitary pursuit, Lisa ran up to her, startling Elaine out of her reverie. "Hey, Elaine! I was looking all over for you."

"Hello, dear!" Elaine laughed. "You surprised me! Back from your latest trip already?"

"Yeah, I flew back in this afternoon. Took a little nap and decided to head over. Whatchya doing over here?"

"Just creating clues for a scavenger hunt. Very important business, you know."

"It sounds like it! Do you need some help?"

"Surely! Do you want to help me come up with clues, or would you rather fold some papers?"

"I'll take the folding part. My clues would probably just confuse people." She laughed.

They made a neat assembly line—the two of them cross-legged on the floor, writing and folding. In an hour's time, they managed to produce dozens of the little clues, which lay scattered on the floor around them.

Elaine stood up, brushing off her skirt. "I suppose we should get a basket to carry these over to the front."

"Or we could just do this instead . . ."

Lisa winked, grabbing a handful of clues and tossing them up in the air. The papers fluttered all around them, like so many snowflakes.

Elaine stared in disbelief. "Did you *really* just do that?"

"I do believe that I did!" With a smirk, Lisa assumed her own proper accent and grabbed a greater handful, scattering them farther.

"I don't know that I should have introduced you to this place. You're trouble!" Elaine squealed. The two of them scooped up bits of paper, raining them down on each other, until the other ladies saw and had to join in too. They all laughed wildly and created a mess, and Elaine even delighted in her own cries: "It's a blithering disaster! A disaster!"

By the end of the evening, she was caught up in it all. The Starlite had worked its magic on Elaine yet again.

She stayed overnight, bunking on a cot like a giggling member of a slumber party. Cynthia kept arranging her hair into various braids and giving Elaine a pocket mirror to see what she thought.

But her voice soon changed in fright. "Elaine," she hissed suddenly. "I think I see something."

"What?" Elaine bolted up.

"I just saw something in the mirror."

"What?"

"I think it was a rat."

"Where?"

"Look down there!" She pointed to the shadows, at the feet of some-one's cot in the far corner.

Elaine closed her eyes. "That's just a ball of stockings."

"That ball of stockings sure has a long tail!" They stared, and the ball with the tail scurried into the shadows. "We need to catch it!" she hissed.

"And do *what* with it? We're locked in for the night."

"Yeah."

The two of them repositioned themselves on their cots and squeezed their eyes shut, not daring to open them until daylight illuminated their lids.

With all the chatter, Elaine got an hour or two of sleep. At the break of day, she stepped out onto the sidewalks of Brooklyn Heights, unsteady on her feet. But she exerted herself to drive with caution, which required her to stare at the road almost unblinkingly.

Back in the brownstone, Tommy was asleep in their bedroom, his shirt stained, atop the blankets.

Elaine undressed and gingerly got into bed as a sleeping Tommy rotated his body toward her.

His scent was alcohol and fried foods, and he was snoring. She inhaled his breath as though she might determine how much he'd drunk.

Elaine's eyes adjusted, and she caught sight of his face in the light that filtered in through the blinds. She drew her breath in horror; a sizable gash glistened red on his forehead. In the shadows of the early morning, it didn't seem that the blood was fresh.

Wordlessly, she rose from bed to get a bandage. She went back to him, and his glossy hair slipped through her fingers as she tried to get a light hold on his head.

Still asleep, Tommy tilted his body away from her.

⌒

The next evening, Elaine's friends sat in the small circle of chairs in their literary circle.

"So good to see you, hon." They kissed her cheek, and for the moment she was enveloped and safe.

Normally she led the circle, but in the two weeks since finding out about her job, Elaine hadn't visited the Starlite as much, so Gloria had taken over for her. "I figured we would all take turns reading," Gloria said. "Then we could get to some books."

There was an art to deciding what to share, how much to reveal. The women had decisions to make each time they removed scraps of paper from their purses and unfolded them, each time they flipped through well-used notebooks, trying to find the right things.

"Does anyone have anything?" Gloria asked.

"I think I do—let me just dig for a little bit." Elaine's purse had become a mess, full of bits of scrawled poems on napkins. "I have a little something."

At the same time, in the back of the Starlite, the women danced, joked, and gossiped, and the volume grew louder. Madeline stood by the door in a defensive upright position—arms crossed over the finely tailored bodice of her dress.

There was an edge to the air that night. The ladies talked louder than usual. Their movements were more exaggerated, demonstrative.

"I wrote this piece the other day." Elaine cleared her throat. The women in the circle leaned in, trying to hear her.

The Magnifying Glass

Underneath the sharp focus,
Inside the curve of your mouth,
There is an intention,
Which I lose,
Or maybe you've never given it to me.
Each day it's something else.

She had more, but she didn't read it. Everything was about Tommy, the tempestuous roller coaster of his moods, his magnetism. Everything was encoded into metaphor but obvious to someone who really knew—like Catherine, who was nearby, warming up her voice before she sang them some jazz.

She got the commentary from the circle:

"That was great, Elaine!" Cynthia patted her on the back.

Gloria was lost, pondering. "It left me with this strong feeling, like a sort of longing."

"I think it's like when something draws you towards somebody and you can't stop yourself, you just can't get enough." Harriet nodded knowingly.

"It's like Bernard, like that character I'm dating. There's something crazy about him, but I just can't help myself!" Cynthia continued. "He's so on and off, all these highs and lows. I hate it! But he's gorgeous, and so romantic! What should we do with these men?"

They had understood, though she hadn't said anything direct. Elaine excused herself and made her way through the clusters of women and clothing racks to Madeline.

Madeline was sealing the door shut. She tightened a series of dead bolts and triple-checked the lock on the doorknob. She startled to see Elaine hovering over her shoulder, but she flashed a cheerful smile as her hand rested on the knob.

"I had to catch you before everyone else." Elaine was breathless. "I was wondering if I could talk to you—about Tommy, you know . . ."

"Of course, darling." Madeline was gracious and brought Elaine aside, behind the cash register. She lifted two cocktails from the top of the counter. "Care for a sip?"

"No, thank you."

"What can I offer you, dear?" She sounded distant.

"I need your advice. I just got this stellar job, so now I can leave Tommy. But I don't know how to do it. I mean, what if he comes looking for me and tries to get me back? And what if I leave him and he—I don't know, gets hurt? Or hurts himself? Then it would be all my fault."

Madeline shook her head. "You're always welcome here, whenever you need to stay—if it's a social club night or not, you can feel free to bunk at night until you've got yourself a steady place." Her eyes flickered away, and then she smiled at Elaine again.

"Thank you, Madeline. Because—" She paused. "I'm not happy."

Elaine bit her lip and turned away.

"If you're not happy, you need to change something." Madeline turned to face her fully; Elaine finally had her complete attention.

The small creases near Madeline's eyelids were the marks of someone wise. Someone who understood. Someone who had gone through it all and survived.

Yet soon Madeline's eyelids fluttered back to the door in wariness, and the spell of her attention was broken.

She had done what she could to barricade them in for the night.

The ladies were light and carefree, twisting and twirling like there was nothing to fear.

Once the song finished, Madeline wandered over to the record player to shuffle through the albums. The women called out their requests, but she shook her head and continued to riffle through the pile.

Then there was a sound. Something unnatural.

A high-pitched disturbance—

A sharp, metallic clang.

A sickening crash of glass. A split-second assault on the eardrums.

The burst of something shattering.

Near the feet of a window mannequin: a pointed lump of concrete. It was a chunk of asphalt, with tiny sharp stones that poked out from its edges.

The explosion of glass had deafened them into silence.

Shards of glass glinted up from the carpet, cutting a swath in the sanctuary as nighttime air blew in through a large, jagged hole in the window.

It was dark outside, with nobody to be seen.

The ladies stared at Madeline, who was quiet.

She was ghastly pale, and so were they.

18

Madeline

They didn't leave.

Anyone could have been out there, and none of them dared to go out on the streets.

They huddled in a quiet mass in the back of the storefront until the cops arrived.

It had been an attack on the face of the Starlite.

The front window had shattered into bits; the chunk of concrete lay stone-cold at the foot of a mannequin.

The cops had arrived. "You're in New York City, ladies, not at some barnyard soiree." They were shocked that a group of women would gather late at night without some sort of guard. But they agreed to put an extra officer on duty for the remainder of the night, especially when Madeline told them that men had been peeking in over the past several weeks.

She didn't say that one of the men might have been Fred.

She wouldn't be a paranoid ex-wife.

After the police left the Starlite, the ladies bunched together again, in a silence interrupted by whispers, as the frigid air entered through the hole in the window.

Harriet was the first to speak: "I think maybe we should all chip in for a guard. Then we'll have the protection we need."

Next to the glass, Madeline hunched down.

She crouched with her knees together, picking up shards. She examined the fragments as though something might change—as though the glass would magically form once again into a front window. Then she reached for another shard, which pierced her skin.

"Shit!" Madeline shrieked. The ladies gaped at her in shock as the illusion of her composure shattered into bits. She sucked on her bleeding finger and knotted her hands together, pushing in the wound. But soon she looked up at them and drew her lips together. She assumed her normal voice once more, speaking to Harriet. "I don't know about a guard, darling. That sounds very expensive."

Everyone continued to stare at Madeline as she grew quiet. She closed her eyes and rested her forehead on her hands.

She looked small as she sat on the floor.

Silence overtook them once more.

Inaction struck the group. Exhalations of quiet followed the shock.

The women shuffled in place—some of them sat in the back of the storefront, far away from the glass.

We have to do something . . . They whispered to each other, and they watched her as she sat frozen, her hands seemingly sewn together as she stared unblinkingly at the jagged hole.

Then at once, a current swelled upward, spurred by a single offer:

"I can give a dollar!"

Then: "I'll give twenty-five cents!" "I can give two dollars!"

Offers of money flew around the room in a cascade of generosity.

Madeline kept her head down, unable to meet their eyes. She didn't answer at first; then she struggled to speak. "That's very beautiful and generous of you, ladies. But I don't want to take your money individually." She wouldn't be a *cause*. "I might have to charge an entry fee instead. We'll see what I'll do. Maybe I'll get a guard."

But now she had declared them defenseless, in need of outside protection.

"I can ask my brother!"

"I can ask my boyfriend!"

Offers of guards popped up in quick succession, but she couldn't talk about it.

One of the cops had parked his squad car outside, providing surveillance for the rest of the night and an endless loop of silent red sirens through the broken window.

19

Elaine

Elaine arrived back at the brownstone in the wee hours of the morning. Next to Tommy, it was stuffy in the bedroom. The old radiator pumped with too much intensity; she could barely breathe, and the heat of his sleeping body put her over the edge.

That rock could have smashed one of their skulls. Elaine held her own head now.

Madeline was obviously a target; they all were. Who were they to frolic in the moonlight and believe they could?

Madeline always gave pause at the doors, at the windows. She was always on the lookout, but Elaine had missed the signs because of her own distraction.

She was under her own daily siege, as a moth to Tommy's flame.

He shifted over with a pained grunt, and his bloodshot eyes confronted her with eerie intensity. "Why, oh Elaine, why?" he mumbled, then closed his eyes again. His arm rested on the bandage.

It was the day before she started her new job. But her blood was clogged with Tommy; at the same time, her head was frozen on that concrete near the foot of the mannequin.

She crept downstairs to escape, to have a sit in the front room. The soft glow of the sun suffused the entire room in light yellow. It could almost be peaceful; she could almost lounge on this padded chair in the quiet of the morning; but instead she closed her eyes, and the deep red of her lids turned into an image of Tommy's forehead.

Nearby, Catherine was sprawled out in her skirts, asleep on the couch.

Outside, the day had started—some neighbors scraped ice from their windshields, others walked briskly down the sidewalk. Elaine would be out with them tomorrow, off to her job to contribute to one of the world's most important newspapers.

She made her tea extra strong this morning. Three tea bags in one cup, steeping for ten minutes.

She would ring her parents in England; they would be proud to hear of her new job. It would at least be a distraction to talk to them.

The operator patched her through, with the usual broken rings as her call pushed through the transatlantic cable.

"Fabulous timing, Elaine! You seem to have a knack for knowing when to call. We were just about to leave the flat for a little tea."

Elaine twitched her nose. "Sounds great, Mum."

"What brings you to calling, dear? We haven't heard from you in a while."

Yet her mother had sent her and Catherine to America when they were teenagers—to a boarding school, to "teach them independence."

"I have some good news to share. I've gotten a job at the *Chronicle*. I'll be a fact-checker."

"Oh—really, dear?" Her mother seemed distracted.

"I start tomorrow."

"I suppose that means you're finished with Tommy, then?"

"No—why would it?"

"Usually an engaged woman doesn't just look around for work. Especially, well—Tommy has some money, doesn't he, darling? Didn't you tell me about an inheritance?"

Always about the money. Never about her.

"I've always wanted to work for the *Chronicle*, Mum. I'm really excited," she said, as the joy fell out of her in clumps, like cotton from a stuffed animal. "Can I talk to Dad?"

Her father always read the *Chronicle*; he always had it air-mailed to London so he could check the prices of commodities. He would certainly understand the enormousness of her accomplishment.

"Your father's a bit occupied at the moment, Elaine, but I'm sure he'll send his best wishes."

Tommy was waking up; his heavy steps led him down the stairs from the bedroom.

"Look out for my package in the post, dear. A birthday gift. And be sure to give Catherine our regards. Tell her to ring us up one of these days. Very sorry, Elaine, but we really have to get going—we told our friends we would meet them at two thirty sharp."

" 'Bye, Mum." An emptiness hovered inside the bulk of the receiver as soon as she set it down.

Tommy had moved to the breakfast table, where he was cradling his bandaged forehead. "You're up early, Elaine. Aren't you still on your *vacation* time? I'm surprised you're not using it."

"Why don't you just go back to sleep, Tommy?"

"You just want to get rid of me all the time, don't you?" Tommy laughed. "Well, guess what—I'm going to stay with you this whole day. Gotta spend some time with my lady before she heads out on her own."

Elaine shrugged. "Fine. It'll be a lot of watching me clean."

"I'll do some cleaning too. I guess I need to do my fair share around here, right?" He smiled, rubbing her shoulders.

"Suit yourself."

He was trying to prove something to her. It was another game. She pulled away from his touch.

Then she made them breakfast. Sausage links and eggs. They dined in the dawning light of day. Tommy removed the bandage from his head and placed it on the table. The thin red slash across his forehead glistened in a coating of sweat.

Elaine gulped; her eyes locked on his head. If he wanted to tell her, he would. She was also hiding the truth of last night. The attack on her social club.

"If you're wondering about this on my head—I had a little fight with some of the boys. I think they understand my point now," he laughed. "They surely won't mess with me tonight."

A shiver passed through Elaine's body, yet she smiled brightly.

"So, first, I'd like to give a good scrubbing to the bathtub; then we need to organize our bookshelves, and do the ironing for the week."

A smile of mischief played across Tommy's lips. "Absolutely, my darling."

He sprung from his chair with a sudden movement, and Elaine watched wide-eyed as he opened the linen closet, grabbed one of her aprons and a pair of her cleaning gloves, and donned them with gleeful abandon. "Tell me what to do, boss!" He smirked.

Elaine formed her lips into a straight line, like his scar. "The scrubbing soap is under the sink."

"You didn't know how well I can clean. I can be your regular man of the house."

Soon he had scrubbed their claw-foot bathtub in vigorous circles. She observed the same kind of intensity he brought to their lovemaking, his gadgets, and his benders.

And she scrubbed their sink. His magnetism kept her watching this damaged but concentrated specimen of a man.

The rest of the day followed in housekeeping tasks, and somehow as the dinner hour drew near, they laughed together, and she watched herself drift to him again; they hugged and kissed, and it all was natural and easy, like nothing was wrong at all.

Then the sun set and it was evening. In the fading light of day, he started to run his hands over her waist.

But she glanced through the window, at the darkness, and pulled her body away from him.

"You know I'm starting my job tomorrow. I'll have to wake up very early."

"That's right, Elaine. I guess I'll be seeing you around, then." He gave a half smile, poked his fork into a chunk of tomato on her chopping board, and tossed it into his mouth.

Then he donned his coat and left.

⌒

Elaine tossed and turned all night. And at one point she started to dress, to head over to the Starlite, even though it was almost midnight and surely Madeline wouldn't have opened the social club so soon after the vandalism. But her skin itched from all sides, as though thousands of tiny ants surrounded her, trying to lift her up from bed.

The hours shrunk, closing in on the time when her alarm would ring for work, and she screwed her eyes shut, fading in and out of sleep. She would tell the ladies at the Starlite that she hadn't gone to work. Tommy was unaccounted for.

You're not married to him. That's what Madeline would say, if she told her the full truth. *You can leave. You can stay in the Starlite until you get on your feet.*

Madeline would make such a generous offer; she would even welcome her company, though Elaine didn't need the help. Elaine wouldn't take it, anyway.

She could do this job. She'd set herself to do this job.

But she got very little sleep.

⌒

When the alarm clock rang, Tommy was still out.

It was her big day.

Elaine wrenched herself out of bed; she looked nothing like somebody ready for their first day at the *Chronicle*, with purple circles beneath her sagging lids.

She gave herself generous dabs of makeup to cover the exhaustion. It didn't conceal all traces, but it was an improvement.

She couldn't eat breakfast; she didn't even try. She packed up a little lunch, took a few sips of tea, and headed out the door.

The morning chill bit her exposed nose sharply—but here she was, on the sidewalk like everyone else, walking to the bus stop as her heels clicked on the concrete. She was heading somewhere important.

But once she was seated on the bus, she took furtive glances at every bar or pub on the route. In the distance, a tall man with dark hair stood outside one of them, smoking, but he wore the apron of a bartender.

Her bus neared the outskirts of Brooklyn and picked up speed. All around her, the other passengers flipped through their copies of the morning paper.

She was almost at the *Chronicle*, her dream job. This newspaper carried significant import for the States, for Great Britain—her motherland—and for nations around the globe.

She was doing something *big* with her life.

As the bus zipped over the bridge to Manhattan, Elaine allowed herself to stop looking for him; instead, she focused her gaze on her own destination.

PART THREE

Indiscretions

20

Lisa

March 1962

The plane's engines roared to life. Lisa usually froze during this moment to linger in the anticipation of lift-off. The passengers were always subdued as they waited to ascend.

But someone next to Lisa buckled a seat belt, and the metallic clink echoed with the vibrations of the shattering window at the Starlite. She had been searching the Starlite for Elaine when its window exploded. Someone had screamed about an attack. Her legs were frozen into place as others ran toward the back of the store. A thin shard of glass cut into her knee as she knelt down to help Harriet, who was bent over in shock.

The storefront glass had detonated on impact; any one of them could have been killed.

Now, Lisa's plane began its ascent. The ground below seemed to shift as the wing started to turn. A deep shudder jerked her back, but she had to commence her usual services; the passengers would need her attention momentarily. Taking a brief opportunity to pause as they flew higher and higher, Lisa gazed out over the bay, and something caught her eye: a dark wisp of something above the marsh, like a plume of smoke. But their jet tilted in the other direction, so she couldn't see.

"Did you see that?" Lisa nudged Betsy, who was otherwise occupied. Then she dismissed it, and turned her attention instead to the first round of drink service.

On the whole, the flight was uneventful, other than the disturbance of a screaming baby, whose wails sent the passengers in her section into a foul mood. Lisa dug for the supply of earplugs in a back cabinet and handed them out to everyone, then searched for some plastic cups to give the baby as a toy. "Here you go!" she cooed to the baby, handing her one of the yellow cups.

The baby smiled and grabbed for it, and her young mother seemed relieved. They were seated in the same row where Billy's father had sat with his mistress, and the seat was now covered in spit-up, an appropriate liquid to mask the scent of Billy's father's cologne, which hadn't yet faded off the fabric of the headrest.

They landed in London in the early evening. A buffet supper awaited the flight crew in the dining room of their hotel.

When it was time to eat, the group sat down for their meal together, as they always did, but the head pilot sat at the head of the table. This wasn't a man of particular pretention; he usually reserved his position of command for his seat in the cockpit.

He wore a grim expression today.

After the crew had gotten their food, he tapped his glass with a fork, making some loud *ting-tings*, and everyone sat at attention.

"I have something to tell you all." His usual grin was nowhere to be seen, and his eyes were blank. "There's been a crash. A plane went down in the swamp at Idlewild. An American Airlines flight."

Lisa had seen the plume of smoke.

A crash.

Her skin erupted in dozens of prickles.

"I don't have any further details. Control didn't want to create additional fear."

She had been oblivious for the entire flight. Not knowing what she had just seen in the bay, her ears had still been ringing with the scene at the Starlite, pieces of glass shattering into the club.

She had hovered over the baby in the seat of Billy's cheating father and inhaled the musk scent of a blouse covered in a sheen of spit-up.

There was a plane crash. That could have been her, going down in the swamp, in a plume of smoke. She had applied to work at American Airlines some time ago.

"Oh my God."

Betsy was the first to start sobbing. The copilot drummed his fingers on the table. Even Jane was incredibly pale.

"What happened to the people?" Lisa asked, in a small voice.

"We don't know yet."

The pilot put his head down on the table and held it between his hands. He started to choke—an unidentifiable sound. It was the second time in her life that Lisa had heard a grown man weep.

None of them could eat.

Lisa trembled, and her fork fell to her plate in a spasm. Soon she withdrew to her hotel room.

A small envelope was attached to her door—a telegram from her mother, asking if she was okay.

Her mother must be in a frenzy; telegrams weren't cheap.

There was nothing from Billy.

She turned on the television and switched the dial to the BBC.

A catastrophic crash. No survivors.

"I don't want to," she said out loud to herself. Then she picked up the phone and had the operator put her through to her mother.

"Lisa?" her mother hyperventilated. "I'm just so happy that you're okay. I don't know how I could have gone on." She cried, in chokes that rushed through the static of the phone line. "Those poor people. Those poor people."

It could have been me. "I'm sorry, Ma."

She was in a dangerous line of work, far away from home, every other week.

Her mother didn't respond to this, gulping, catching her breath. "This phone call is expensive, I know. Let's hang up now. I love you, Lisa."

They hung up.

The BBC switched to another topic, something about Parliament. Things didn't seem to matter much to people unless they lived right near where it happened.

She had seen that plume of smoke.

The fire of the dying.

There was still no word from Billy. She got out of bed, gazing out the window over London, at lights that sparkled all around. Life still went on somehow—people here across the Atlantic, with all the other things that they were doing.

Elaine was from London. She could have grown up in one of those buildings. Lisa had seen Elaine briefly at the Starlite last night, before the window exploded. She had talked a bit more about her fancy new job at the *Chronicle*, speaking in a strangely distracted way as she twisted the huge rock on her finger.

Elaine's man had given her such a beautiful ring. He definitely would have checked to see if Elaine was okay.

21

Elaine

The *Chronicle* lobby was packed. People milled everywhere, and Elaine moved through the crowd to board the elevator.

Nobody talked, as everyone seemed to be in a strange, quiet rush. They stared at the ceiling, the elevator buttons, and their watches. They exited the elevator in a hurry to their respective floors.

She got off at the fifth floor. Nobody was in plain sight.

The corridor was empty and smelled like a cleaning chemical.

Elaine peeled her ears to search for signs of activity. The sound of a few voices filtered through a doorway. She meandered down a hallway and stumbled upon rows of women crammed in one room.

They sat with long pads of paper, scrawling notes in shorthand as a tall, blonde woman announced names and subjects from a roster. There had been a horrific plane crash at Idlewild, and most of the articles would be about that. Everybody raised their arms as the woman announced the specific topics of each article and made the final assignations.

They were all fact-checkers, getting their work for the day.

"You must be the new girl." The blonde woman shook Elaine's hand with brisk efficiency. "Mr. Stephens told me you were starting today. You arrived in the midst of our article assignation. Whoever doesn't claim an article gets stuck with whatever's left over."

"I'll gladly take the leftovers!" Elaine's voice was too high-pitched; the other women glared, and her neck grew hot.

The blonde woman spoke curtly. "After these ladies have picked, you'll have yours."

Elaine took a step back. The *Chronicle* was not a friendly social club; she would need to tame her outward eagerness. She was now employed at a significant newspaper, reporting on important topics.

The others got their articles and scurried to their duties, leaving Elaine and the head fact-checker alone. "I'm Mrs. Ainsley," she announced. "I'll be showing you the ropes for the first half of the day. You should be ready to go at it on your own after lunch break—you seem like a bright enough girl."

She led Elaine out of the room, to a desk near the back of the main space. It had a phone, a lamp, and a typewriter—catty-corner to another desk, where a woman held a receiver to her ear and fluently chatted in another language.

"You speak French, correct?" Mrs. Ainsley tossed a look over her shoulder to Elaine, who nodded with a thin-lipped smile. "Next to you will be Nia—she speaks Greek. We have a multilingual staff so we can field calls with non-English speakers." Elaine hadn't used much French since she graduated from college eight years prior, aside from the poetry she sometimes read with Tommy. "I'm going to walk you through your day: you'll get your article, as you saw happening this morning; then you'll return to your desk and ring the reporter of the article, whose extension should appear on the slip of paper. If the reporter doesn't answer the phone, you'll locate him in the building. If a reporter is occupied when you approach him, you must not interrupt; instead, flash him a hello sign and return in ten minutes. Reporters *do not* like fact-checkers who lurk around their desks."

"Yes, madam," Elaine replied.

"Once you've ascertained your sources, you're under strict deadline. You know we have our early and late editions, and everything needs to be checked and approved well before printing."

They went off on the tour of the building, which had ten floors. Elaine's head spun at the convoluted alleyways of desks, chairs, hallways, and offices.

Afterward, she attempted to work on her article, but soon she got lost, and her eyes darted through the unfamiliar building in a hopeless state, as though she would never find her way through the mazes of halls and desks. It took nearly thirty minutes to track down the reporter. Finally, she completed the assignment and began to fact-check another article about the governor's race in New Jersey. She called the campaign offices multiple times before reaching a person who could answer her questions.

She ate lunch at her desk and absentmindedly scrawled words on a scrap of paper.

Lost.

Empty.

All at once, her phone started to ring off the hook. She typed notes with studied taps of her fingers and yanked the papers with quick pulls from the typewriter. She scanned to check the accuracy of figures, budgetary estimates, and percentage points. The familiarity of detailed work flooded back to her senses—this was something comfortable, at least.

When it was all done, she gave a quick exhalation of accomplishment. She ran down the stairs to the sixth floor and speed-walked to the desk of the news editor.

He bellowed out, "Cutting it close to deadline!" The portly man had a cigar between his teeth, and he seemed to be laughing and shouting at the same time.

Elaine blushed. "Sorry, I'm new."

"Of course, dear! I remember you from that interview—lost your shoe in the Rockaways." He took the cigar from his mouth. "Don't mind me. I get all the girls confused sometimes."

She nodded, as if she understood *perfectly*; then she handed over her work with a clammy hand and rushed back to her desk.

The Greek woman at the next desk was off the phone. "Looks like you had a busy day!"

"I did!"

"Well, that's usually every day around here!" The woman gave a friendly laugh. "I'm Nia. Pleased to make your acquaintance! Hey, do you want to head down to the pizza parlor when we clock out? I have a hankering for a slice."

Elaine fingered the scrap of paper on her desk, the one with the words *lost* and *empty*. "I'm really sorry; I can't."

She would go back to the brownstone—see if Tommy had returned.

"All right then. Maybe another time! We're so busy around here, we usually don't have time for socializing during the day. We try to get together after work if we can."

Elaine had rejected her first social invitation at the job, but none of the other fact-checkers could possibly have a man like Tommy at home.

Then she looked down at herself, taking in her own professional ensemble, her neat skirt and polished heels. Nobody could surmise anything based on *her* appearance, so it might be impossible to make guesses about any of them.

⁓

When she arrived back to the brownstone, Tommy was in bed, sleeping. He didn't budge in response to her footsteps.

She stood over him, searching for bruises, any telltale signs of what he'd been doing or where he'd been. Her only evidence took the shape of scents: cigarette smoke and booze.

He woke, hours later, when at last she laid herself down to sleep. He shot up from bed as though startled by her gentle presence. He coughed and sputtered.

Elaine's own voice was slurred with exhaustion. "Oh God. Where were you last night?"

It took him a moment to respond.

Then he laughed. "What's there for me to do if you're not around, Elaine?"

"How about you get a job? That'll be something to do."

"You actually think I could hold down a job?" He laughed again, briefly.

The other *Chronicle* women had seemed so content. Smiles nestled into the corners of their lips as they made phone calls with professional ease, and their fingers danced gracefully as they typed up their notes with tall-postured efficiency. They couldn't possibly be well postured if they had to deal with something like this.

But she had looked efficient too, even as she scrawled her chaotic feelings onto pieces of scrap paper, prepared to read it all later—in literary code at the Starlite.

It was dark and late. If she told Tommy she was leaving to make her own life, he would promise to change. He might even apply to jobs, just to placate her. Then it would be the same thing all over again. No job could be enough for him. He thought he was *beyond* any work that would be offered to him.

Or, if she just stayed put, she might become so disgusted that she would forget to want him.

If she could learn not to want him.

She struggled to speak as exhaustion gripped her with steely fingers.

"What are we doing, Tommy?"

He was wide awake, intent on putting his shoes on in the dark. He laughed. "I'm not sure what you're doing, but I'm going out now."

She gulped. "Drinking some more, I assume?"

"As a matter of fact, you're right. I'm going to drown my sorrows." He pulled his long coat over his arms, with jumpy movements and taps of his feet. His voice was unsteady, and his hands shook as he tried to button his coat. "I'm really not sure why you're still living with me, Elaine. I guess you just want to sleep here after your hard day at work and have a place for your sister to stay. I guess I'm almost like your landlord now. Maybe I should start charging rent."

"So, you want me to quit my job and drink with you all day?"

"Maybe you just need to consider things, Elaine."

He slammed the bedroom door behind him as he left.

As he stumbled down the stairs, she rolled over to the warm spot in bed where he had slept—where she now trembled.

Downstairs, she heard the slam of the front door. The vibrations of his exit came to a quick stop—to a heavy silence, broken only by the ticking of the grandfather clock.

She put a pillow over her ears, to muffle the sound of the steady rhythm.

Then—with a sudden move, she got up.

She lifted herself with a force that was barely her own.

She turned on the light.

She was packing her bags; she was shoving in dresses and night-clothes, everything in lumpy knots.

When she finally filled the luggage, it was midnight, and she trembled, in uncontrollable shudders. There was an emptiness on her shoulders, no reassuring arms. Catherine wasn't downstairs—she was out somewhere.

She found herself dialing Madeline. It was midnight, but that wouldn't matter. But nobody answered, so she closed her eyes and hung up.

Somehow, under her pulsating eyelids, she managed to nod off for a few short hours, even with the empty spot in the bed next to her, now cold.

In the morning, Tommy hadn't returned.

Elaine found herself back on the chilly sidewalks, walking to the bus. Everyone else walked with resolute strides as she made her way to her destination in spasms and shivers.

⁓

The *Chronicle* was chaotic, with more reports about the horrific plane crash. Fatigue rushed over her in waves, but she gathered her notes together and began her typed confirmations.

A courier stopped at her desk. "Ms. Huxley, a delivery for you."

The package didn't have a return address. She ripped open its plain brown wrapping paper to find a shiny box. It was a package of chocolates, with a note printed on the candy store's gift card. *Thank you for taking care of me. Love, Tommy.*

She uttered a curse under her breath, and fat, intrusive tears slipped down her cheeks. She knelt behind her desk to hide her face.

She had to type up her notes. She had a deadline. He wouldn't distract her, trying to stop her from being effective at her job. She worked as fast as she could, typing in a frenzy, making her calls, finishing her notes and handing them to the editor upstairs, and working on the second article. The office air smelled of metallic typewriters, crumpled papers and sweat. It was a dirty but purposeful smell accompanied by *tap-tapping*, quick footsteps and murmured voices.

She made it to five PM. On the bus, she made moves to write a poem, but nothing would come out.

As the bus neared her stop, her eyes locked in a trance.

He was at home when she got there, at the kitchen table, with his disheveled hair. The sharp line of his jaw bit the tip of a cigar, his lip curved over its brown top. He was messing with a gadget on the table, something with twisted wires.

He looked normal. Like any man doing work.

"I spent a lot of time on this today." He turned animated as he got up from his chair and paced around the room. "I really think I got something here!" He jumped around like a little boy.

Elaine took a sharp breath inward.

Now, his sudden lightness.

He was so many people at once.

"Oh?"

He had asked nothing about *her* work. And she was at one of the most important newspapers in the city.

"Yeah. I figured I would have a nice prototype to show the guys who interview me."

"Interview?"

"I've got a job interview set up for Friday."

"Friday?"

"Yeah, I figure I should start bringing in some more money too. After all, we're burning through my inheritance pretty quickly right now. And I'm hoping . . ." Tommy grabbed her and drew her close to his chest. He smelled like clean aftershave, with only a minor trace of alcohol on his breath. "Well, I'm hoping that we can save up a little. For our wedding, you know." He held her hand, and his fingers encircled her engagement ring. "After all, you deserve something nice."

Elaine's packed bags remained on the floor upstairs.

22

Elaine

Elaine watched the stricken, soot-filled faces of the search crews on the news.

They interviewed the firefighters who had arrived at the scene of the plane crash, only to find no survivors.

Tommy wasn't home, as usual. He could have watched with them—seen the people whose struggles burned out in front of their faces instead of in their souls.

Catherine was there—coming in with her food, settling down on the settee. "Isn't it horrific? Hey, what about your friend, that blonde girl? What's her name, Lisa? That one who went to the Starlite in her stewardess uniform?"

"She works for Pan Am."

"Golly gee, that lucky girl." Catherine shuddered. "By the way, have you seen Tommy? I owe him a couple of dollars."

"He gave you money?"

"You know, my wallet was empty, and I needed some money that day. I had to go buy a pair of shoes for my job interview. It was too bloody freezing to walk to the bank."

"Sister dear, if you need money, ask me—not Tommy. All right?"

"What's the big deal? He is your fiancé, isn't he?"

Elaine's throat was craggy; she struggled to speak. "I'm not married to him." She ended the sentence on a sharp note to stop the conversation.

She hadn't told Catherine the beginnings of her plan.

The evening before, after he left, she had carefully unpacked her clothing—she had returned each item to the closet. She had readied her things for the next day.

There were places for men to go with problems like his. During her lunch break, she had looked in the archives at the *Chronicle* and found a recovery center in Manhattan.

He would be sure to laugh at the foolishness of her idea. He would never admit to a problem.

Sure, put me away in a place somewhere, Elaine! That's a handy way of disposing of me!

It was sure to go like that. Then he would leave the house again and find more to drink somewhere.

After a sudden creak, the front door opened. She heard Tommy's uneven footsteps heading inside the house, with one of his drinking buddies.

"Hellooo!" he bellowed.

She didn't respond, and Catherine gave her a look.

On the television, they were interviewing witnesses to the plane crash. Tommy swung into the room with a loud whoop, his buddy at his heels.

Tommy plopped next to Elaine on the sofa, throwing his arm around her. His voice was high-pitched and unnatural, as though he was trying to sound sober. "This is my lady right here!"

Elaine edged away from his arm, keeping her eyes fixed on the horrifying scene on the screen.

The friend, Peter, had found his way into her fruit basket, and he loudly chomped an apple in the doorway. "Tommy told me that you've been going to that women's club, Elaine. You know, my police officer buddy told me that it was vandalized the other day. Maybe you should lay off your visits to dangerous places. You know, your guy here is quite, *quite* worried about you."

She couldn't help but laugh out loud. Drunken Tommy tapped an invisible drum on his knee, with that great big scar on his forehead from Lord knows where. Stupid Peter was glazed over, with glassy eyes and an idiotic face.

Yet she responded anyway—as though she had something to prove.

"I heard the Starlite is getting a guard. They'll charge a bit of money at the door, and we'll be very safe in there."

⁓

Later, Tommy and his friend were engaged in a game with wires and cigarette lighters. They guffawed and cursed as pieces of the wire caught aflame, then snuffed them out between their fingers.

Elaine smelled plastic and metal burning and ran up behind them, hissing in Tommy's ear.

"You need to stop."

"Stop what, baby? We're having a little fun." He flickered his lighter and giggled. His eyes were bloodshot, with spindly veins.

"It's dangerous. You need to stop. Maybe you could come inside and have a conversation with me and my sister, like a regular person."

"All you're doing is watching the news. That crap depresses the hell out of me."

"It's real life." She changed to a regular tone—no more hushed hissing. His friend wasn't paying attention, immersed in their little game.

Tommy squinted at her. "That's life? Looking at a whole bunch of death?"

"I have a friend who could have perished in that plane, you know. She was lucky." He didn't respond to her; he only grunted out expletives as his fingers blistered. "Do you even care? Do you care about what's going on?"

He paused his work with the wires. "Of course I care, baby. But I can't think about anything like that too much, you know?"

For a moment, he looked sad, even earnest. As though things were just too much for him to handle.

His eyes were glassy and she had to turn away.

⁓

Hours later, he was going out again. His buddy had already left.

"When will you be back?"

Tommy made a cocky half smile. "When the sun shines and I'm feeling good."

It was an English translation from a French poem they both loved. He was sober enough.

She got sharp with him, suddenly—as an energy swept over her, something unlike her usual self.

"Get the hell out, then, if you're going."

"Get the hell out of my own house? Ha!" His voice was slurred again. He kicked the ironing board as though it were a misbehaving animal.

The steaming-hot iron nearly fell on Elaine's arm, plate down.

She screamed, with a fury she had never held on her own.

"Get the hell out!"

He scurried out and slammed the door, hard.

The brownstone shook, and her lip began to quiver, like gelatin pushed back and forth by childish thumbs. But this time she didn't retreat. She made herself continue amid intermittent shakes in her body. She ironed her clothes as though nothing around her were happening, as if she were in some sort of humdrum, normal existence. She made her lunch for the next day, deriving a small pleasure from the sane and predictable elegance of placing a slice of bologna on bread. Life would go on. She had a job; she was making her own money again. She had even managed to save some of the money, stashing ten-dollar bills into balled-up nylons in the back of her sock drawer. When it came time to leave, she would have a deposit for an apartment.

She would wear a large hat to hide her face, so he wouldn't know her if he saw her on the street.

He was impossibly good-looking, so he would find another girl quick enough—maybe a lonely lass who liked to drink as much as he did. He would impregnate her, quickly. His new girl would fret away at home with a baby while he ran amok elsewhere.

Now he was off, to do whatever he did.

Catherine seemed to be staying at the brownstone that evening; there were sounds of her puttering around in the guest room.

Elaine would join her in the guest room for a chat. She would grab a few blankets and sleep in the guest room on the floor as they talked themselves to sleep, like it was all very casual, a nostalgic slumber party—like when they would sneak into each other's rooms and chit-chat the night away as wee ones. Of course, she wouldn't tell Catherine the truth, because one day Catherine would have a few drinks or get too tired, and then she would blurt out the wrong thing.

Tommy could only find out once she was *truly* gone.

Now she sauntered into the guest room as if nothing was askew, with an upright, casual gait.

Yet Catherine eyed her suspiciously. "Don't you have to be getting ready for bed now?"

"Are you trying to be Mum or something?"

Elaine brought a pillow down from the sofa, which became an invitation to play fight, as though they were children. They chased each other around like mice, bashing each other with velvet pillows, and she threw herself into an anarchic frenzy. They collapsed on the floor in a breathless heap; Elaine was even giggling, before she turned quiet.

Having thus exhausted herself, she laid her head on a pillow like it was a cloud, near sleep. But her sister interrupted her quiet daze.

"Did I tell you I got a singing gig?"

"That's stellar! Where at?"

"Well, it's some ways out, in Hoboken, actually. Have you heard of Hoboken? In New Jersey? Anyway, it's just for a couple of nights, actually. At some executive's penthouse, I guess. He's having some fancy get-togethers for his associates."

"Maybe some of the executives will hire you after they hear you sing."

"Maybe. It would be nice to not have to mooch off you and Tommy forever."

"Oh, well, that's all right."

Catherine would have to leave the brownstone anyway, along with her.

It was late on a work night—around ten thirty. Elaine got up and turned off the light. She curled up on a nest of blankets on the floor as Catherine sprawled out on the velvet couch.

"You know what, Elaine? I've been saving up. Soon I'll have enough to get a place of my own."

"Maybe I can move in with you," Elaine whispered, in a voice soft enough for Catherine to miss. Soon, a shroud of sleep descended over her, and she shut her eyes.

They were both quiet, drifting off.

Then, through the walls, there was a squeak of the front door.

A clatter. A crash.

A splintering sound and a moan.

Elaine pricked her ears.

There was a sharp gag, a spilling of some kind, then more gagging.

Then nothing.

Silence.

Catherine was still asleep.

Tommy would have left the door ajar, in his state. Anyone could have come inside.

Her breathing was fast and heavy. Her ears were peeled.

She hunted for sharp objects—books, candles, a transistor radio.

There was a sculpture on the table—a small, leaden statue with a pointed edge. She held it close to her chest and opened the door in one fell swoop, plowing toward the front hall.

There had been a spill. Globs of sickness spewed across the carpet.

Elaine's nose seized up with the smell—after that, she could barely see.

He was on the carpet, not moving.

His body lay twisted near the fragments of a broken vase.

Tommy was faceup, with his eyes rolled up in the back of his head.

Time stood still for a moment, along with the image of his frozen face.

23

Elaine

Madeline had never met Tommy.

But when she heard of Elaine's loss, she strove to do something.

"We'll have a remembrance day. Bring any writing you've done about him. I'm sure you've done something. It will give you an opportunity to think about his life, to talk about it in a public way." Madeline waited a full minute for agreement before prompting her further. "So what do you think, dear?"

Elaine's crisp, lively voice had been steamrolled. "Whatever you say."

⌒

Everything was red, bleary. Elaine was a mass of eyes and headache and filth; she had not bathed in several days.

The police had come on the night she found him. The coroner came, too, and they took him away. Catherine went to buy a bottle of bleach. With the flick of her wrist, she had doused the red and brown stains with bleach. The two of them sat in stunned silence and stared as it all turned white.

A sudden end to it all.

"I'll tell the girls to wear black. I'll call them up now, tell them about the memorial. I'm sure they'll all be there. Have you left the house? Have you gotten something to eat? Where is Catherine?"

Madeline kept calling. She kept asking questions, checking in. But nothing was regular or normal. She kept calling, as though she could help.

The coroner declared it asphyxiation; it was rare, the result of alcohol poisoning. Elaine admitted to Catherine that she had always worried that Tommy might be killed in an altercation with another drunk, or that he might get hit by a car, dancing across the street in the darkness. Not this.

It was a plunge into something incomprehensible.

She was on the verge of throwing up with every movement she made, as it all flashed before her in each moment—his lifeless flesh, which lay in their entryway in a grotesque stilling of his passions, of his fraught inclinations.

She had loved him, though it didn't make any sense.

"What was that?"

She had to shake herself, make herself listen to Madeline, who was trying in the best way she knew how. "Do you need any food, darling?"

"No, I'm fine. There's plenty in the refrigerator." There were a few moldy things on the bottom shelf.

"Make sure you let me know. You need to keep your strength up."

Elaine was frozen in place, yet her fingers ached to release the receiver. "I have to get going now."

She would go to their room—to the quiet, velvet enclave of the bed she had shared with him. The area where he had last slept still smelled like him. She curled up for a fitful nap, then woke, darting her head around like she might hear him in the background. It was always a guessing game, deciphering his next moment of unexpected behavior—would he be silent and brooding, affectionate and manic, or intellectual and chatty? Maybe he would be hopeful and brilliant, building some gadget.

He had said he had an interview scheduled. He was going to turn his life around. That's what he'd said.

He had said so many things.

The phone rang, and it was his aunt Mary, the only family he had left. She lived alone on the Upper West Side of Manhattan and was bitter, widowed, and sarcastic. Elaine had met her once, at Tommy's father's funeral. She had shaken Elaine's hand and asked if Elaine was "the girl" who was "shacking up" with her nephew.

Elaine had asked Catherine to call his aunt Mary with the news that morning. Now she was calling back.

"I thought you would be calling to tell me you had a wedding date."

Elaine didn't respond. Tommy's ashes would be returned to her next week, and she wasn't sure about services. His aunt sounded confused and said something about calling again; then they hung up, and the phone rang once more.

Elaine was talking from the end of some distant tunnel.

"Hello?"

"Madeline again, dear. I need to keep calling you to make sure you're okay. I know what it's like to suffer a loss, dear. I don't have either one of my parents, you know. And it was a loss in its own way when Fred started doing his behaviors and all of that happened. I know about the solitude."

"Uh-huh."

"Listen, dear—why don't you do some of that writing that you do so well? You know, I think it will help you. And then you could share it with us at the Starlite. Give it a try."

Elaine's tongue stuck to the roof of her mouth, parched like the desert.

Her words came out coarsely. "Right."

"Great, I'll see you at the service." Madeline sounded settled—like she had done her duty.

"Thank you." Elaine hung up the phone. In a spate of weakness, she sat on the floor.

She was dizzy; she hadn't eaten anything in three days. Food would make her retch uncontrollably.

She hoisted herself up to the kitchen counter and instead grabbed a tea bag; she brewed a scalding-hot cup.

The liquid fire of the brew bit into a portion of her mouth—she screamed at once, and the cup released itself from her hand, its searing contents spilling down her legs.

Elaine ripped off her wet clothes and crawled upstairs to the bed, where she cried in choking sobs until she was bone-dry and nothing remained.

She hadn't been able to save him. All that she had given hadn't been enough—though maybe if she had given *more*, he could have come out on the other side. Maybe if she had just given one extra piece to him—something that would appeal to him, or even all of herself, devoted to him and nothing else—she could have changed him. Saved him.

24

Lisa

When Lisa arrived back at her Brooklyn apartment, her mother almost lifted her off her feet in a tight hug.

"It's just so good to see you in one piece, honey. The news keeps showing that area of the bay—the area of the crash. They're trying to figure out what went wrong."

The television blared in the living room. Lisa averted her eyes, heading into the kitchen for a snack. Her mother had made cookies. Lisa dunked them in milk; they were sweet and buttery. She stopped after eating two, as there would be another weigh-in soon enough.

"I don't know, Lisa." Her mother was still watching TV.

"What's that, Ma?" Lisa ogled the cookies and their crisp edges.

Her mother entered the kitchen. "You eat when you get nervous, don't you?"

Lisa hid her shaking foot under the table. "I'm not nervous."

"I don't blame you; I would be nervous too, going up in the sky every day. What do you think? Is this something you want to do for the rest of your life?"

"I don't know, Ma. I love to travel, but they won't let me be a stewardess for the rest of my life, remember? There's an expiration date over my head, anyway—I'm toast after age thirty-two. I knew this when I signed up—I can't do this forever."

One more cookie. She popped it into her mouth with a satisfying crunch. She didn't say her other thought aloud—that she would have to quit if she got married.

She would work until she got engaged; she would be forced to quit when she got married anyway. It shouldn't be too long until the engagement—maybe six months, tops.

"Maybe you should—" The phone interrupted her mother on the verge of something. "Hello? Yes, she's here. Hold on."

Her mother handed Lisa the phone with a grimace. It was Billy.

"Hello?"

"Babe! It's so good to hear that gorgeous voice of yours."

She giggled. "Hi."

"Listen, are you off tomorrow? I was thinking you could come by the bridge at the end of my shift, and we could grab pizza or something."

"Okay, I guess. What time?"

"Four thirty. Just look for Joe if you don't see me. He always knows where I am."

"Okay."

In the background, Billy's mother informed him that dinner was almost ready. His mother would be setting the table now, carefully placing dinner forks on napkins. Her husband could be anywhere, with anyone.

"See you soon, babe."

" 'Bye." Lisa hung up and jetted to her room, where she sat down on the floor, thumbing through *Seventeen* magazine. She wasn't a teenager anymore, but it was still her favorite.

She slung her uniform over the top of a tall chair in her room. There was a stain on it that she would have to clean, but not just yet.

When she switched on the radio, the dial was set to the news. Her mother must have come into her room and listened to it while she was gone. The announcer was talking about the plane crash.

She switched it off.

Maybe if she quit being a flight attendant, if she stopped leaving all the time, it would change their relationship. It would be just the thing to make him think about marriage.

But then she would be stuck in Brooklyn, without the release of travel.

If she was bound to her parents' dingy apartment, there would be nothing to distract her if Billy wasn't ready to commit.

There would be nothing to do but sit on her narrow bed and wait.

⌦

The next day, she visited his construction site. The official name was the Verrazzano-Narrows Bridge, but it was the Brooklyn-Staten Island Bridge for now.

She always drew a sharp breath to see the work in progress—the platform in pieces, the cables suspended from the frame. One day it would become the longest suspension bridge in the world, right here in Bay Ridge.

Billy's demeanor seemed odd when she approached him. It wasn't a sort of affect she had previously seen; he darted his head around—distracted, lips slightly drawn. But soon enough he was gregarious and full of energy.

"Check out what I did today!"

He put his arm around her waist and led her to the other side of the work site, to a piece of platform he had welded together. One of his friends—Mack—interrupted. Mack jumped off the back of a little truck to come punch Billy's arm.

Billy punched him back. "You son of a gun!"

Mack went for Billy's head and held him down in a headlock. He wore an ugly smirk on his face as Billy struggled to crane away, and his pale eyes gleamed with the primal satisfaction of holding another man down. Mack was like an animal, with exaggerated movements: giant puffs of his chest, a wide-legged swagger. He would rapidly sweep his arm when he threw down a cigarette butt.

Not much mattered to Mack, including personal hygiene. Half the time he smelled like something not usually found in civilized society.

And he would always mix Billy up in his trouble. Six months ago, Mack had brought Billy to a party at a house he claimed was abandoned. But the house wasn't abandoned—the elderly owner was still monitoring it. Mack and Billy almost got arrested.

Mack never called Lisa by her real name. "Hey, why don't *you* and *you* come out with me tonight?" He spat on the grass and spoke through wads of chewing tobacco. "I'm going to catch a flick in Manhattan."

Billy turned to face Lisa with a hopeful eye. "What do you say, babe?"

She sighed. "What movie is it?"

Mack gave a ghoulish laugh, then ran his fingers up and down her spine to simulate spiders. "It's a horror flick. You know—one of the ones that makes you scream!"

Lisa jolted away from him, her blouse now tainted by his grease. But Billy barely registered anything as he lit a cigarette.

"No, thanks. That's not my sort of movie." Lisa gazed in the distance at her parked car, a long walk from the construction site.

Billy whispered to her under his breath. "Do you mind if I go, babe?"

"Sure." She gave a close-lipped grin and shrugged. "I'm going to the Starlite, anyway. You boys have fun."

Mack scrunched up his face like a little boy's, then affected a nasal voice. "Oh, the *Starlite*. Is that your *women's* club? Billy told me you ladies go there for some good *girdle* talk."

Her hand almost rose up to smack him—she used the other hand to push it down.

"I didn't say that, babe. I promise!" Billy turned away and stuck out his foot to kick Mack's work boot. "You'd better quit trying to cause me trouble, or I'll wallop you!"

With a hoot, Mack twisted his body away, then ground his cigarette into the dirt. "I guess I'd better leave you two lovebirds together to sort things out!"

Then he left them in a cloud of his smoke, laughing so much that he choked in a series of coughs.

"Hey, babe. You know Mack is a loon." Billy stroked her arm in apology. "Do you still want to get pizza?"

She shrugged. It was almost time for dinner.

"I guess so."

On the way to the pizza joint, Billy talked a little about Mack. Once a month Mack would go to Billy's apartment and the two of them would play poker with Billy's father. Mack was a talented poker player—he made breathtaking bets. Once he'd even won a cool hundred from Billy's father.

As they walked, Billy kept trying to slip his arm around Lisa's waist. But she would pull away, so he started to tickle her in the middle of the sidewalk. She almost fell to her feet with the ridiculousness; she laughed and couldn't control it. She giggled like a maniac. His jokes and breezy, casual way made her susceptible. A woman with a baby carriage tried to get past them, but Lisa was doubled over and Billy was almost on top of her as she yelled for mercy.

When they arrived at the pizza shop, it was hot and crowded. The doughy smell from the brick ovens was too comfortable. Familiar.

Every time they went out for pizza, he would get three slices and she would get just one. They always sat at one choice booth, right in the corner of the restaurant, the one near the jukebox. Billy would let the gooey cheese drip all over his hands as he took quick, ravenous bites, while she dabbed her mouth with a paper napkin after every greasy nibble.

Billy spoke with his mouth full of food. "So, the plane crash."

"Yeah."

"Did you see it?"

"Just the smoke."

"Do you still want to do the job?"

"It's my job right now."

"Well, I'm getting a raise at the site soon," he said. "And I'll be making more money, so that's good."

She was oh-so-casual. "That's good."

"Yeah. The raise starts in two months."

"Uh-huh."

His eyes were set right on her as he chomped on his slice. "You gonna keep flying?"

"That's what I'm doing for now."

Soon they left the pizza parlor, and Billy went off to meet Mack at the movies. It was dark outside, and Lisa made initial motions to drive back home. But instead she made good on her alibi and headed up to Brooklyn Heights, to the Starlite.

⁓

A tarp was stretched over the broken window, and a man was positioned by the door, straight-backed like a guard.

Lisa observed the entrance from her parking spot, and she waited in the driver's seat, listening to the radio. She hadn't checked to see if Elaine would be coming.

She stepped out of her car. Under the streetlights, her heels made dents in the powdery snow.

At the door, the guard wore a poker face.

"Is this, uh, establishment still open?" she asked.

"Yes, ma'am. Are you one of Madeline's friends?"

"Yeah," Lisa replied, with some hesitation.

He looked her up and down, then opened the door.

She held her breath as she entered the Starlite, alert for its usual noise and excitement—the dancing, singing, laughing. The joking around.

But tonight, everyone sat in neat rows, hands folded on their laps. In the back, there were teetering rows of cots, stacked beyond the edge of a burlap curtain.

She squinted in the dim light to look further.

In front of the crowd stood Elaine, head bent down.

It was dark and melancholy in the Starlite. Something serious must have happened while she was overseas.

25

Madeline

Alone at her shop, Madeline stitched a custom-made ensemble—a detailed, embroidered piece for one of the society ladies.

She had done for Elaine what she could do.

Elaine had joined them for nearly every social club soiree since its inception, along with Madeline's other customers who had turned into regulars—and friends. She never talked too much about her fiancé, yet her poetry and the faraway look in her eye had said it all.

Madeline knew something about hiding problems, and she understood why Elaine might not have been forthright about her relationship issues. Some things weren't easy to reveal.

Madeline sat up suddenly, drawing in a deep breath. The rhythmic clatter of the sewing machine had nearly lulled her into an afternoon nap, but she kicked herself awake. She immersed herself in her handiwork as she glided the fabric up and down. It was always smooth and easy when she sewed. Her hands would move of their own accord, and sometimes hours would pass before she noticed the time.

The bells on the shop door rang, and she checked the clock. Diana had arrived early—the dress wouldn't be ready until five PM.

"I see you're hard at work!" Diana called over.

Madeline smiled delicately. "Yes, things are coming together! But you're a little early, dear."

It was all about the *experience*.

Diana smiled. "Oh, I know! I came to have a little chat."

Diana had golden hair and the whitest teeth in Brooklyn. She was the wife of a former councilman.

Madeline spoke through a pin in her mouth as she scrambled to finish her dress. "Sure, I'm always up for a chat!"

Diana's lips curled in some anxiety. "Okay. I don't know how much you'll like this, though, Madeline." She spoke as she looked down at her heels. "I've been debating if I should even be telling you this."

Madeline's teeth clenched together on the pin.

She would finish making this dress. She concentrated on the stitches, wrapping her focus in its twisted threads. "Well, I do feel I *must* know, dear. Please share." She punctuated her request with a laugh, like it didn't matter too much.

"It's just that—well, Fred was talking to Lenny, you know? I mean, he always visits him at the law firm and chats him up for advice. Anyway. I don't know how to say this, Madeline." Diana folded her arms across her chest and cleared her throat. "Do you really want me to tell you what he said?"

One more stitch. Madeline yanked it from the machine and looped it by hand. Her frantic assessments of hem height and bodice length had resulted in an astounding creation.

She held the dress up in the air and stared at it.

It was perfect.

"Tell me," she said.

"Fred told Lenny that you're stealing money. He said that you still have his bank account number and that you're taking out cash. He says he drove by your shop and saw that big hole in your window, and he figures that you must need money to get it fixed, so you're stealing from him little by little. Fred asked Lenny's advice, because he says he doesn't want to go to the police about it."

Madeline would rip the dress she was making in half.

She would pull it apart, seam by seam.

"I'm sure the ladies have told you the truth about Fred by now, dear. Do you honestly believe he would be telling anyone the truth about *me*?" Madeline controlled her voice as she trembled.

It was his word against her word. Always the same.

"I was positive he wasn't telling the truth, darling. I actually came here to make you an offer. I'm friends with a girl who writes under a pseudonym for the society pages. I wanted to see if you wanted to do a reveal. Once Fred's campaign heats up, he'll probably smear your name in the dirt. I wanted to give you an opportunity to preempt him, darling." She paused. "What do you think?"

The dress lay on Madeline's sewing table. She fingered a crease in its fabric, a wrinkle that had formed when she hastily set it down.

Another complication.

It had been perfect for a moment.

The tarp was still draped over her store window. The memorial for Elaine's beloved had been held under the shadow of its brown ugliness. It was like Fred's filth—his lies—an overlay that polluted it all.

A society-pages reporter. Madeline had made it a point to never read those pages. There were too many names she knew from her old life.

"Do you want her phone number?"

"How about this: have her call *me*, at her convenience."

Madeline wouldn't call of her own accord; she wouldn't beg for sympathy through the newspaper pages.

"Absolutely." Diana gave another huge smile, with gleaming teeth. "I have to run now, darling. I need to pick up some things before I make my way back here for that dress." She sneaked a peek at the fabric bunched between Madeline's fingers. "The dress looks fantastic. I can't wait to wear it, darling."

"Thank you." Madeline hid the crease under her index finger. It measured almost the exact width of a newspaper headline.

26

Lisa

Lisa readied herself.

Billy's parents were at a social function, and she was in his bathroom. She applied some powder to a stubborn pimple, then dabbed her armpits with a damp tissue to make sure they smelled decent.

Billy was in his room, completely naked.

It was very first time she had seen him totally unclothed. She had seen glimpses in the back seat of his car before, but never everything like this.

He had stripped himself down as they were kissing; he'd stepped out of his trousers, unbuttoned his own shirt, and undone her brassiere. At the quick unfastening of that latch, she'd excused herself to the bathroom, where she was practicing the art of extending time, finding more things to do.

There was a draft in the bathroom, entering through the frosted window, which was cracked for ventilation. The air smelled like cologne—that cologne she'd smelled on the airplane seat, the one that Billy and his father both used.

She would need to make a choice.

In eighth grade, her friend's older sister had had a boyfriend. The friend had reported all the details, telling her about her sister's *first time*. "It hurts, but then it's over pretty quickly," she said. "The rubber feels strange in there, but you need to wear it so you don't get pregnant."

If Lisa got pregnant, she would be ousted from the airline. Her mother would classify her as a whore and disown her, and she would

163

be left penniless, with nowhere to live but a house for unwed mothers. Unless Billy were to marry her—but that wasn't the beginning of the marriage she had planned.

She took a deep breath as she stepped back into Billy's bedroom. He had thrown a blanket over himself; he was sprawled across his bed, flipping through a magazine.

When he saw her, he beckoned her closer, and she leaned in for a kiss, his warmth close. He wasn't wearing a rubber. He wrapped his arms around her, pulled her down to the bed, and started to lift up her skirt.

A strange tug in her throat caused her to roll over. "We're not married," she whispered.

"Maybe that can happen soon." He bit her earlobe, which hurt, but she stayed in the area of his warm breath.

Then she sat up suddenly, with some power in her abdomen—upright and still dressed as he sat fully exposed. "Well, we'll see, I guess," she replied.

Then she slid off his bed, onto his floor.

Billy jumped off the bed and headed toward the bathroom, by himself.

She was left alone in his immaculate bedroom. His mother cleaned it every day, even polishing the lightbulb in the ceiling fixture.

They watched television for a while after Billy got dressed, eating food from cans they had found in the pantry. He was relatively quiet with Lisa, but he laughed uproariously when the comedy hour came on.

When she left to go home, he gave her a peck on the lips.

Lisa went down to the sidewalk, toward her car, though she needed a moment before she could drive.

27

Madeline

The store was so busy that Madeline barely had time to eat. As she lost weight, she had to quickly let in the seams of her own dresses.

And then he was mentioned again, and it was two days before she could touch a bite of food.

She had been pinning up a skirt for Mrs. Morello, another one of the society ladies.

"That ex-husband of yours really is a cheating liar, isn't he, dear?"

"What?" The measuring tape fell from Madeline's mouth. She hadn't breathed one word about Fred to any of these ladies.

"You don't have to act surprised, dear. It's really obvious that he was cheating on you."

"What do you mean?" Madeline stammered, unlike her.

"You know, honey, Fred was trying to get at *me* during one of those galas a few years ago. I was fixing my makeup in the powder room, and when I went out, he was right there, as though he were waiting for me. He smiled and just so casually put his hand on my rear, rubbing it like I was a little puppy. I slapped him and ran back towards my husband. But Fred gave me his warning, that he would crap all over my husband's reputation if I were to tell anyone." Mrs. Morello sighed. "I was really relieved when I heard you were divorced from that man."

"Oh, God."

In the dozens of reflective surfaces around her shop, Madeline caught her image and hid her face. Mrs. Morello stepped down from the fitting pedestal and clutched Madeline's shoulder.

"I'm sure this is something you don't want to confront, dear."

The tears came fast, and she turned away. "I'm sorry."

"You know—the things you may tell me now may help other women. What do you think about giving me a little ammunition? I might as well add some truth to the fight and bring justice to your name." She grabbed Madeline's hand. "I'm sure you wouldn't want him to win another term of office, would you?"

"What's he been saying?" Madeline asked, though her ears strained inward, as though she could block it out.

"Are you sure you want to know, dear?" Mrs. Morello glanced at her sideways.

Madeline tightened her jaw. "You can tell me."

"Well, dear, he's telling everyone that you got divorced because . . ." Mrs. Morello paused, clearing her throat. "Well, he's saying it's because you wanted him to do—*things*—that he didn't want to do."

"Things?"

"Like things with another woman. Bringing another woman into the house and all that. Whatever the French call it—a *ménage*, or something like that."

Madeline's eyes opened wide like saucers, and she flinched as if she'd had a punch to the gut. Suddenly her spine rolled inward as something airy and absurd hit her tongue. She giggled out of control—so loud that she almost couldn't hear Mrs. Morello. "You're serious, now?"

"He said that you thought all of us ladies were beautiful, darling, and that's why you started a dress shop—so you could better, well, *access* us in our beauty. So you could give one of *us* an invitation."

"Ha!" she heard herself scream, and then she threw back her head in laughter, cawing like a bird, pushing all of the ridiculousness out of her chest—the tight knot she had contained for years, since even before the divorce.

Mrs. Morello laughed along with her, as if she didn't know what else to do. The two laughed like sea gulls in a beach of trash, and Madeline laughed so hard that tears streamed from her eyes.

Once their laughter died down, it all became silent, and Madeline returned to pinning fabric. She was back to where she was.

"I'm sure you know how early these campaigns start," said Mrs. Morello. "If you want to really give me the details, I'll be sure to spread the information, so Fred doesn't have a chance."

"Uh-huh." Madeline nodded. Anything else stayed buried in her chest. "I'll let you know."

"Of course, dear. When you're ready."

⌇

March was months ahead of the election, but signs of Fred and his propaganda machine were popping up all over the borough, with glorified stories appearing in the papers about what he had done for Brooklyn.

Something within Madeline was welling and growing. It was something that had lain dormant until heat pushed it through its dark root chamber.

She wouldn't be the one to suffer again.

When the bells jangled again on the Starlite's door, she took in a sharp breath. She stood up from her sewing machine, and the unfinished sleeves of a dress fell to the floor.

"Mrs. Morello—I'm so glad you're here."

"Of course! I apologize that I'm back so soon! I know I was *just* here yesterday. You must think I'm rushing you. But tell me—when do you think the skirt will be ready? I had forgotten to ask you, amidst all our other talk."

"It *is* ready, actually. Though you just might want to try it on and make sure."

She had completed the alteration with a rush of fire in her blood. It had been ready since the previous day—within a half hour after Mrs. Morello left her store. Now she rustled through the rack of finished alterations and pulled out the jade-green organdy skirt—a statement piece with tiers of tiny ruffles.

Mrs. Morello accepted the skirt from Madeline's shaky hand and adjourned to the fitting room. Soon she shrieked, from behind the door, "It's amazing! A perfect fit, Madeline!"

Madeline smiled weakly. Mrs. Morello had redressed herself and emerged from the fitting room with her organdy skirt in hand, ready to pay.

Madeline attempted to stride to the checkout counter with her posture straight and upright, the confident proprietress of her shop, but her heel snagged the edge of a rack, and she stumbled.

She ungracefully caught herself as sweat pooled beneath her arms. She cleared her throat multiple times, but the words were stuck, lodged in her windpipe like burs.

She coughed; she attempted to swallow.

Mrs. Morello, unaware, ran her fingers through the ruffles of her skirt on the hanger.

Then Madeline gripped the edge of the counter behind her cash register and gulped, finally making a space in her throat for the words to come out.

"I have to tell you something."

"Hm? What is it, dear? Don't worry if it's a little more than your estimate. You did beautiful work on this piece; I'll gladly pay for it."

"Not the skirt, actually. It's about . . . Fred." She could barely eke out his name from behind her teeth—it was like an expletive, something she couldn't say lightly.

"Yes, that buffoon! Tell me, darling, what is it?"

Madeline drew in a breath and glanced out the remaining window, next to the ugly tarp. A young bicyclist raced past her store with the strident sound of bells; her shoulders jumped upward.

"The elections . . . you wanted anything that might help him . . . not to win . . . right?"

"Oh! So, you have something for me, then?"

Madeline's voice cracked, but she cleared her throat. Her neck was frozen in place, her pupils fully dilated.

Then she made her decision.

"He was cheating on me, you know."

"Oh, really?"

Madeline drew in another breath. "I'm going to sit down for a moment."

"Absolutely, dear."

She settled on the wobbly counter stool—something to hold her, to keep her from getting too dizzy.

Then she spat her words out all at once, as though saying them quickly would mean she wasn't saying them at all.

"It was with different women. He was cheating with different women."

"Oh?" Mrs. Morello leaned in toward her, over the counter, her hazel eyes growing wide. Her breath smelled like peppermint, and a hard candy clinked against her teeth. She brandished one from her purse. "Would you like one of these, dear? You look a little faint."

"No, thank you."

When she had seen Fred at the bakery, his chuckles with his crony had chased her out the door.

His teeth had been stained with the mud brown of his coffee; he had smirked as she fled amid his hyena-like laughter.

"How did you find out he was cheating, dear?"

Madeline took a sharp breath inward. "There were always women trying to reach him . . . and I saw something happen one day."

Then her breath sped up as she peered through the intact window. Passersby roamed innocently past on the sidewalk. She squinted as if to see whether Fred might be among them, watching every word she said, but their faces were too far away.

"You saw . . . ?" Mrs. Morello paused expectantly, a blast of peppermint shooting in Madeline's face.

But she shook her head. "Yes, I saw—" She paused as she hunkered down on her wobbly stool, her foot tapping against the bar. She had an audience of only *one*, but the news would spread to all the society women, so she might as well have been onstage, under the white-hot lights. "I saw something. Then he was living with one of the women, but he made me pretend . . ."

Fred could do whatever he wanted; he had enough friends in high places. She had been keeping a low enough profile, not talking about him publicly. Yet he still had sent his warning sign.

A break through her borders. A smash through her territory.

It had taken only a moment for the ice-cold air to enter from the street.

"What did he make you pretend, dear?"

Madeline gulped and held her face in her hands. "I had to pretend that we were okay. That nothing wrong was happening at all."

"That must have been impossibly hard—to pretend. So, you had to act like his wife?" Mrs. Morello leaned in, and she gently touched Madeline's elbow.

Goose bumps prickled up Madeline's neck. "I knew I would have nothing left otherwise."

Then she bit her tongue; she couldn't say any more.

She locked her eyes on a clothing rack. Something stable. Her presentation to the public: a beautiful row of dresses.

"It sounds like he was almost holding you hostage, in a way . . . for his crimes." Gently, Mrs. Morello set her fingertips on Madeline's chin and tilted it upward; then she paused for a long moment before stroking Madeline's hair. "It doesn't seem to me that a man like that should be a Brooklyn councilman. What do *you* think, my dear?"

Madeline gulped and shook her head. Then she broke into a sweat, her eyes locked up front again on the tarp that shrouded the gaping hole in the broken window.

The news would spread among the society circles.

When he found out that she had told, a shattered window couldn't be enough for him.

28

Lisa

Lisa remained in the driver's seat for a while, wide-eyed with her experience after leaving Billy's apartment.

Elaine might appreciate some company. But she still didn't know where Elaine lived. She'd tried to call Elaine on the phone after the Starlite memorial service, but her sister had answered and reported that Elaine had retired to bed.

It might be too soon for Elaine to have visitors after all.

Instead, she would go see if the Starlite was having a function.

As Lisa drove, her shoulders slackened with the excitement and strain of her experience. She had never before seen Billy so up close, or as clearly, as in his bedroom, when he had fully revealed himself.

When she arrived at the Starlite, a security guard was once again stationed outside the door. She found a parking spot, then stepped out into the crisp air. A fine mist of rain showered her exposed face.

As she neared the entrance, the security guard smiled and motioned her inside. A silver cash box sat on a little table next to him. The Starlight was becoming a swanky spot now, with a guard and apparently an entry fee too.

"Lisa!"

A voice—someone else. She jolted and turned around. Some ways down the street was Billy.

He looked taller than usual, and his brow was furrowed with some sort of anger.

"Hey," Lisa said, taken aback. The security guard was watching them; he shot her a strange look. "Why are you over here?"

"I called and your mom said you were here." Billy squinted at the Starlite.

"Why are you here?" she asked again.

"I wanted to make sure you were safe. And not coming here."

"You came here to wait for me?"

He cleared his throat. "It's icy out. You shouldn't be on the roads."

"It's not icy."

"I don't think you should be here, Lisa. I heard that the owner of the shop is a . . . well . . . that she . . ." He leaned toward her, out of earshot of the security guard, and stuttered, "I heard that the owner likes, uh, women."

Lisa laughed. "Who told you that?"

"My father. He heard it from some guys at the office. He told my mother not to come here anymore to shop."

"That's ridiculous. And even if she does like women, so what? I go to plenty of stores owned by men, and men like women. So, what about that?"

He was following her like a little boy.

Since she wouldn't go all the way with him, he'd come up with some silly stories.

Pathetic.

She shivered. It was chilly, though not icy like he'd said it was.

She watched him cast an eye at the Starlite, at the tarp over the front window.

The security guard eyed them.

"I was gonna play cards with Mack and my father tonight. But I thought I should stop here and make sure you weren't out in this weather." He took her bare hands into his own gloved ones, rubbing them to keep them warm. Lisa allowed her fingers to flood with his heat.

Carefree laughter from within the Starlite leaked through the tarp.

Billy continued to hover over her; Lisa slumped down.

She wasn't a little girl.

Then all at once, icy bits pelted down on their heads. Lisa cleared her throat sheepishly. "I guess we'd better go home now."

Billy flashed her a smile. "I'll follow you home."

She exhaled, and he threw an arm over her shoulder. He walked her to her car, steadying her as she hopped over a patch of ice to get to her driver's seat. He drove behind her on the way to her apartment, trailing her on the slippery roads.

The yellow beams of his head lamps featured prominently in her rearview mirror. They each parallel parked outside her building, and Lisa went to his car. He unrolled his window for a kiss. Little pellets of ice melted between their lips, tasting like chilled metal.

"Good night, babe," he said, then drove away.

Lisa bounded up the steps into her warm apartment.

Her legs bounced as she headed straight to her room. Breathless, she plopped down on her bed. The latest issue of her brand-new wedding magazine lay on her dresser. She grabbed it and went directly to a page she had dog-eared—the dress with a six-foot train.

The epitome of glamour. She would look like a movie star.

But soon the pages of white dresses grew blurry, and her eyelids drooped low. She went to her daily calendar to rip off another page. She was scheduled to fly out in a few days.

She would quit after this next flight.

By then, he might have the ring.

29

Madeline

The security guard had a hacking cough, so Madeline sent him home.

It was the evening of the relaxation oasis. As Gloria entertained them with her piccolo, they sipped citrus drinks and looked at glorious pictures of exotic destinations. Madeline had a full-color book she'd gotten through a special magazine offer— "From Hawaii to Indonesia"—with stunning scenes of sunsets and other pictures from nature. She kept the lighting down low to create a calming atmosphere for herself and the ladies.

Madeline glowed under the dim lights with her extra application of rouge, hastily applied. Underneath it all, she was pale, as she worked the cocktail shaker in quick flashes of silver.

"I'll help." Cynthia leaned in and grabbed some glasses.

"We're doing something called a Singapore Sling. I'm mixing in the booze. You can craft the virgin version."

"I'm still living with my parents. I *am* the virgin version!" Cynthia laughed.

In a cascade of laughter, Madeline handed over a series of bottles: juices of lime and pineapple, soda water, and bitters. "Here, I'll pop you a cherry!" she whooped, and slid Cynthia the bowl of maraschinos.

Cynthia took another shaker and got to work. "Hey, do you want to hear something so awkward? My parents are trying to set me up with an orthodontist from New Jersey. They're trying to get me off Bernard. This orthodontist guy is my uncle's friend's son, or something like that.

My parents had him over for dinner three times last week . . . He takes out his floss right at the table—it's so disgusting! And he had the nerve to call me *hon*." She sighed. "Ugh, my parents think I'm past my prime . . . that I'll *settle*."

"Maybe you need to invent a fictional fiancé so they'll lay off." Madeline poured out the drinks with rapid reversals of her wrists. "Mr. Fake Fiancé could be named after our next imbibement: Tom Collins." Madeline plucked more bottles from beneath a shelf of hair ribbons and slid them over the counter.

Cynthia splashed unmeasured amounts into a stemmed glass and took a sip. "*Oof!* Tom Collins is intense!" She laughed. "I'm not sure about him, Madeline. Maybe some of the other girls want a taste!"

Then Cynthia was off, proffering her drink to any takers.

Madeline continued her work, placing sprigs of mint on the rims of cocktail glasses. The music and voices were a heavy blanket over her ears. It was tropical; it was different; it was perfect. Madeline worked at a fast pace, until Lisa pulled her aside. She was asking for some advice about her boyfriend—was he going to ask her to get married soon? What did Madeline think? Funny how anyone would want her advice about men—but they always did. She was the matriarch of most evenings, and they came to her.

Lisa hovered expectantly, breathlessly. Madeline gathered her words as she chopped thin stems of herb, her palms damp.

Then she paused.

Her eyes flickered to the front of her store, as they did automatically now, throughout the days and nights.

There were a pair of eyes at the bottom of the intact window, peering through a tiny exposed sliver to the side of her mannequin display.

Then there was a flash of forehead. The tip of an ear. The side of a face.

Madeline left Lisa by her lonesome and bolted toward the door.

She strode with an upright posture, prepared for confrontation, as an itchy rage swept her body.

She no longer trembled. She was mobilized. She was ready to end it—to do whatever she had to do.

But the lurker darted away before she could get there.

Now there was only the still sidewalk.

Empty. But she wouldn't just *imagine* men spying on them.

The man in the window hadn't looked like Fred. The tip of his ear was a little pointy.

Nothing like Fred's big old boxy ear.

It could have been someone sent in Fred's place.

⁓

Madeline had never been able to understand Fred's fixation with politics. He had been a post office clerk when they first met, but even then, he was always obsessed with promotion, and he worked his way to the top of their neighborhood post office. After they got married, he took a few law classes, switching jobs to become a legal clerk, then becoming an assistant to his boss, who was running for councilman.

He was obsessed with that campaign—much more enraptured with *it* than with her, though they were newlyweds at the time. Every night he ran through the newspapers, looking for mentions of his boss.

He would constantly mutter to himself, "I'll be the one in those papers one day." He was always on the lookout for someone writing "slander"—something he could tell his boss about, to "catch" them on. "More slander," he would hiss. "But James will take care of it."

She would always freeze in place when he said that. Fred wasn't in the mob or anything of the sort.

Now she would become that voice he muttered about.

The voice of "slander."

But she had spoken only the complete truth. And now the wives of Fred's cronies had learned.

When these society ladies visited her store now, they acted more natural. Friendlier.

One lady even admitted that she was living a similar sham to the one Madeline had been in—married to a man she felt she couldn't leave.

It wasn't easy to leave a man who was in politics.

But the Starlite would continue.

Last night, after the other man peeked in, Madeline had given a hand signal to Gloria to stop playing the piccolo. She got the ladies' attention by jumping up on a chair and tapping a spoon to her glass.

"I have an announcement to make." Her voice quivered even as she worked to steady it. "We're going to need to start putting in place more security features."

The women exchanged glances. A flash of concern burned through the group, evidenced by their crossed arms, their nervous laughter.

"There's a possibility we're being spied upon." She pressed her hands together to stop the shakes. "A couple of times now, I've caught men peering in through the window. Tonight was the second night, which makes me concerned. And I want to ensure the safety of all of you."

"Maybe the cops are onto you, Madeline!" Harriet quipped.

A couple of women laughed. Most just glared at Harriet. Madeline ignored the joke and stared through the intact window again.

If she covered that window up, no one could peek in; but that might not be safe, because someone could be right outside.

"Do you think one of the men was Fred?" Cynthia asked, in a low voice.

Madeline didn't respond. "Here's our plan, ladies." Her voice rose, strident above a song on the record player. "No more entering the Starlite after eight PM. When you travel here, you must arrive in groups, so you're not walking around alone. We'll go through and figure out who lives near whom and set up rides." Her voice cracked; she cleared her throat. "And nobody can leave until the sun is up. I'll order more cots for those who want to sleep. I don't want that door opening and closing late at night. Anyone can come in, and anyone can be followed."

The ladies' nervous giggles were replaced by a strange silence, offset only by the ticking of the clock in the back of the Starlite.

Madeline kept the same brisk voice. "I understand if nobody wants to come anymore."

She scanned their faces. Many of them bit their lips, staring in the distance.

None met her eye.

Their fun was over.

Madeline got down from the chair, her feet unsteady. She tripped a little; it was so dim in the storefront.

Then she began to cry.

She covered her face.

Her breath came in choking sounds—in convulsive sobs.

She knelt down on the floor, and the heaviness of her blood kept her down as it churned through her veins like sludge.

Catherine Huxley raced to her, patted her head. "It's okay, darling! Of course we'll still come."

Then other women ran to her—at first only two or three, but then all fifty or so, surrounding her in a mass of comfort and concern. Harriet squeezed her arm in little pulses as Cynthia stroked her hair. Even Lisa put her hand on Madeline's shoulder, looking doe-eyed and worried.

Madeline's face was splotchy as makeup dripped down her dress, and she cried even more, looking at the beautiful faces of her best friends.

She had done something good, making the Starlite.

Her tears dissolved and melted into her sweat. Even if it ended and nobody came back, they had grown these connections.

They had experienced something together.

"He can't have the power anymore," she whispered to nobody in particular.

Some of the women heard and nodded, which helped her more than they could imagine. Her sobs stopped for the time being, replaced by something resolute.

She had either done too little, or she had done too much.

But she hadn't done anything wrong.

Madeline's body trembled in waves beneath their reassuring hands, which gently patted her arm, her shoulder, and her back—until she reached stillness.

30

Elaine

April 1962

Elaine volunteered for extra work at the *Chronicle* whenever she could. She rotated her activities: she stayed late, did research, organized her desk, and went out for bites to eat with Nia or another coworker.

In the brownstone, nighttime was different. Chilly and silent. Every move she made magnified itself. A climb upstairs was a toil up a mountain. Efforts to make her own simple supper carried the drudgery of concocting a feast for ten.

Yet Catherine was free and easy, without a care in the world.

Catherine had earned a full-time gig, singing at an upscale jazz restaurant in downtown Manhattan. She belted out the hits in front of a five-piece band—swoony covers and originals composed by the band's leader, a man she was dating. She stayed at his place most of the time, if she wasn't at the restaurant. Though sometimes she stopped by the brownstone on her evenings off; at those times, she would forcibly drag Elaine to the Starlite.

But at the Starlite, things were too illuminated. The sounds of chatter ground on her ears. When someone turned up the volume on the music, it was like an assault. She would move to the quietest corner of the room and seek shelter among the tightly clustered racks of clothing.

But the ladies never failed to check on her; they always noticed when she was missing. They were so good to her. They stopped by to bring her casseroles and pound cakes. They gave her hugs on her fragile shoulders, though she puffed as the air squeezed out of her lungs.

She didn't tell them that her freezer was full, and she didn't avoid them. That would be ungrateful of her.

She slept on a fold-out cot in the storefront—she would change what would otherwise have been a long night alone into an easier-to-digest close to the day, surrounded by the snores and laughs of the ladies.

Tommy had never made a last will and testament. She knew his aunt Mary would claim the brownstone as her own. She was his only surviving kin.

The call finally came over two weeks after Tommy's death.

His aunt was brusque; she was ready to assert ownership. "I didn't want to bother you during the mourning period. But I think it's time now for us to discuss some business matters."

Elaine's eyes snapped open as she rolled out of her torpor for a moment with a quickening of her lungs. "Business matters? Such as, Mary?"

"The house, the car. I just want to check—you never legally married Thomas, did you?"

"No, I did not."

"I wanted to make sure. As his spouse, you would have had property rights. But there is nothing legally binding here. You know that I am the next of kin. Everything should have been mine already. My lawyer kept prodding me to call, but as I said, I wanted to give you some time. And I'd like to give you a little more time now. You'll have a month to vacate the brownstone. Feel free to take any personal items that belong to you. But in a month's time, I will be having my broker come to make an assessment, and everything will go on the market."

Elaine bit her tongue, without recourse. "All right."

"Also, I have to ask, Elaine, dear. I heard that Thomas died of intoxication. So, you weren't monitoring him? Making sure he didn't drink too much?" She cleared her throat. "Since you were cohabitating as lovers, you must have been very *close* to one another."

A familiar tremble took its hold on Elaine's arms. "He wasn't my puppy, Mary. I couldn't control him."

"Oh, but that's not what I'm saying at all. I just thought you might have been able to exercise a little more *influence* over the boy. He was really a boy, darling. After all he had been through with his mother dying so young, and his father having died more recently."

Elaine's breath fell heavy on the phone receiver. Her cheekbones receded, slack in her skull. "Mary, you know—"

"I'd better get going; I have an appointment with the beautician. But write down the date of April thirtieth. The broker will come on that date, and anything you want out of the house needs to be gone by then. Let me know if I can assist you in finding another place to live. I have a friend who owns a house who might be able to provide you with assistance."

Elaine grasped the phone receiver and stifled a scream.

The restricted expression cut like a knife, deep into her chest. "Yes. All right. Ta-ta, Mary."

She hung up the phone.

She got up, started to wander around. To straighten things—bring something back to the parlor. Wash a dish. She would leave the house, but she stopped short of the entryway again.

Instead, she would call Lisa. Though she had been surrounded by people on recent nights at the Starlite and during her time at work, she hadn't spent much one-on-one time with a friend.

Lisa was always a breath of fresh air; she was uncomplicated, somehow. Innocent and rosy-cheeked. Interested in new things.

Lisa answered the phone on the first ring. "Hello?"

"Lisa, dearie. I hope I didn't wake you."

"That's all right. How are you? I haven't wanted to call and disturb you."

"That's fine. I was wondering, would you like to come and visit? Have a spot of tea?"

"This morning? That sounds nice! I'll get dressed and be over."

"I'll give you the address." The brownstone was still a mess, things strewn everywhere. Elaine didn't have any sugar, or cream, or milk. But having a guest would be an excuse to tidy up, to pretend that her surroundings still mattered.

She was breathless as she raced around the house, picking up stray articles of clothing and running the carpet sweeper over the rugs.

She paused when she drew near the front door, the zone of the bleach stains.

She went to the washroom and yanked out some bath mats to throw on top of the stains. She took some from the upstairs too.

No matter how she attempted to hide it, it was all still there.

❦

The doorbell rang as Elaine scrounged in the cabinets to find a tin of tea.

She stepped down from the kitchen step stool, brushed off her skirt, and opened the front door.

Lisa was all smiles on her doorstep. Innocence shone through her eyes, a pure light from within.

Elaine was wistful. "You look gorgeous." Lisa still had her youth, and although at age twenty-nine she was only seven years her elder, the gap could be measured in decades. "Come in; I'll make us some tea."

They stepped over the bleached patch of carpet, still visible between the bath mats.

In the kitchen, Elaine opened the freezer. "Care for a little tea cake?"

"Sounds scrumptious."

Elaine gestured to the kitchen table, which she had made an effort to clean. "Have a seat, darling."

"So how did things go—" Lisa hedged, then paused. "Did you end up having a funeral?"

"No. He was cremated. He has no family to speak of, save his aunt. I have the urn. I have to check with his aunt on what she'd like to do with the"—she gulped, then continued—"ashes."

"Ask his aunt? But aren't you—?"

"We weren't married. His aunt is next of kin, so she makes the decisions. She'll be getting this house soon too."

"And how do you feel about that?"

"I'm happy to leave."

"Do you have a place to stay?"

Elaine struggled to open her eyes fully, as though she were having this conversation from beneath the ocean. "I'll go live with my coworker for a couple weeks. But she only has one bedroom, so I'll sleep on a bedroll in the living room. We'll see what comes after that." She sat up in her chair, and she coughed. Her next words came in a high-pitched burst, almost a falsetto: "So, how is your work going? Visit any new places?"

"Well, I was just in India for a week. We went to the Taj Mahal and all that. It was gorgeous. But exhausting. And I really miss my boyfriend when I'm overseas." Suddenly Lisa drew a sharp breath as she glanced up at her surroundings in horror. "Oh gosh, I'm so sorry, talking about my boyfriend and all!" Her cheeks turned cherry red as she curled her lips inward.

Elaine moved forward with weak shoulders and patted Lisa's back. "That's all right, dear. I can imagine it must be tough for you and . . . Billy? Is that his name?"

Lisa reddened even more. "That's right. Anyway, as I always said, I want to quit when I get married."

Elaine's teapot shrieked from the stove. She excused herself to prepare the cups and saucers and the tea cakes, which she had reheated in the oven. Even after being frozen, they had maintained a good texture.

Unlike Elaine, the tea cakes, when prodded, had quickly bounced back.

She sat back at the table and sank her teeth into a tea cake; her salivary glands pricked in pain. The taste evoked a moment from earlier in the year—a night when she and Tommy had been home at the same time. She had baked those tea cakes as they listened to his new records. Tommy had put his head on her shoulder as they watched the record spin, around and around.

"These are wonderful." Lisa finished hers, then grabbed for another. "Maybe you could give me the recipe."

Elaine got up. She had a task to do. Her hand ached to do an activity. She brought out a recipe card and penned the ingredients in her best handwriting. She had been frozen for activities, aside from work, and had written her last poem weeks ago, for Tommy's memorial, at Madeline's entreaty.

Lisa smiled at her hopefully. "So, what do you think about going to the Starlite tonight?"

"Don't you have a hot date? It's Saturday, isn't it?" Elaine was sarcastic—not her usual tone.

Lisa laughed. "Billy's working overtime today, and he told me that he'll be exhausted. But I'll go visit him at the construction site this afternoon. Maybe you and I could go to the Starlite afterward?"

"Maybe I'll try and make a showing of it."

She would just close her eyes when she walked out of the brownstone, past that stain.

31

Lisa

Lisa shed her cardigan before the walk from her car to the construction site. Springtime had arrived in Brooklyn. She had downed so much tea that she almost jumped around the streets, rabbitlike. The outside air was fresh after the stifling atmosphere of Elaine's brownstone.

Billy would be happy to see her for this surprise visit. She wouldn't have to wait too long—unless he was out on a crane.

The water had a different feel during the springtime. Boats sluiced by in the distance: pleasure crafts, high yachts and low motorboats.

Nearer to the site, Mack worked in dusty, baggy pants that drooped from his waist. He hoisted a big bag onto the back of a truck with a loud grunt.

"Hey there, Mack." Lisa smiled; Mack was Billy's friend, after all.

"Oh, hi." Mack's pale eyes strained against his scarlet cheeks as he pushed the gigantic bag to the front of the flatbed. He hopped off the truck and spit a wad on the ground, strutting over to her with one cheek puffed out. "I guess you're looking for Billy."

"Yep. Have you seen him?"

His face grew redder. "Billy's pretty busy right now. I think he's talking to someone." He stopped in his tracks as his eyes swept down her body, lingering on her chest and arms.

Lisa felt her waist for her cardigan, but she had left it in the car. She folded her arms over her chest.

Suddenly, Mack whistled, piercingly loud. Lisa covered her ears as Mack spun to face the other direction. Billy was heading their way in his construction overalls.

He was joined by his father, who wore a business suit.

Lisa gulped and took a few steps back. It was her first encounter with Billy's father since the airplane ride.

"Mack, just tell Billy I came to say hello."

"Hey, wait up—he knows you're here. He gave me the hand wave when I whistled." Mack grunted and hoisted up another large bag.

She stood in place, tongue-tied; then she tried out different faces for Billy's father as she kicked around some dust:

A foul stare of disapproval.

An angry gaze of retribution.

A neutral look of casual disregard.

"Hey, babe," Billy shouted.

The two of them walked toward her. His father's clothes were always tightly tailored—impeccably neat—and today was no exception.

Billy's father approached Lisa directly, with a firm handshake, followed by a peck on the cheek. "Good to see you." He smiled. "A fine day. Gorgeous weather."

Her facial muscles tensed into another smile. "A nice day." She reached up to wipe off a drop of saliva he had left behind on her cheek.

"I've been taking Dad for a tour of the yard, introducing him to some guys here. Dad is now Fred Abbott's campaign manager, so he wants to get a feeling for the constituency and introduce himself to the laborers." Billy puffed out his chest, a proud son.

"Fred Abbott?" The Starlite ladies sometimes mentioned him—Fred was Madeline's ex. She had heard Madeline utter his name only once, in an unexpected blast of expletives, while drinking cocktails.

Two pieces of scum are better than one. Lisa's tongue silently formed the words, and she almost giggled out loud at her ridiculous unspoken joke. She smiled, inquiring, "Is Abbott the borough councilman?"

"He's been in office for some time now. And he's done quite well, bringing extra money into Brooklyn." Billy's father grinned and cocked his brow upward.

Lisa turned away to scan for an escape route. "Yep. Well, better be going. I'm starved. Haven't eaten all afternoon."

Billy grabbed her hand to pull her back. "Where are you going? Let me come with you."

"I'm just going to grab some pizza."

"That sounds great, babe. Hey, Pops—do you want to join us?"

His father chuckled. "I'm not going to be the third wheel! And I have a few more places to visit this afternoon. Have a great time, kids. Pizza on me!" He stuffed some bills into Billy's hand and gave him a hearty pat on the back.

Lisa's ears turned pink.

⌒

The pizza parlor was crowded, swarming with guys from the construction site, and Billy seemed to know each and every one of them. He went around and gave everyone handshakes as Lisa sipped a Coke, alone, at their booth.

She watched him flit his eyes briefly to a slim blonde girl in the corner.

Then he slid into the booth next to Lisa and slung his arm around her shoulders. "Five slices, coming right up!"

"Five slices for us?"

"*Two* pieces for you today, babe. Does it feel good to see pizza again? I wonder what sort of food they have in India. Or where did you say you went? Beirut?"

"Beirut. It's in Lebanon, far away from India. I didn't see any pizza there."

"Humph." He slurped down long strings of the hot, melting cheese, then switched topics. "Hey, you wanna catch a flick tonight?"

"I can't. I told my friend Elaine I would join her at the Starlite tonight. Remember, she's that girl whose fiancé passed?"

"You mean the one who drank himself to death?"

She gaped at him. "Yes, if you put it like that. She's still recovering, so I'd like to help cheer her up."

"Why don't you bring her to the movies with us?"

"I don't think she'd want to be a third wheel. Besides, Elaine and I already made the plans, and we're going to the Starlite."

A sudden look crossed Billy's face, as though he had tasted something unpleasant, but it disappeared as quickly as it had arrived. Their conversation shifted to other things: the Mets' upcoming season, the upgrades he wanted to make to his car.

Lisa had planned to meet Elaine, so before too long, she gave Billy a good-bye kiss. Some of his work friends noticed and wolf-whistled at them.

Lisa blushed, exited by herself, and walked back to her car, which was still parked near the bridge construction site.

At this hour, the sunset cast a fiery orange glint on the metal frame of the incomplete bridge.

32

Madeline

The security plan had reached the next level. The ladies arrived in small clusters, like Madeline had instructed, between seven-thirty and eight PM.

From her post at the front entrance, Madeline watched the guard screen each visitor before entering.

"Fabulous to see you, darling!" she sang out upon each woman's entrance.

This night would be a return to basics, with sandwiches from the deli and a pile of new books and magazines in the reading and discussion area. The corners of Madeline's mouth could barely keep from turning upward.

So many ladies had ventured out, even under the restrictions.

Things looked different at the Starlite, more like a secluded enclave. A heavy curtain hung from hooks in the ceiling. A dozen extra portable cots revealed themselves in a bumpy outline at the back of the storefront. It would be a big slumber party tonight, once they entered the wee hours of the morning—the biggest one yet.

She wouldn't be a pawn in Fred's game; she would find ways to win it.

"Elaine! Wonderful to see you, darling! And Lisa, hello! Thank you both for joining us!"

Elaine seemed much thinner, frail since her fiancé's passing. Her complexion was always fair; this evening she was distractingly pale. But her black hair was neat, carefully parted to one side. And she had arrived with Lisa, so she was making an effort to stay social.

"Wonderful to see you too, Madeline." Elaine's eyes seemed to glisten with moisture, but she brushed it away, smiling. "Always wonderful to see you. Looking forward to telling you more about my job later."

"I can't wait to hear about it, but I'm on door duty right now, dear. At eight PM, we're locking up, and then I want every detail." Madeline took a peek outside the door, past the security guard, and spotted a man across the street, walking with a shopping bag. She leaned out the doorway to scan the sidewalk, but her own security guard nodded her inside.

When the clock struck eight, she inhaled deeply.

"No more newcomers, dear," she instructed the guard, and then she shut the door—hard. The wall vibrated with the intensity of the slam, and the revelers on the dance floor froze their movements, wide-eyed. She laughed it away. "Carry on, ladies!"

Then she threw off her heels and joined them in her stocking feet, slipping into the rhythms of the music. Cynthia slid to her side and grabbed Madeline's hand, and they made little box steps that ended in single claps, which only grew in volume.

⌒

Breathless from the dancing, Madeline poured herself a spiked cider, and a sip of spice danced across her tongue as she stood behind a side counter for a moment.

Taking another sip, she glanced over to a display of handmade bucket hats, where Elaine and Gloria were chatting. "Hey! Girls—do the two of you want some cider?"

Elaine was pale—giving Madeline only a halfhearted smile—but Gloria grabbed her arm and pulled her toward Madeline's counter.

Madeline brandished the pitcher of cider with a spark in her eye, and the two of them sat down on two high stools in front of the counter, pushing aside stacks of hand-drawn dress patterns to make room for their feet.

"So this is just cider?"

"It's a special cider, Elaine. You'll love it." Madeline held out the pitcher toward Gloria, who accepted a full glass.

Elaine bit her lip, appearing nervous. "I don't know—I've only been having tepid tea these days—not much more than that."

"Don't worry, darling. I'll just give you a tiny taste." Madeline smiled with reassurance, splashing a miniscule amount into the glass on the counter in front of Elaine.

Gloria playfully clinked her cider cup against Elaine's. "Delicious, eh?"

Elaine took another sip, almost in guilt. Her skin assumed a faint glow. "Yes," she conceded. "Tell us about your job." Gloria sidled close to Elaine, talking above the hubbub of the social club. "It sounds beyond amazing. I would do anything to work at the *Chronicle*."

Elaine's lips edged upward. "It's fast-paced. I stay busy most of the time. It can be high intensity if there's a lot of breaking news." She paused. "It's fine to be a fact-checker, for now."

"For now? Are you considering something else?" Madeline asked.

Elaine looked around, at the women who chatted in tight groups. "I always dreamed of being a reporter." She gestured to her handbag and squeezed her journal inside a leather pocket. "But there's not much room for poetry in journalism. And I think there's maybe . . . a grand total of *three* women who work outside of fact-checking."

Gloria gave her an encouraging pat on her back. "Well, you could be number four!"

Elaine seemed in a daze; she didn't respond at first, and then she laughed, sadly. "That's right." She paused, her eyes locked—trance-like—at something in the distance. "How about you? What do you want to do?"

"Well, I'm trying to break into writing, any way I can. You know, I don't have a college degree, so nobody's going to hire me to be a reporter. But I'm making the news bulletin for my apartment building. It's called *The Jacobs Tribune*. I made that name up; doesn't it sound professional? I have a copy here." Gloria went to her purse and pulled out a carefully folded paper. "It's not much, but I'm thinking I could make it bigger. I might even do one for my whole block."

She handed the thin brochure to Elaine, who read it carefully, then handed it to Madeline to read. The brochure lacked photographs or illustrations, but a quick read revealed agile prose and a subtle sense of humor.

"I love that headline: 'New Elevator Uplifting Residents.'" She handed it back to Gloria.

Elaine nodded in agreement. "It's quite well done." Her voice emerged stronger than it had in some time. "Save it. It would be perfect for a portfolio."

"Portfolio?"

"Just keep it together with anything else you do. It will impress employers to see examples of your work."

"Oh! Thanks for the advice!"

Gloria beamed at Elaine, ear to ear. Her smile opened up new dimensions of hope, which registered so acutely that Madeline had to look away.

⌒

Madeline stared at the tarp over her broken window as the women snoozed intermittently in their cots.

It was late. Too late.

She found an empty cot and at last lay down to rest amid the others. In the semidarkness, women whispered to each other as they tossed and turned on their hard cots.

Nothing was comfortable.

It might happen again, if men lurked outside. Sharp pieces of glass, hurtling in. They could take down the guard if they needed to.

Her backed ached as she repositioned herself in dozens of revolutions, but she couldn't settle comfortably.

It would be easy to shut it down.

It would be safer to shut it down.

It would be more comfortable to shut it down.

Madeline rotated, over and over, as the rough blanket scratched her skin.

It was so late at night.

If the social club ended, she could focus even more on her dressmaking. Put all her stock into sewing and her business.

It would be easier.

But then Fred would win.

He would check her intact window and see it darkened, night upon night.

It was four AM, cold in the storefront. Chilly air wafted in through the break in the window, beneath the tarp. She would need to secure the tarp to make the room warm. She made her way through rows of half-sleeping women, pulling a bedsheet from an empty cot to stretch over the tarp.

Back at the window, she tried to tape it, standing on her tiptoes to reach the window frame.

Through the darkness of the storefront, Harriet approached her, speaking in a sleepy whisper: "Here—let me help." She stumbled over in a half sleep and held the corner of the sheet. "I can't sleep, seeing you do this all by yourself."

"Thank you, dear."

The two of them worked quietly. They spread the sheet taut until it stretched fully. The cold air still had an entry point, but at least the cloth blunted the frigid winds.

Madeline cupped her face in her open palms, still in her dress clothes and jewelry. Her lids refused to close, even though the guard was still outside.

"Hey, how are you?" Harriet whispered.

"Fine."

"I hope so." She patted Madeline's shoulder. "You know, I think it's a great idea to get a security guard. I'm glad you did this so we could keep coming. I would go insane if I had to spend every night at home."

"Yeah? Why?"

"Frank drives me crazy."

"What? What does he do?"

"He makes me do the deed every day, even if I'm not in the mood. He thinks it's his right. And sometimes I just need some time away. Like tonight, I told him I was spending the night at my sister's. That's where he thinks I am."

"What does he do if you try to stop him?"

"Well, he's really tall, you know, really big. And the way he stands over me—I just don't want to try anything. I don't want to get him mad." Harriet was small in the corner of the window, hunched over, and her profile made a curved silhouette against the wall. Not more than twenty-two—but aged. "I know that other women are dealing with things like that. Or completely different things. Or maybe they're all alone and have no one. But whatever the case may be, I think it's a good place here."

"Thanks, my dear." Madeline gave her a wan smile.

Harriet looked at Madeline, young and hopeful again. "It is. We need this. It's a place just for us girls. A place to have fun. Because, you know, we need to have fun in life."

Madeline looked out over her store. Most of the women were sleeping, but she heard whispers; others were wide awake as they told each other their secrets.

They existed in that moment, no matter what would come.

If she took the Starlite away from them, the ending would be her doing.

⌒

It took a couple of days for her to decide for sure.

Madeline's fingers ran down long spools of thread, winding and unwinding the notion until the thread lay flat, in perfect circles.

She was struck with round after round of violent chills, as if a deluge of ice water had been sent through her veins.

She crouched down onto the floor and huddled into the skirts of her puffy dress.

Nothing brought comfort.

Even her decision.

She cradled the phone receiver with a hand of ice.

The society-pages reporter was friendly when she answered, almost neighborly. "I heard you might give me a ring. Good to hear from you, Madeline. You're making the right choice." She chatted with Madeline like an old friend and congratulated her on her bravery.

Madeline huddled beneath her skirt. "I'm a little nervous. I don't know what the retribution will be."

She couldn't stop looking outside, as if another rock would hurtle through straightaway.

"Nobody's going to try anything once you've made the society pages, darling. Don't you think it would be a little too obvious?"

Madeline nodded and fingered the edge of her skirt. Her chest rose and fell quickly. "So, how much do you want me to tell you?"

"Every single detail." The reporter coughed. "Hold on, let me get my notepad."

Madeline gulped as her throat started to swell. When the reporter returned to the phone, she coughed out some distorted syllables, unable to speak.

Then she began.

"It was a slow buildup with Fred . . ."

Then she continued.

She remembered him staying out late a lot, claiming he had to go to functions "with the guys."

He was always out. Getting gas for his car. Going to appointments for "aches in the back." Picking up "stuff" from the store—"more packs of cigarettes."

Always in and out, in and out. Sometimes he would smell different, like roses or heavy perfume, feminine scents. She asked him and he said it was hand soap. *All the hand soaps at my office smell like women these days!*

He always laughed.

She checked his collars when she did his laundry and always checked his pockets. But there was never anything, and he was his regular self otherwise, chatting up a storm at dinner, taking her out to shows on the weekend.

He was always so friendly to everyone and anyone—a real man about town. She felt silly to be suspicious, because she had such a sociable, charming husband who was politically engaged and locally powerful.

With Fred being out and about so much, she had a lot of free time, so she took up sewing projects when she wasn't cleaning or cooking. She had always been good at sewing. Before she married Fred, she had worked at a little dress shop in downtown Brooklyn. So, once she had all this free time, she toyed with the idea of opening her own dress shop in a nice part of Brooklyn Heights.

Fred encouraged the project, and he gave her some starter money. She became busy when he was, and in that way she found plenty of things to do when he was at work, or at another "male-only" function.

"Too much detail?"

"Not at all. You're showing me that he was building a facade around himself, trying to be the Fred that everyone thought he was."

"Okay."

Then she told the society-pages reporter more—about the day when she climbed up the stairs to her apartment and saw a woman scuttle out through her own door.

Fred claimed that this woman was a missionary, knocking on the door to try to convert him. But she sure didn't look the part in her form-fitting attire, pointy brassiere, and high heels.

But there was no evidence. Nothing was out of place in the apartment.

"I thought you had a late day at work today," she told him.

"I thought you had a late day too. Why are you home so early?"

He was an expert at flipping things around.

He got craftier after that first time. She was pretty sure the other liaisons didn't take place in their apartment, though she received phone calls from women sometimes. They asked for Fred but wouldn't give their names. She told him about the calls, and he said they must be "sleazy reporters" trying to pin him for something.

The day when she finally confirmed her worst fears was an unexpected one. She was at a gala function, a political fundraiser in a large hall overlooking the East River. It had been a gorgeous day, and she was in a great mood, looking at the sunset and sipping a perfect cocktail creation while having a lovely chat with the district attorney's wife. The district attorney's wife had just invited Madeline and Fred out to her estate on the East End of Long Island.

Madeline wanted to check to see if that date worked with Fred. She searched the reception hall for him, to no avail.

She went to get her coat so she could search outside for him, but the coat check girl wasn't at the window. So she opened the door to the cloakroom herself, grabbing her woolen coat from its hanger.

That's when she heard him.

"Quickly," he said, behind a closed door.

She opened the door, and there was his naked backside, hairy and pale, with the coat check girl kneeling in front of him.

She didn't say anything.

She only saw streaks of white.

Fred turned to face the open door, and she slammed it, running to the ladies' room, where she vomited, over and over again, as if willing her insides to get rid of this horrific thing. She wanted to stay in that stall forever, but other women started banging at the door to ask if she was all right. When she coughed out that she was okay, the women whispered to each other that she must be pregnant.

She emerged from the stall about an hour later. A fully-dressed Fred was back in the ballroom, chatting with his cronies, puffing on a cigar. She was about to rip the cigar from his mouth and tell him that she was leaving him, right in front of everyone.

Before she could do it, he gave her his big Fred smile, putting his arm around her. "We'll be going now, dear," he said.

She wrangled herself away from his grip as party guests looked on in curiosity. Madeline kept silent for aching, choking minutes, and on the walk to the car she nearly passed out, but she got in the driver's seat.

Fred didn't dare argue, as he took the passenger's seat. She wouldn't let him drive her anywhere. She left the car idling.

"I'm leaving you."

"Maddy, let's not be silly now. You must have known, dear. I've made it quite obvious. You can't really be that dense."

He'd done it again, flipping it around on her. "I hope you burn in hell," she said.

"I thought you were more forgiving than that, Maddy. And believe me, I'm not the only man in that ballroom who's guilty."

Inside her beautiful, purple coat, her inner core was boiling and blistering—like she was a nothing, a wrinkled crab inside a pretty shell.

"I'm leaving you. When we get to the apartment, I will remove all of my stuff."

"You won't be getting any of my things, Madeline. People saw the way you acted today. I can easily say that it was you who got in some trouble."

"Nobody will believe you."

"Everyone will believe me. I sell promises for a living."

She started up the car and drove home in silence, mechanically. She was dead but still moving. She didn't have anywhere to go but home. All her friends were wives of Fred's cronies.

When they got back to the apartment, Fred put his hand on her arm.

"How about we make this easy on you—I have a few places to live. You can have the apartment. You can still play the role of my wife. You'll have every material thing you want from me. I'll do my thing, and you do yours."

She didn't respond.

Once they got to their apartment, Fred packed up a few bags and left.

She wanted to leave too. It felt filthy at home, though she kept it sparkling clean. But her dress shop wasn't making enough money, and she had nowhere to go unless she wanted to live in a tenement. She didn't want to be a woman alone in a tenement—so she stayed.

She worked long hours. She continued going to social functions, playing the role of wife, dead-eyed as Fred came to pick her up in his town car. At the functions, she tried to drum up more business for her shop to give her some savings, so she could move out on her own to somewhere that Fred couldn't find her.

After months of loneliness, she started the social club. Then she met these lovely women, her friends, and Brooklyn didn't belong to Fred anymore.

❦

She told the reporter about the divorce, about the lies he spread.

And she told her about the broken window.

"You think he's out to get you?"

"He could be. I'm sure he would love to see me disappear." Madeline paced, and the telephone cord dragged around the carpet, picking up little pieces of lint. Her voice slurred with the effort to talk. "When will the article come out?"

"It shouldn't be more than a few days," the reporter answered. "You better get ready. I have a feeling that a lot more women will be coming to your shop and club, now that you'll be public."

"Public?"

" 'Owner of the Starlite Dress Shop Reveals All.' That's our headline!"

"Fred's name won't be in the headline, will it?"

"He'll get his fair share of headlines after this comes out, darling." The society-pages reporter laughed.

It was too late to keep quiet.

33

Madeline

A few days after Madeline made the phone call, she decorated the storefront in paper cutouts of stars and moons, created from pieces of discarded fabric patterns.

Celestial accents shimmered everywhere: on the carpet, shelves, and racks. Early arrivers to the social club enjoyed a telescope positioned between the blinds of the intact window.

"Have you heard?" Madeline announced. "We're going to send a satellite to the moon this week."

She was paying strict attention to the news now, buying a paper each morning. She would turn through the pages with sweaty palms, looking for her name, but she hadn't found it yet. There were headlines about space instead. Lots of speculations about the grandness of it all. It reassured her to read these pages of something magnificent and large, beyond herself.

Elaine's lips drew upward with effort. "Oh? The satellite will launch straight from the Starlite, I presume?"

Madeline laughed heartily. "Well, the U.S. government has a big part in it!"

"Those Americans! They're always up to something." Elaine gave a more earnest laugh—seeming to surprise herself as her eyes twinkled.

"We're a hoot, aren't we?" Madeline smirked, with a sudden sassy lightness of being. "If they find little green men up there, maybe they'll send them down here. I'm looking for a new green man!"

A certain kind of moonshine was burning through her veins now; she glowed with something new, and her spirit soared in release.

Lisa smiled. "You look great! Hey, let me check out what you have tonight. Is that a new rack of clothes?"

"Oh, darling, you have to see this newest thing I just got in! It would look perfect on you!"

Madeline flipped through a rack and pounced on a pastel-blue flounced skirt. Lisa slipped it on over the skirt she was already wearing and spun around in front of the mirror. Then she went around the Starlite and modeled it in twirls; the tulle expanded like a blossom in its burst.

34

Lisa

Elaine's crew—the regulars—had started to make their literary circle. Lisa joined them; though she wasn't yet a regular, sometimes she did a bit of writing.

She could only imagine Billy's reaction if he saw her, with her little notebook on her knee, sitting with the other ladies. Though her flouncy skirt defied any image of *beatnik*.

"What's our topic tonight?"

"We're doing something about space. What do we all imagine that it's like out there?"

The women in the circle scribbled with their stubby pencils, focused in their reverie, as others nearby enjoyed laughter and dancing. Lisa eyed the partiers on the dance floor a bit wistfully as she struggled to begin writing.

Elaine had frozen up again. She made a gaunt shape, hunched over her notebook, unable to generate anything new. Lisa tried to make a show of her own writing to encourage Elaine; it was slow going, but she tried to scrawl down some words.

"I think I'll write about when I was a kid," Lisa whispered suddenly. "My parents couldn't pay the electric bill one month, and I woke up from sleep one day with icicles up my nose. That's what I imagine space is like. *Freezing* and bleak."

"Icicles in the nose?" Elaine lifted her head, taken aback. "I've never heard of that happening to someone. That must have been terrifying."

Lisa nodded slowly. Then she started to write.

In the middle of the circle, Jackie came and sat with them. She hadn't been to the Starlite since the day the window was smashed.

Jackie accepted a pad of paper from Elaine and got to writing. She bent over her work, writing without saying a word.

Lisa tapped her shoulder and whispered, "I'm happy to see you here." Many weeks had passed since Lisa had last seen Jackie, that day at the dry grocer's where her husband publicly bullied her. More obvious bruises now covered Jackie's arms, which were draped in a shawl of green lace.

"Thanks. My husband's visiting his brother in New Jersey. He'll be there overnight and into the morning. He's going to move us to Jersey soon. He says he doesn't like me walking around Brooklyn—there's too many men on the sidewalk, and he doesn't like how they look at me!" Jackie laughed bitterly.

Lisa leaned over to squeeze her arm. "Really? He said you have to move because of that?" But Jackie didn't respond, pulling back from her touch, so she modulated her tone. "Oh, goodness. I'm so sorry to hear you'll be leaving us."

Jackie kept her head down, looking at her work. "Yes." She bit her lip. "Thanks."

Lisa bent her head down too and whispered, "It must be hard for you."

Jackie was silent as her eyes skittered across an empty page on her lap. She turned away, and a tear fell on the paper. Then she cleared her throat.

Lisa put a hand on her arm for comfort. The other women in the circle didn't notice, absorbed in their work.

"Thank you," Jackie whispered, her head still down.

She made a motion to go back to writing, and she and Lisa each wrote only a few words between them before the ladies started up again with their reading.

Gloria raised her arm, as if in school. "I'll read first!"

Starlight.
Twinkles.
A great big glittering mess in the void.
A mind bereft of Earth.
Sing, baby, sing, going into the unknown.

Madeline had come over to the circle to listen, perched next to Lisa. Her eyes also glistened with tears. This display of emotion was too thick for the moment, so Lisa shifted the dynamic after Gloria finished reading. She talked about a photograph she had once taken from an airplane, high up in the atmosphere. It was a clear photo of the edge of Europe—thirty-five thousand feet up in the air.

"I'll go get the photo—I think it's in my car!" Lisa dashed toward the door to go get it. It would be her contribution to the literary circle, a beautiful photo. Nobody would cry; they would look at it in awe.

But at the door, the guard stopped her. "Not a good idea to be running off, miss. Too dark outside. No good to be out there by yourself."

"I just need to run to my car. It's right around the block. I'll be right back."

"Do as you may. But you be careful now," he warned.

Lisa shrugged, though it *was* exceptionally dark out that night.

She scurried quickly across the street, toward her car, in the thin beam of the streetlight.

It was only a moment before someone grabbed her arm.

A large presence pulled her aside.

He was bigger than her.

She let out a shout, before the light reflected off the man's face.

Lisa craned up at him, in the long shadows of the streetlights.

"Billy! What are you doing here?"

He looked strange. Older. Gruff and angry. "I can't believe you're just walking around by yourself!"

"What? What are you even doing here?" she sputtered.

He had an unsettling air about him, on this dark street corner. His usual casual tone was gone, replaced with a sort of glazed distraction.

He shot glances over his shoulder, like he was keeping his eye out for someone. He was urgent as he drew her close, darting glances all around. "I need to take care of you."

"I'm not five years old, you know. You don't have to supervise me."

"I'm not supervising you. I'm watching out for all of *them*."

He gestured with his chin. There was a couple, hand in hand, and a man pushing a hot dog cart. Other stray pedestrians walked past and paid the two of them no heed as they strolled briskly to their destinations.

"Why are you acting like this all of a sudden?"

He cleared his throat and coughed. "I need to make sure that you stay safe."

She gazed longingly at the Starlite, silent in the distance. The security guard stood smoking with a little hunch in his back—without a uniform, he looked just like a man who had found a convenient doorway to provide shelter from the wind.

She took a subtle whiff of Billy's breath. No alcohol.

"I have to get back inside, before the girls start wondering what happened to me. You'd better get going, Billy. I'm spending the night here with the rest of the ladies. There's a guard, you know. I'll be fine."

"Fine." Billy released her from his arms abruptly. "See ya later, sugar cakes."

Then he strode into the darkness, rounding the street corner.

No good-bye kiss.

Her shivers came in a rush as she stood alone on the sidewalk.

She scampered back toward the Starlite, fast as could be.

When she neared the door, the guard looked her up and down with a question in his eye. "Everything all right? That took a little while."

"Everything's peachy keen."

Back in the Starlite, everything was vibrant, bright and buzzing. Warm. Ladies chatted and played cards among the paper stars. Others practiced a new dance step.

In the literary corner, there was an air of focus, with everyone attentive to their writing—even Madeline was writing something. Usually

Madeline didn't sit still for even a moment at the social club, as she perennially mingled or served as the mistress of ceremonies.

But Madeline interrupted her rare state of silence to whisper to Lisa, "You have to be careful, my girl. You can't just run outside into the dark."

Lisa cringed. Everybody was treating her like a child. "Listen, I know about the incident with the window, but things happen. Street vandals, right? They're not always around."

"The vandal who I believe it to be will be getting wind soon, darling. Because there's a story coming out in the papers tomorrow."

"A story?"

With the word repeated, Madeline flinched, and her beautiful long nails turned white above her cigarette holder. "Yes—I spoke to a reporter. So certain things will be said. I just hope they get the story right. I'm not even sure of the things that will be said. I just can't have things be one-sided anymore."

In confusion, Lisa scanned Madeline's face. "I'm not sure I understand."

"Fred would love to have everything be his way. But I'm not going to let that happen. This—" Madeline swung around her long cigarette demonstratively. "This all matters too much to me. And I don't want people to think things about me that aren't true. So now they're going to know the truth."

Lisa pushed back her cuticles; her own nails were painted a five-cent shade of pink. "The truth?"

Madeline grew quiet. She had looked much younger an hour ago, when she had greeted everyone at the door with a sense of sensational vibrancy. Now her face dimmed as she cleared her throat, deflecting the question. "So, what do you have there?" She flicked the photograph in Lisa's hand.

"Oh!" Lisa brightened. "This is the picture I took from my trip to India! The tip of Europe, from way up high. Can you make it out? I think it's Spain. Isn't it amazing?"

"It's beautiful," Madeline answered, and she seemed to mean it. "What's it like—going all these different places on an airplane?"

"I love it. Have you ever been on a plane?"

"Never. Fred went on trips, but he never wanted me to come with him."

"Oh."

Madeline smiled. "Maybe one day I'll take a trip. I've always wanted to go to England, you know. Wouldn't it be a delight to be surrounded with so many beautiful accents at once? I know I just can't get enough of listening to Elaine."

"Yeah." Distracted, Lisa glanced toward the front entrance. Billy could be roaming the neighborhood, just stewing. She let out a large exhalation as she moved to the dance floor for another dance.

When she turned back to the literary circle, she looked for poor Jackie, to say good-bye—but Jackie had already disappeared from the Starlite.

35

Elaine

Elaine had completed her thousandth delay tactic of the evening—cleaning out her wastepaper basket, riffling through her drawer.

The brownstone would be empty if she went home.

She dawdled on the sidewalk, looking in the windows of Midtown shops. Outside the movie theater, she stared at the marquee. Women didn't usually attend the pictures alone, but the images generated by Hollywood loomed so large on the screen that it would be an escape to allow herself to fall right into them.

She stood outside the movie theater and got in line to pay for her ticket.

A hawker moved past the ticket line, selling the late edition of the rival paper to the *Chronicle* at a discount rate because it was the end of the day. This other paper had a bit of a lowbrow feel with its "society pages"—a gossip column in disguise—but Elaine could immerse herself in some dirt now. Dirt was a distraction.

The society pages were a few pages in; she flipped to them and gasped.

There was something in here about Madeline.

A story about her and Fred. No lurid details, yet the implications were clear. Fred had been cohabitating with another woman for many years while Madeline played the role of his innocent wife. There had been other women, too, for years before their divorce.

Madeline was a skilled actress, then. Even better than the ones in the pictures.

There was even a suggestion in the story that Madeline suspected Fred in the vandalism to her shop.

Elaine's own friend—in the news!

She would telephone her, but she knew how abrasive the ring of the phone could be during a time of turmoil. It would do her a service to give her some space. She would see Madeline soon enough, in person.

The article was sure to bring her friend a lot of attention. Madeline's style would likely be to minimize it all—to enact the role of proceeding as normal.

Elaine didn't have those skills of an actress. She was "emaciated," according to everybody. She was "extremely pale." Everyone continued to hover over her with worry, even though it had been weeks since Tommy died.

Elaine would eat some extra popcorn at the film tonight. She would force herself to navigate the greasy kernels, though eating anything left her doubled over in cramps later.

But even as she paid for her movie ticket, she couldn't stop staring at Madeline's name in the society pages.

The Starlite would get attention.

It wouldn't be their enclave any longer.

36

Madeline

Madeline hadn't seen the article yet.

After a full weekend of being a social butterfly and dress shop owner, she needed a day to herself to get organized. She had started closing the shop on Mondays. Harriet was happy to have the day off.

As the surrounding commercial district buzzed with business and activity, her shop was quiet. Only muted sounds of car horns and pedestrians entered from the outside as the racks lay undisturbed. It was a stark contrast to the thump of the social club in full swing, when the rest of the neighborhood sat empty, silenced for the night.

On this Monday, she lolled about in the silkiness of her satin robe as she applied cold cream to her face in her back room. She had finally saved up a little money to get her own apartment, but for now, she would stay here. To move somewhere else would require a great upheaval.

Though Fred had to know her whereabouts, and she had told that society reporter everything about them—about him.

Everything would come out soon.

Madeline flipped on her little television in a flash. But her own story wouldn't make broadcast news. Instead she watched a startling scene from Cape Canaveral of the satellite that had been launched earlier today, headed straight to the moon.

Life was becoming so big, everything so expansive. Things used to be small.

Inside her own beautiful little shop, she could rest. She could shut out the outside world. Though she didn't have much in the way of food—only a can of beans, which wouldn't suffice for a full day.

The local luncheonette was always good for a sandwich and a soda. She would exit her enclave and head into the world.

It was raining. Even with the protection of an umbrella, her fresh curls lost their bounce. She shook her wet head like a puppy to dry out as she walked at a brisk pace. Cars splashed water from the edges of their wheels and soaked her stockings.

"Late edition! Late edition!" The newspaper man barked extra loud underneath his roomy umbrella as he brandished copies of the paper, wrapped up in plastic. Madeline handed him a dime, which she passed beneath their umbrellas.

Her fingers shook in the cold rain as she carried the paper beneath her poncho, making her way to the luncheonette.

It was almost empty in the restaurant, so she took a little booth for herself, then pulled out the paper. She kept to the front page at first, her eyes on the space shuttle. But soon she moved in a rush of flips to the gossip section as her soggy fingers smudged the newsprint.

HE DID WHAT? INDISCRETIONS OF COUNCILMAN UP FOR RE-ELECTION!

It was the lead story.

Everything was in black and white for the world to see:

Fred's dalliances with other women. The way he had made her pretend to be his wife. The way he had mishandled their divorce.

Even the fact that he might have been snooping at the window of the Starlite a couple of weeks before the rock was hurled through the window.

The Starlite, a private social club for women, was violated by this act of vandalism, which may or may not be connected to Mr. Abbott. The club's loyal patrons continue to frequent the establishment. Many of them say that "the Starlite" is a necessary fixture in their lives.

A necessary fixture. She reread the last five words again and again. The reporter must have interviewed some of her ladies. Her family. She was crying.

A necessary fixture in their lives.

They were her family.

The newspaper grew soggier, damp from the rain mixed with her tears. Nothing would be a secret.

Nothing. Including her own social club.

The waitress brought over her salami sandwich, and Madeline closed the newspaper, as though she could be recognized from a passage of text.

The waitress served her without comment. She ate her lunch, eyes locked in a trance on the crusty bread, on the yellow mustard in its squeeze bottle.

The Starlite would be *known*.

And she was the one who had made the phone call to the reporter; *she* was the one who had made it happen.

She shuddered, her breath quickening.

Madeline pushed aside her food, unable to eat.

37

Lisa

The ring was a little loose on Lisa's hand.

She felt for it often, making sure it hadn't fallen off.

Her left thumb kept the diamond pressed inward, hidden in her palm as she danced with the ladies. It was the most expensive thing she had ever touched, and now she wore it on her very own finger.

Billy had proposed a few days prior. He did it at Woolworth's, near the soda counter. He gave her a balloon that you had to pop to see if you had won a free soda. She used a pin from the soda jerk to pop the balloon; then her engagement ring fell to her feet. The soda jerk went into hysterics when he saw the expression on her face.

Billy grabbed the fallen ring, and then he crouched down on one knee, next to her high stool.

"Will you marry me?"

Customers nearby stared, wide-eyed, as though they were in a movie or a television show. Lisa said, "Yes," and she and Billy kissed; everyone clapped. A cashier at the other end of Woolworth's dabbed her eyes with a tissue.

She hadn't told anyone yet. They might still remember the day he left her at the airport and disappeared from her life back in February, and although she had been back together with him for several months now, they wouldn't have easily forgotten.

It was too soon for her to share the news. But he had apologized for everything, so it was all in the past.

Everyone made mistakes sometimes.

The stone on her ring was round-cut, beveled. The diamond spoke of a substantial outlay of money, of enough to care for her—and even her family—in the future.

Though when Billy had called her on Wednesday to ask for a date, she lied, saying that she had plans to celebrate that night with her friends.

"Are you going to the Starlite?" He was gruff, expectant.

She replied, in a chipper voice, "Yep, that's where I'm going!"

"That's a bad idea, babe. You know, my father is working for Fred Abbott right now. You really shouldn't be going to the establishment of his ex-wife."

He bossed her, as though he were telling a worker on his site to move a plank from a pile.

"Give me a break, Billy. Besides, you saw all of that stuff in the paper? I understand that your father's working for him and all, but Fred Abbott seems like a monster. What a hideous man! Did you read about all those affairs he had?"

"You actually believe all those lies? I don't even read the paper. Who can trust reporters?" Billy scoffed. "You should hear what my father tells me about the press. They're a bunch of fiction writers!"

His father.

His father spoke about the press only with his cigar in the corner of his mouth, his hands scented with something Lisa wouldn't repeat.

She would keep her mouth closed.

Instead of responding to Billy, she sighed. "Well, I'm still going to go spend some time with my friends. A girl has got to celebrate after she gets engaged."

"I guess so. I guess I'll go celebrate with the boys, then, and we'll call it even."

"Sounds good." She was short with him.

For a moment, neither of them said anything.

Then he chortled. "Well. I guess that was our first compromise as man and wife."

He laughed, earnest and funny again, and she couldn't help but to laugh in response, albeit delayed.

They hung up shortly after. Lisa would go to the Starlite. Madeline's sad story was in the newspaper; she would be in a state.

She would need the members of her club.

38

Madeline

Madeline would now be known as "the woman who was cheated upon."

But she was more than that. Much more. Everyone had to see that she was fine. That her business and club were doing fine—even *better* than fine.

She kept the dress shop closed on Tuesday and Wednesday so she could make things look beyond perfect. She tidied everything from top to bottom, shined every clothing rack, set out extra tables and chairs, and added plentiful pops of color—she tucked sprigs of flowers tied with ribbon into every available niche.

Her finished space looked not only gorgeous; it was breathtakingly fresh.

Madeline also looked breathtakingly fresh. She had given herself a mud mask the night before the club would meet, and her skin was radiant. She was bedecked in a dress she had never worn—an emerald-green number, with a beautiful new brooch to match.

The soft hairs on Madeline's arms stood on end as the time drew nearer. She rubbed the back of her neck as her skin erupted in goose bumps.

The security guard was the first to arrive, at six o'clock. He took his station outside and yelled through the doorway. "Looking gorgeous!"

"Thank you!" She checked her reflection and fixed her lipstick.

She scurried to and fro, cleaning and settling everything. It would be their Spring Fling. She waffled through her pile of records, contemplating several choices.

"Madeline! I can't even believe it! You're famous!" Harriet bounded through the door, early as could be, like an excited schoolgirl. "I had to come as soon as I could! I can't believe it! Wow, Fred's gonna get it now, won't he?"

It would be the first vibration of the ongoing theme of the evening: the buzz of scandal. Madeline kept her lips closed as she continued flipping through her stack of records.

The familiar faces entered first. Then, all at once, more ladies flowed in. These were unfamiliar women—friends of friends—women who said they'd heard about the Starlite in the paper and wanted to check it out. The social club had been invitation-only up to this point, but Madeline allowed these new women inside. They chatted a million miles a minute, and she served up little petit fours on plates, which allowed her to circulate, avoiding conversation where she could.

The air quivered with something different; everybody was quicker to laugh. They gathered in groups, circles of old and new patrons.

Her small storefront could barely contain these throngs of women. Madeline greeted each of them warmly, but soon there was more and more, and she lost track of all the new faces.

At the same time, her friends surrounded her—to get her attention, to make conversation:

"That scumbag sure has it coming now!"

"I can't believe you dealt with that for so long!"

She nodded, like they weren't talking about her but about someone else.

She set herself on the organization of things, to get rid of all the chairs, to make standing room for everyone and push back the clothing racks. She enlisted the help of a few ladies to move some heavy tables over to the side.

Elaine came over. She was white as alabaster, and she lightened in color even more as she tried to lift a bulky rack.

"Quite a crowd," she commented, as her frail body strained with effort.

"I can barely believe it," Madeline said, and then she told Elaine to stop. Elaine did so without protest.

Elaine's eyes glazed over as she gestured to the crowds. "It seems as though you've become famous."

"Famous for what?"

The three-ring circus swirled before them. A group of unknown ladies caught sight of Madeline and waved from the other side of the room. Madeline waved back.

"Making top headline on the gossip page is a big deal."

"I know that." She eyed the cots piled in the back. There wouldn't be enough sleeping accommodations for the crowd that evening, and even if there had been enough, the new women wouldn't know about the rule where they had to spend the night.

She couldn't guarantee everyone's safety if the ladies filtered out into the streets at odd hours.

They would all be targets, especially now that the story had broken.

"Damn it!" Madeline exclaimed. She never used such crude language.

"What's wrong?" Elaine whipped around to face her, in a bit of shock.

"There's no way everyone could sleep here tonight! This is a mess!" A choke hold of a sob overtook her, and she dashed to escape prying eyes.

She ran off to her back room.

She would be alone for a moment.

The women knew her secrets, but they didn't know Madeline.

She crumpled into a ball, sobbing at the feet of her back-room sofa. Her hairdo was moist and matted as the wet salt of her tears dripped on the skirt of her dress. She was alone in her close confines behind her little door. Her face was down, smushed into the crevices of her arm, where it was dark.

Soon enough, someone came behind her and interrupted her damp isolation.

It was Elaine, treading with light feet. "Does that feel better now?" She spoke in low tones, in her beautiful British accent.

Madeline's bloodshot eyes balked at this delicate creature in the shadows. Elaine was so skinny that she looked barely able to stand.

"Thank you." She accepted the tissue from Elaine's thin fingers. "I feel like I made a big mistake. Or more than one mistake. And there's nothing I can do about it now."

"I don't understand. What did you do wrong?"

"Everything! First of all, I married Fred—"

"You didn't know he would go with another woman."

"Of course I didn't!"

He had been a boisterous, jovial guy when she met him. He had chatted her up so charmingly, giving her flowers on every date. After he expressed his political aspirations, she had latched on further, excited to have met an ambitious man.

Elaine gave Madeline a sad smile. "They're not always who we think they are, right?"

"I guess not. I guess it's impossible to tell sometimes." Madeline gave a deep sigh, a precursor to sitting up, straightening herself. She pulled at her skirt to get out the wrinkles. She inhaled deeply, and a snort escaped her nose. It was a funny sound.

The two of them laughed in spite of themselves.

They were so separate from the din of the party, tucked away in that tiny back room.

"Care for a petit four?" Elaine had brought in a plate.

She seemed less pale, with a smile on her lips. Madeline tried to smile too and accepted a small square of dessert, allowing her teeth to sink into the sugared, delicate crust. "These are good. I usually don't get around to tasting the food."

"I guess things are different tonight."

"I guess they are."

☙

Elaine gave her a gift later; it was a new record for the Starlite's collection, a jazz album that had belonged to her fiancé. Madeline set it on the turntable, and the din of voices dipped down as the opening riff came on—the clear sound of a trumpet piping, soaring up, up, *up*.

It was a stunning, clear sound. Elaine's fiancé had had good taste.

She stirred to the beat in her hips, with quick steps of her feet. Some other ladies gathered around her, everyone in a rhythm, moving around. The music bounced and rolled, coming to a full crescendo as old and new faces assembled, grooving and shaking, twisting and turning. Women picked up the little bouquets of carnations she had set out, waving them around to the music, and they threw off their shoes, casting them into a big pile on the floor. Madeline caught sight of Lisa, who grabbed her hand, getting her up to dance. Lisa had dropped that flight attendant posturing and was letting her body move to the music. They laughed, and Madeline giggled like she was twenty-two again too.

She was herself again.

Then there came a slow song. Catherine Huxley sang in a tremolo, like a little bird, and the whole giant group gathered around her in awe. Cynthia grabbed one of the silk scarves from her new collection and waved it around in circles that floated and shifted—graceful movements, like water. Catherine's voice soared higher to the heavens, and Harriet swayed back and forth, her arms twirling to match the sound. Even Elaine allowed her guard to go down in front of the others, holding her face up as though the sun had burst through the night, lit up with an unearthly beauty. Together they glowed, in a type of transcendence, and it was all grand, wonderful fun.

Madeline found another album, and they all kept dancing. They took breaks only for sips of water and nibbles of petit fours, and even though it was a weeknight, nobody asked about sleeping, or cots, and nobody tried to leave, and the energy kept them going until the sun rose in the morning.

39

Lisa

By the time Lisa left the Starlite, it was five thirty AM. She blasted the radio as she drove home, turning the knobs in pulses of volume, jolting herself awake.

At home, her mother slept upright beneath a throw blanket on the living room couch. Her father was in the kitchen, making his own breakfast, a rare occurrence for him.

Her father sipped coffee as he read the sports pages, not looking her in the eye.

"Your mother stayed up almost all night waiting for you."

"I didn't want to be walking home too late, so I stayed over." The exhaustion suddenly hit her, and she yawned. Her hand moved in front of her mouth.

"Are you—?" Her father froze suddenly, looking up from the sports pages. A dumbfounded look struck his face.

"I'm engaged, Dad."

He sputtered on his coffee. "You're *what*? When were you planning to tell your mother and I?"

"It just happened on Tuesday. I wanted to wait until Billy could come over so we could tell you the news together." It was a lie she had invented quickly, and she gulped.

Her father set down his coffee, which splashed out on the table. "We'd better wake your mom and tell her too." He got up from his chair as Lisa frantically shook her head.

"No, no, no—let's just wait, Dad—*please*. I need a little time."

"You're going to hide your engagement from your mother?"

"No. It's just . . . I'm so tired. I need to go to bed. I know, I stayed out too late." Her lids were too heavy; she stumbled inside.

In her room, she soon fell asleep, with the ring still on her finger.

A few hours later, Lisa rose, dizzily. She had gotten her period all over her new skirt from the Starlite.

She trudged into the other room. Nobody was around. She cleaned up in the lavatory and put on a sanitary napkin with a belt around her waist.

Then she stepped on the bathroom scale. She had crossed the line. One thirty-one. Weigh-in would be in two days. Adding to that, she was engaged, with an airline expiration date on her head. Her ring would be an invitation for Jane to treat her with even more disregard, because she would be gone from the airline soon anyway.

Some time ago, Lisa had waited tables. She could do it again.

⌒

"Hi, this is Lisa O'Malley. I'd like to know how to go about offering my resignation."

She spoke to someone she had never talked to before.

The lady on the phone was aloof as she gave her her personnel information, like it couldn't matter to her less. Another girl down.

Afterward, Lisa called her friend Betsy—she would barely see her anymore—but Betsy wasn't home, so she left a message with Betsy's mother.

After this whirlwind of activity, Lisa sat in the living room by herself. The sun shone through the windowpanes, making rectangular patches on the brown carpet. Cramps clutched her lower half, and she hunched down in the corner of a chair. Drained—but in too much pain to go to sleep—she gazed through the thin, gauzy curtains on the windows, facing the brick building next door.

She would be sentenced to a life inside Brooklyn.

No more Paris. No more chances at Rome or London.

Lisa moaned.

She'd had too much to eat. She was too heavy for the airline.

She would marry the son of a cheater.

He could abandon her again, like he did at the airport.

The sparkling new diamond on her finger rose upward in its perfect cut. It was exactly the sort of ring she would have chosen for herself.

At least Billy had a good job. That counted for something.

Lisa's mother was coming back, ascending the creaking steps. She shouted upstairs: "Will you help me bring these groceries upstairs?"

"Okay."

She roused herself from the chair, taking a moment to collect herself. Then she trudged up and down the stairs with armfuls of bags, sprinting back to sit when she was finished.

Then her mother shouted from the kitchen as she put away cans. "Your father tells me you're engaged."

"He told you?"

"Why didn't you tell me first?"

"You were sleeping when I came home."

"He said it happened on Tuesday."

"I know, Ma."

"Why would you be embarrassed about being engaged?" Her mother came inside, holding a can of peas.

"I know what you're thinking, Ma—that . . ."

"Didn't you say that he had apologized? You told me that everything was okay, didn't you? That he apologized. You've been fine since, right?"

"Sure, but . . ." Lisa ran the edge of her diamond across the part of her lips that met her skin. It had no give; it was a tough stone—hard proof that Billy loved her. She spoke quietly. "Well, I don't know what my friends will think."

"Why do you care about what your friends will think?"

Lisa didn't answer. Nothing about Madeline, or about Fred Abbott, or about Billy's cheating father. She said nothing about quitting the airline.

"I don't know! Oh, God. It's hard to be a girl." A mumble dropped from her mouth as she seized up in cramps and doubled over on the fraying chair.

She began to cry, and her mother came over with outstretched arms, squeezing next to her over a piece of patchwork, stroking her hair like when she was little.

⌒

Billy wasn't home when Lisa called his apartment.

His mother spoke to Lisa.

"Oh dear! I'm so excited! We need to plan a special dinner in your honor! Billy told me how he popped the question, too. I didn't know he would do it like that! A balloon at Woolworth's! Isn't he a riot?"

Lisa fingered her ring. "Yeah, I know! I'm so excited, too." Her eyes locked on a piece of peeling paint in her kitchen.

Billy's kitchen was always meticulous. His mother changed their wallpaper every six months. Lisa imagined that one day her married home with Billy could be just like the one he'd grown up in: spic-and-span, updated with the latest trends.

"Billy is out right now, honey," his mother said. "He's out with some friends, I think. I'll have him call you when he gets back home, if it's not too late."

"Okay." She didn't ask if he was out with Mack.

For two hours, she lay with a hot-water bottle on her stomach, watching game shows on television until her cramps dissipated.

Then she readied herself to go to the Starlite.

40

Madeline

The Spring Fling had been a free and clear night with no signs of danger. No signs of lurking men.

But Madeline needed a night to recuperate. She shut the doors to her shop for the evening, drew the blinds, dressed in her nightclothes, donned her eye mask, and put herself on her cot in the back room. In a matter of seconds, she entered a deep, dreamless sleep, the black void of exhaustion.

When she woke, it was dark beneath her eye mask.

She startled.

A knock.

The knock turned to a pounding—an insistent rhythm—from the front of the store, someone from outside. She ripped off her eye mask and padded across the floor in her bare feet. After her short, interrupted slumber, she walked dizzily, stumbling between the clothing racks.

She jammed her toe on the edge of a metal bracket and yelped as she moved toward the front door in a haze.

Someone was still thumping.

She moved aside the curtain on the front door just a little bit.

Outside was a tall man. A dark mask covered his features. He must have seen her shadow through the curtain as he leaned toward the glass.

Madeline backed away from the door. The man turned quickly and darted his head over his shoulder, perhaps to see who was watching.

She felt around for the phone in the dark. She stumbled over her own feet.

"Come on out!"

He thumped louder and yelled.

It wasn't Fred's voice.

She searched for the phone, knocking over a pile of clothes, tripping, kicking things around in the dark.

Outside her door, he shouted, loud and sharp. "Come on out before you get hurt!"

An orange light flickered behind the curtain.

"Come on out!"

The words were blurred together. "We're gonna torch it!"

She ran up to the window.

He was poised with a pointed stick. A fire stick, near her window. His hand was in position, ready to throw.

"Come out now!"

The carpet in the Starlite was shag. Easily burned. Reams of fabric in flammable cardboard lined the walls.

The store would incinerate. She would be inside, aflame.

She would be safer in the open, on the street. She could flee. Someone would see her.

Her breath almost stopped as she ran to the door. He was still there, trying to peer in. She braced her hands. She would push the door hard, push the door fast and move, move, move—

She would run.

Her hand gripped the doorknob.

Now.

She was outside.

She ran fast, so fast. In her bare feet, on the sidewalk. He wasn't behind her. She was in the street, far away, stepping on glass. Her feet were bleeding. He wasn't behind her.

Her heavy breaths mixed with the smell of smoke, which trailed from the Starlite.

She didn't look.

He would chase her, come next to her. She hadn't seen if he had a gun. Or if there were others.

She turned around; she didn't know.

All at once, there were headlights in her face, blinding her.

41

Lisa

Lisa was a few blocks away from the Starlite. With a backup on the avenue, she waited. It was nine-thirty at night. The traffic was heavy, and her car stood at a complete standstill.

An ambulance squealed around the corner. It was natural to hear the wail of an ambulance in Brooklyn. Cars drove between squeals; there was always a person in an ambulance, or a person about to be in an ambulance.

As her car inched forward, Lisa moved to make a right down one of the street blocks. She might be waiting for another half hour; instead, she would turn around and go back home.

She had come all the way up to Brooklyn Heights, and she hadn't even asked Madeline if an event was scheduled for tonight. She had been too hasty.

She made the right turn, then another right, and another right, and soon she was cruising in the opposite direction, with traffic backed up the other way.

There was a car up ahead of her, ahead of other cars, in the dark. From the distance, it almost looked like Billy's convertible with its roof rolled up, but the shadows under the elevated train obscured a full sweep of the street.

Billy would assume she was tailing him as he went out with his friends. Engaged not even four days and already stalking him like a possessive woman. Mack would roll his eyes and snort with tobacco in his cheek. *Desperate woman you got there, Billy.*

She beeped at the car anyway, but the vehicle moved into the next lane, made a quick turn, and was gone.

Lisa seized up, trying to sit straight, her cramps squeezing; she cringed.

PART FOUR

Locking Up

42

Elaine

Elaine woke every morning in the early hours, tossing and turning. She would feel the empty spot in the bed—the crevice where his body had sometimes curled around her own.

After her own twisted ruckus above the sheets, eventually she would get up to douse her face in the sink.

She had begun to make use of the early mornings these days. She had started to pack boxes and make strides toward getting free of the house. The bedroom was crammed with boxes, hastily thrown together tangles of clothes, shoes, and other sundries. She had packed some gadgets Tommy had made, things she didn't know how to use but would keep.

As packing material, she used a stack of newsprint that she had gotten from a friend in the printing room at the *Chronicle*. The dry skin of her palms was irritated from crumpling up the paper as she shoved wads between the breakables.

Elaine packed in the yellowish light of a small lamp, as the sun had yet to come up, but the *brriing* of her alarm was her cue to get ready for work—to stop the packing.

Then came the numbing familiarity of pulling on her nylons, putting powder on her nose, and setting her hair.

This morning she took out the dress she had worn at the Spring Fling—the dandelion-yellow number. It was a little soiled, but that was nothing a dose of perfume wouldn't fix.

On the bus ride to work, Elaine nodded off and nearly missed her stop. She jolted awake just in time.

She rushed into the office, heading to roll call for the daily dispersal of articles.

She took a seat in the back of the room, her recent post. Other fact-checkers jostled for the easy assignments, but Elaine took whichever jobs required the most tedium.

Once upon a time, this had been her dream employment, to be at the *Chronicle*.

But these days she found it impossible to dream of anything.

A few articles were about the effects of the continued embargo with Cuba. Others were about space. Explorer 11 had launched into Earth's orbit to study gamma rays.

She was falling asleep again in her chair as the long list of assignments continued. Her eyelids fluttered down as Mrs. Ainsley read the headline toppers in quick staccato.

EX-WIFE OF BROOKLYN COUNCILMAN KILLED BY SPEEDING CAR

The words didn't connect at first.

Then her eyes opened wide, with a jolt.

She repeated the headline under her breath, as though it might make sense if she spoke it aloud.

Her arm shot up in the air, and she claimed the article in a trance, dashing to the front of the room and snatching it up.

Madeline Abbott, ex-wife of B'klyn councilman Fred Abbott, died yesterday evening in Brooklyn Heights. She was hit by a car on the street in front of her own dress shop. The driver, an unnamed resident of Bay Ridge, was going at 25 mph above the legal limit. He claims to have not seen Ms. Abbott as she dashed across the street.

Ms. Abbott is reported to have died instantly, upon impact.

The driver of the vehicle was inconsolable at the scene of the incident. Police are holding him for further questioning. There were no eyewitnesses to this incident.

Councilman Abbott was asked for a statement.
"I express my deepest condolences to the family of my estranged wife."

⤳

"Elaine?"

"I don't think she hears us."

"Elaine?"

"Yes?"

Bunches of faces gathered around her.

"Oh, honey." Her office friend, Nia, was stroking her head. "You knew her?"

"Yes."

When Elaine opened her eyes, the room blurred in a bending light, as if she were underwater.

She could sleep now, take a nice rest. Change to a new nightmare. She had been having nightmares since Tommy died.

"Do you want any water?"

Mr. Stephens bent down near her head, and Elaine accepted a small glass.

She took small sips.

There was the reality of her tongue and the cool liquid.

"Can I have the article?"

She would read it again, to parse out the reality.

She jerked with a spasm; she needed to be the one researching this, to call people.

"Oh, God."

Sobbing, she couldn't do anything. Couldn't move. Until she ripped off her tight heels and threw them across the room. She had never shed a tear in front of her office mates after Tommy's death. She'd cried only when alone. She had taken pride in holding herself together in front of people.

Later, she would call Madeline, of course, who would answer and tell her about the event at the Starlite tonight. An event, and Elaine would lead the literary circle.

"I'm sorry." Her eyes were a flood. She coughed on her own efflux, on and on, and she apologized as she made a scene, everyone gathering around. She was at work. "I'm sorry."

You have to be calm to work for a newspaper. Calm in the face of any story. Her journalism professor at Briarcliff College had often repeated this mantra.

Calm in the face of anything.

"Let's take you home, honey." Nia put her arm around her shoulder and gently lifted her from the floor.

"She was a friend," she whispered.

They nodded, like they understood.

43

Lisa

"Lisa!" Her mother called her inside and pointed to the TV. "Is that the social club you go to?"

It was the Starlite, right on the news. Police tape crisscrossed the entryway. A dour anchor reported from the studio.

"Brooklyn Heights is in mourning for the owner of the Starlite Dress Shop, which also served as a woman's social club. Madeline Abbott was hit and killed by a car yesterday evening. She was forty-two years old. She was the ex-wife of Fred Abbott, who has offered his condolences to her family."

Lisa's eyes were broken. They wouldn't blink.

She stood in a stupor.

The ambulance.

The traffic.

Madeline wouldn't have been out on the road if Lisa had been there.

She wouldn't have been crossing the street if Lisa had been there sooner.

44

Elaine

Madeline's urn had a pearlescent surface. It was topped by gold filigree and encircled by a ring of low candles. Thin flickers of the flames reflected in golden streaks that hopped up and down the curved lines of the porcelain, illuminating it in bursts as if it were a holy object.

Elaine knelt on the floor, hands clasped, knees bare.

Madeline would have come behind her to compliment her on her dress, an elegant black number she'd brought over from London last year.

You look very sophisticated, darling.

With a drink in her hand, she would have twirled Elaine around to dance.

She had tried many times to twirl Elaine.

To release her.

But Elaine had accepted only a few times. Now it was too late to dance.

❧

Madeline had just one family member who could be located, an elderly aunt, who had paid for the public wake. Madeline would have hated it. It was in a stark hall with heavy black curtains, and there was a layer of dust on everything. Madeline's aunt couldn't afford much, and there was a horrific smell; nobody could breathe too well. The ladies kept filtering in, and every time another arrived, Elaine would shake uncontrollably.

Fred had made an appearance at the wake. He'd knelt in front of her coffin and said something in a voice nobody could hear. Elaine unknowingly asked Harriet if he was another one of Madeline's relatives, but Harriet gave her a horrified look—the man was Fred.

He stood in the corner of the room, in the pretense of looking at the memorial program. He stroked his waxy moustache and glanced up at the ladies in the room; Elaine even felt his eyes examine her body. He seemed to be sizing them all up, and they edged to the other side of the room, skittish, grouping together.

He left after a few minutes, and none of them could even talk about it.

They couldn't talk about anything.

When everything was said and done, the service wasn't enough for Madeline.

They took up a collection and rented a hall for another memorial service not too far from Green-Wood Cemetery, where her ashes would be interred.

None of the regular Starlite ladies had much money, but Cynthia donated to pay for the headstone, using the money she had saved to move out of her parents' apartment.

The ladies chose Elaine to write the inscription. Elaine ground her pencil to a nub and wrote a bunch of empty words throughout the night, barely breathing.

She fell asleep in the early morning.

She awoke an hour later, and there was something at least—a *Hamlet* quote she had memorized at age twelve.

> *Doubt that the stars are fire,*
> *Doubt that the sun doth move.*
> *Doubt truth to be a liar,*
> *But never doubt that I love.*

～

The women of the Starlite stood and knelt in lines behind the urn, their faces streaked with red that wouldn't fade.

Their tongues were dry from their stilted speech.

Harriet came forward and wrapped the urn in a piece of cloth. It was an unfinished dress, a shimmery piece of cloth, intended for an unknown customer. Now it served as a shroud for the vessel that held Madeline's remains.

They were silent, vibrations passing through and between them. The past revelries of the Starlite throbbed as a taste in their mouths, echoes of what had been lost in the rose-scented air of their last event, their entire group together, laughing, Madeline in her beautiful dress.

They trembled and shook.

Nobody was ready to act.

After the time on the hall rental expired, they left. Harriet and some others blew out the candles. The candles and urn went into a beautiful rolling valise that someone had once purchased from the Starlite.

The women huddled on the wide patch of concrete, under a green awning. They grouped together like shaky tree branches tied together with ribbon.

"Maybe we could get together again sometime."

They all said the same, though no one could mention a place or time.

45

Lisa

Lisa hadn't attended the public service, because Fred Abbott would surely be there; a councilman would need to be present at the wake of his ex-wife. Lisa had never met him in person, only seen his picture in the paper, with his waxy moustache, his grin—the same grin Billy's father had, a closed-lip smile of being pleased with oneself.

Now, however, she was on her way to the memorial hosted by the Starlite ladies. The spring weather was warm and humid; Lisa's knit black dress was too thick. She was running late. Sweat made her palms stick to the hanging strap of the bus, to which she held tightly as the vehicle bumped ahead.

The driver called out the stop, and she exited. She walked the few blocks to the hall, dripping with perspiration.

But she was too late. The service was finished. Women were already filing out the door. They stood in a group out on the sidewalk, talking to each other with glazed eyes, and Lisa formed her lips to say something, but nothing came out. She had been to only one funeral previously—her grandfather's—but he had been very sick before he died, and everyone had expected it to happen.

As she stood with the group, Lisa once again hid her engagement ring by turning it into her palm.

Elaine came up next to her and gave her a gentle pat on the back. Someone dug a pen from her purse, and someone had paper, and they made a list of all the names and phone numbers, and Elaine took the paper—somehow she had become the designated woman for writing things down.

"We'll find places to go."

This came out loudly, from Elaine's mouth. They turned around, startled—she was so wispy, air rushing through her perfect accent with the ravages of it all; then Catherine chimed in while taking a drag of her cigarette.

"We'll figure it out; we'll get things together."

"Not yet." Harriet's voice quavered. Then all at once she broke into the wails of an animal, something loud and feral. "We never finished the dress!" She yanked the shimmery cloth out of the valise, waving it over her head. "We never finished!"

They all clustered around her, dozens of hands grasping to hold an inch of the fabric, joining them as one.

"We'll wait a little. Until we're ready," somebody said.

"When we're ready."

"When we're all ready."

They all seemed to agree on it, and they nodded their heads up and down. But it was getting late, and a large, bright moon was rising, and they couldn't stay.

46

Elaine

E laine sat upright on a red velvet couch.
    "Lie down. Let your body relax."

"I'd really rather sit up, thank you." She was in a little office with an absolute stranger, who expected her to spill her most intimate thoughts.

The psychoanalyst gazed at her quizzically, cocked his head to the side as if she were some sort of zoological specimen, and jotted down some notes.

He spoke in a monotone. "So tell me, what brings you here?"

"My sister keeps insisting that I'm in a bad way."

"And you don't think that you are?"

"I go to work. I'm quite active socially. I take a leading role in organizing my social group. I'm quite functional."

"Then what does your sister perceive to be the problem?"

"She worries that I've been getting too thin, and that I've been crying. But I've had two people who perished within a short period of time."

"You feel that your reaction has been a normal expression of grief?"

"Yes."

This was a lot of questions for such a hefty sum. At the analyst's request, Elaine talked about Tommy's death—in full detail. She talked about Madeline.

The analyst didn't say much in the midst of this, only: "Yes. Tell me more."

Before she left, she paid the exorbitant fee. Now her wallet was empty along with everything else.

Elaine went back to her new residence, the ladies' boardinghouse, and sat upright on her own hard little bed.

If she had *insisted* that Tommy go to that center for men with problems, she might have been able to save him.

She tried, as she usually did, to write a poem, but nothing came out.

47

Lisa

It was stuffy in Lisa's tiny room. She scratched her irritated skin. She had fallen asleep early the day before after working an overtime shift at the luncheonette, and she hadn't bathed.

A few weeks after quitting her flight attendant position, she had gotten a job at a popular sandwich shop, right near the courthouse. The money was decent enough; usually the courthouse employees were pretty generous with their tips.

Billy would pick her up soon. They were going to a Fourth of July party. She had told the hostess that she would bring a macaroni salad, so she had to figure out how to make it. Her mother would have a rec-ipe. Lisa had made a list of things she needed to learn how to do before she was married, and macaroni salad was on the list.

Now she aimed her tiny electric fan at her face as she lay on her bed and gazed at her ring. The big diamond gleamed like ice, even in the heat. She pushed the ring over her finger, sliding it back and forth.

"Lisa!"

She jolted as a voice came from outside her building. She hoisted herself up, peering out the window at the sidewalk.

It was Elaine and Catherine.

She hadn't seen the two of them since Madeline's service, two months prior. She hadn't made any effort to see any of the ladies from the Starlite. It was too complicated, with Billy's father working for Madeline's ex.

Elaine had phoned several times over the past few weeks, but Lisa hadn't spoken to her. Lisa's mother had always answered the phone, and Lisa had made dramatic hand gestures for her mother to pretend she was out.

Now Catherine shouted up at her from the sidewalk. "Hey Lisa! Do you want to join us for a party at Harriet's apartment tomorrow evening? It's us and some other girls from the Starlite."

"I have plans—I'm so sorry! But thanks for the invitation!" Lisa made her voice bright and cheery, and Elaine uttered an inaudible response. "What's that?" she called down to the sidewalk.

Elaine repeated herself, but Lisa still couldn't make out the words, so Catherine translated: "She said that we would love to see you out and about. We're trying to get the girls together now that some time has passed."

"Oh, yeah." Lisa reached up to her hair self-consciously. "Sorry I'm so sloppy! I haven't curled my hair yet."

The two sisters were dressed neatly, in sharp, tailored little dresses with belts around their waists, and their hair was styled.

"We don't care about your hair!" Catherine laughed, but Elaine turned away, as if she was thinking of something else—then she mumbled to her sister. Catherine vocalized for her again. "We might be having a thing on Saturday night too, if you want to come. A little get-together at one of the ladies' apartments."

"I'm sorry; I'm working then. I got a job at the luncheonette."

"Well, okeydokey." Catherine smirked at her own funny little American accent.

Elaine's serious face seemed to crack a little; Lisa couldn't help but giggle too. Then the sisters waggled their fingers, waving good-bye.

The door to Lisa's bedroom creaked open; her mother poked her head in. "Were you having a conversation with yourself, honey? I heard you from the living room."

Lisa yawned, like it was all very casual. "No, those girls were here. The one who keeps calling me, and her sister. They were asking me to go to some party tomorrow."

"I guess they haven't gotten the hint that you're busy! I'm happy I only have a few friends. Too many can be a bother." Her mother wiped her hands on her apron.

"Yeah, well . . ." Lisa changed the subject. "Hey, Ma, can you show me how to make macaroni salad? I told Billy we were bringing it."

"I'll make it for you, honey."

"I want to learn how to do it myself."

"All right then." Her mother shrugged. "I guess you're growing up, now that you're an engaged woman."

"I guess so."

Lisa brought a brush to her hair.

Billy would be there soon.

⌣

He beeped his horn outside her building.

Lisa's mother threw her hands in the air, still putting the finishing touches on the macaroni salad. "Why doesn't he come in?"

"I told him to wait for me outside. I don't want him to see me until I'm ready."

"After you get married, is he gonna wait outside while you put on your makeup?"

Lisa shrugged and glanced at herself in the mirror. Her hair was perfect, and her lipstick was sharp. In keeping with the day's theme, she was patriotic, in a white blouse and little blue skirt with red stars. Madeline would have approved of the outfit.

Lisa shuddered, averting her eyes from her reflection.

At least Billy's father wouldn't be at the party. No campaign talk of Fred Abbott.

"See ya later, Ma." Billy was still honking outside, so she sped down the steps.

He waited for her in his father's car, the shiny red Oldsmobile with white stripes down the sides. The car was very flashy; her neighbors all down the street gawked from their front stoops.

Billy made a long, low whistle. "You look fabulous, babe. Hello, America, indeed." He gave her a French kiss, running his hot tongue against hers.

Lisa buckled her seat belt and rolled down the window. The car smelled like his father's cologne.

His father could have brought *that woman* in the car. They might have French-kissed in the car, like her and Billy.

"So, why'd you bring your father's car?"

"Pops is at one of his campaign functions. Someone picked him and Ma up in a Rolls-Royce."

"Your father doesn't mind you bringing his car on the ferry?"

"Why should that matter?"

They cruised down to Sixty-Ninth Street with the windows wide open. It was only a little past noon, but kids were already setting off firecrackers in garbage cans. Brooklyn was thundering in small explosions.

The ferry station was packed with cars trying to make it onto the ramp before the cutoff point. Their own car slid into the line just before a man flipped up a sign that read FULL.

Billy rolled the car into the dark underbelly of the ferry and parked in the one remaining spot, a forsaken corner of the boat. The two of them raced up to the deck as the man started to close the bottom of the boat. Lisa clung to her Tupperware of macaroni salad as she ran in her heels.

On the observation deck, they leaned against the railing, and Billy wrapped his arm around her. Lisa watched the long path of water trail behind the boat, a triangular footprint of their ferry. A drop of water fell on her head. She stuck out her free hand to see if it was rain, and Billy tickled her underarm.

"Stop! I'm gonna drop the macaroni salad!"

A little girl dressed in stars and stripes stared at them from across the deck as Billy continued to tickle her.

"I mean it—I'm going to drop this! Stop it!"

A moment before the Tupperware fell to the water, he grabbed her hand and pulled her down to the other side of the deck. "Look, you can see my bridge from here, babe. Check it out!"

He always pointed out blurs in the distance that she was supposed to see, as though she could make them out from so far away.

After the ferry docked, they got back in the Oldsmobile and drove to Roger's house in New Dorp.

Roger had gotten married last year, and Lisa had cried over his wife's gorgeous wedding dress. The two of them made such a nice couple. Roger worked down at the bridge site with Billy.

"Happy Fourth, to an upstanding fellow!"

Billy loved making a grand entrance. He went from person to person, chuckling about inside jokes and slapping all the guys on the back.

Lisa remained in the back of the kitchen. She chatted with Roger's wife, who was pregnant. The idea of pregnancy was very exotic to Lisa. "Do you feel like the same person? Do you feel any different?"

"I'm a lot hungrier! And my back's in terrible pain most of the time." Roger's wife groaned, getting up from her chair. She was pretty, with rosy cheeks—only a year older than Lisa.

The house wasn't anything fancy; it didn't look as if Roger's wife shopped at Bergdorf Goodman. But it was nice and clean. It was a good starter home. Lisa turned on the kitchen sink to wash her hands; the faucet wasn't leaky like the one at her parents' apartment. Roger and his wife even had a little lawn out back.

"Hey, Mack!" Billy shouted across the living room.

Mack stood tall amid the fanfare, puffing out his chest. The other guys greeted him like a king as he carted in a barrel of firecrackers and fireworks.

"Boy oh boy, Mack, you did us well!"

The guys dug through the barrel as though sifting for gold.

"I got this one!"

"That's mine!"

"Hey, buddy, get a load of this!"

Soon everyone switched to eating, serving themselves food from the kitchen table. Lisa conversed with the ladies as she ate, and she became the center of attention as they talked about her trips. Everyone was especially interested in her trip to Italy, and she did her best to describe the Pantheon between bites of coleslaw.

The women of the Starlite had been fascinated with her trips too.

One of the women at the kitchen table reminded Lisa of Jackie, who had never returned to the Starlite after her husband forced her to move to New Jersey. This woman had the same half smile and faltering mannerisms as Jackie, which made Lisa suspect that something was wrong.

Her suspicions were confirmed when the woman tapped her on the shoulder, beckoning Lisa to follow her to the corner of the kitchen.

The woman spoke in a hushed tone, shooting glances around the room to make sure nobody was listening. "I can't believe you got to do all that traveling. My husband would never have let me travel in a plane or taxi with all those other men around, even before we were married."

"He wouldn't have let you?" Lisa gulped, searching the woman's eyes. "What would he have done?"

"I can only imagine." The woman gave a sad laugh. "You're lucky, aren't you? You got to go places."

Lisa was silent, not knowing what to say. The woman gave her another half smile and then walked away, disappearing into the crowd of partygoers.

A chill passed through Lisa's veins as she sat back down at the kitchen table, suddenly afraid to enter the other room, where a bunch of the men were gathering.

She didn't know which one of these men was the girl's husband—and she wasn't sure that she wanted to.

The sky was growing dark now, with low-hanging clouds and the beginnings of twilight. Soon the guys were rushing outside to let loose their fireworks. Lisa nibbled on a brownie and watched the action through the window along with some other women who remained at the kitchen table. Now that she wasn't at Pan Am, she couldn't travel anymore, but she did like being able to eat what she wanted. She no longer had to watch her weight so closely, and being a stewardess felt so removed from her present tense.

It felt good to sit for a moment, though she was getting a little headache from all the noise at this party, with the guys darting around like maniacs, setting off quick successions of firecrackers.

It was better to remain inside the house for the fireworks. The smoke would feel stifling in the humid air, furling upward like the black plume from the plane crash in the bay.

One guy set off a Roman candle, which made a great big plume in the air. There was a burst, and sparks came raining down. There was fire everywhere: in the skies, blasting out of lighters and sticks, falling down in little showers from the silver sparklers. A few guys brandished wooden torches, waving them in the air.

Their rowdy, wild energy turned to concentrated focus with fire in hand.

The men stood near the window, looking inside at the women, the long handles of their torches casting a dark shadow to the side.

"Would you look at that!"

The other halves of their faces were brightly lit, and though Lisa was some distance away, she could see miniature reflections of fire in their eyes. One of the women pointed, and all of the women stared. The guys' lips rolled into laughter, and they spun around, using their torches to light the pyrotechnics. Lisa fixated on that fire, eyes in a deep trance as she watched the sky go aflame.

The house shook with the sounds, as if under siege.

One of the women shook her head and laughed. "Those boys sure are characters, aren't they?"

Lisa turned away, unable to watch the smoke.

48

Elaine

Elaine had been staying in the boardinghouse for over two months. It was on the Upper East Side, a quiet neighborhood in Manhattan. She was familiar with the area, as she had lived there briefly before she moved in with Tommy.

The accommodations were clean, and the food was prepared and served by a hulking, silent woman in her sixties. It was a sparse but predictable place, a short fifteen-minute bus ride to work.

It was a little more of a trek to Brooklyn, so Elaine hadn't been able to be with the Starlite ladies so often. They'd had a little party in Harriet's apartment the other day, and she was trying to organize something else for them with Catherine, but it was slow going, because she lost much of her energy when she returned to the boardinghouse at night.

Talking to the ladies on the phone seemed to send her into exhaustion. One of them would inevitably bring up Madeline, and then all bets were off.

Now it was six o'clock in the evening. The landlady clanged the dinner bell in the hallway, as she did every night, up and down the halls with a strident chime.

Elaine ignored the bell and rubbed her stomach.

A reporter from the *Chronicle* had actually asked her to accompany him to dinner that night, but she had refused, as she had done on three previous occasions. He was nice looking and friendly enough, but the thought of making small talk over steaks seemed impossible.

A mirror image—
My own ideals—

She got her pencil to write a poem, but the yellow stick had turned to an itty-bitty nub. There wouldn't be a poem tonight either.

Together with Catherine, Elaine had gotten several events up and running after Madeline's memorial service. In addition to the recent party at Harriet's apartment, they'd had a get-together at a restaurant and a lunch at someone's house. But the conversation had been stilted, the dancing had been nonexistent, the readings had been dull, and none of the events had had themes to hold them together.

The fear in the group was low level, unspoken. There were no security guards, just women with eyes that didn't ignore their surroundings.

The press had reported that Madeline had been hit by a wayward driver, but given that revelatory article in the society pages so close to her death, it was better to live far from those campaign signs plastered everywhere: RE-ELECT FRED ABBOTT.

Manhattan seemed a world away.

Elaine's boardinghouse room was cramped, but it had a small chair. Enough space for a single visitor.

Her sister had come the previous night. Catherine was full of energy; she talked about moving quickly with her new beau. Catherine guessed that he might even propose to her soon enough. She was enraptured with him, though she insisted that she missed the social club, and she talked about taking steps to resurrect the feeling of the Starlite.

Elaine couldn't work up any fervor to make plans. It seemed to her that the social club was lost.

Yet Catherine buzzed with ideas. "What if we try to organize some get-togethers outdoors? Maybe a twilight reading near Brooklyn Bridge. Or a picnic near the pond in Central Park, just a casual mid-summer thing." Catherine perched on Elaine's little chair, twirling her jazz-singer boa. She had a gig later that evening.

"Whatever you say, sister dear. I suppose I'll ring some of the ladies tomorrow."

The Starlite was gone. Madeline was gone. But it was a mild distraction for Elaine to attend to obligations.

⁓

The next evening, after meeting with her sister, Elaine dialed down the list of ladies, starting with Harriet—she was usually good for an affirmative RSVP.

But Harriet didn't answer her phone, and neither did the next five women on the list.

Without a leader, they would all drift their separate ways.

It was sweltering in the boardinghouse. Elaine tried to get something cool from the bathroom tap, but the water would only run warm. She drank the tepid, fizzy stuff anyway, then sat back down and fanned herself with the phone list.

The next name on the list was Lisa, whose mother always answered and claimed that Lisa was busy. Last week, Elaine had gone with Catherine to Lisa's apartment to try to convince her to join them for the get-together they would be having. She hadn't been surprised when Lisa made an excuse.

Now she was expecting that Lisa wouldn't answer the phone. But tonight, Lisa actually picked up instead of her mother.

"Hello?"

"Hi, dear, it's Elaine."

"Oh, Elaine? Hi! That's so funny, because I thought it might be you."

"Oh?"

"Yes, I was just thinking about you and your sister—Catherine, right? You know, I'm really sorry I haven't been in touch, and I was quick with both of you when you came outside my apartment last week, on the Fourth. I've just been so busy lately. I'm working lots of hours now, and I'm also engaged to be married."

"Oh, well—congratulations! Who is the lucky gentleman?"

"His name is Billy. The one I was dating." Lisa was speedy and breathless. "We're getting married next year, so I'm trying to save up some money."

"It's wonderful to be working, making your own money and all that."

"Yeah, well." Lisa paused. "I *would* like to get together soon, though."

"You're in luck, dear, because I was calling to organize an alfresco get-together for the ladies tomorrow night."

"I'm sorry, I have a date planned with Billy. Are you available tonight instead? Maybe we could have some girls' time."

"It would be a bit of a trek for you. I'm living in Manhattan now."

"Whereabouts?"

"On Eighty-Fifty Street, in a nice ladies' boardinghouse."

"Do they allow visitors?"

"Women visitors, yes. But it's rather late for you to make that trek, wouldn't you say?"

"It's only eight. I could probably get there by nine if I leave now. I'll only bother you for an hour or so. Just give me the cross street and I'll make my way over."

After Elaine give her the directions, they hung up.

Elaine rubbed her stomach; it was past dinner service. She couldn't live solely on tap water, hot air, and loneliness. She sat on her little chair and waited for Lisa.

⌐

"Knock-knock!" Lisa shouted from behind the door.

Lisa had made a speedy trip to Manhattan—quicker than Elaine had anticipated. Elaine felt a bit startled to have a visitor that wasn't her sister, even though she was the one who had invited her. She couldn't help but feel a bit embarrassed about her meager new living space. "It's a plain old room. Come right in, dear." It was certainly a downgrade from the grand old brownstone. "I have tea, if you want. I have this little electric kettle that plugs into the wall, quite the invention."

"I don't know how you can drink tea in the middle of July!"

"Routine, I guess." Elaine poured the steaming liquid into her cup as she sat on her bed, then she watched Lisa shift around on the stiff little chair in the corner of the room.

They were silent for a moment as Elaine took a sip of tea and exhaled. "I've been visiting a psychoanalyst."

"You mean a shrink?" Lisa pulled back a little in her chair.

"I suppose that's the nickname, isn't it? It all seems a bunch of blather anyway. He asks me to talk about these things that I don't want to talk about."

"I guess it's not helping, then?"

"I suppose it's not doing much. Maybe it's all poppycock. But I've paid for the next few visits already; he's lured me in for more tries."

"I understand." Lisa squirmed and repositioned her legs. "I'm sorry. I really don't want to bother you. I guess there's a curfew here, so I probably should leave soon."

"No, no, dear! I really appreciate the company. Sit, sit, please."

"Okay." Lisa's cheeks were flushed. They were both silent as they fanned themselves in the stuffy air. "Listen, I have a confession to make, Elaine."

Elaine stood, adjusting the lace doily on her dresser. It was the room's only decoration. "Go ahead. I'm listening."

She imagined that Lisa might admit that she didn't want to visit her at the boardinghouse anymore—it was just too cramped.

"My fiancé—remember I told you his name is Billy? Well, Billy is the son of Fred Abbott's campaign manager." Lisa gulped. "I don't like keeping secrets, and I just had to tell you."

The tea almost dribbled from Elaine's mouth as she felt a punch to the gut from hearing Fred Abbott's name, but she kept her voice even. "Well. That's an unfortunate coincidence, isn't it, darling?"

Lisa shuddered. "I've just felt so guilty—you know? And then, you know, the night that Madeline . . . the night it happened with Madeline? I was actually on my way to see her. Can you imagine, Elaine? I was right there. If I had been there a little earlier, maybe she wouldn't have been taking a walk. Maybe she would still be alive today."

Lisa's face was bright pink with heat and exertion. Suddenly she leaned over Elaine's wooden table, her head in her hands, and sobbed.

"There, there."

Elaine patted her back, and Lisa cried even more. She was bent over at the waist, unable to speak.

It must have felt quite awkward for the girl this whole time—to be with the son of Fred Abbott's campaign manager. Yet it wasn't as though Lisa's beau was Fred Abbott himself.

Elaine rested a hand on Lisa's back as she cried, doubled over on the wooden chair. Something small and metallic clinked under the table.

Elaine reached under and picked up a sizable diamond ring.

"Yours, I presume?"

Lisa nodded, her face still down on the table. Elaine slid the ring to her, and Lisa felt around blindly and put it back in her dress pocket.

"I couldn't wear it here."

"I understand," Elaine said softly. She stood upright, hands at her sides, and then she brought them down to stroke Lisa's hair, which was damp near her face. "You know, dear, you have nothing to be guilty about. For starters, it's not like you're engaged to Fred Abbott himself. Secondly, there was no way you could have known that Madeline would run out onto the street that night. Not unless you're a clairvoyant and you haven't been letting on."

Lisa picked her face up off the table and giggled a little in spite of herself. "Not that I know of."

"But I understand what it's like to blame yourself. My . . . well . . . *shrink*, if we're going to use that word . . . well, he might very well have been trying to question me to see if that's what I've been doing with Tommy's passing."

"But that's not your fault, right? Tommy just drank too much, right?"

"I suppose so." They were both silent. "What's your Billy like? He's a good man, I'm sure."

Lisa blushed. "He's funny and charming. You'll have to meet him someday."

"Right. Tell me, does he go out a lot?" Elaine quickly flew her hand to her mouth, reddening.

"Well, yes—he has this big group of friends from the work site, you know."

Elaine uncovered her mouth and exhaled. "That's good; he has a job, then. What are his friends like?"

"I get along with most of them all right. A few are a little rough around the edges, but after all, I'm not a boy." Lisa cleared her throat and gestured toward the top of Elaine's dresser. "That's a nice radio you have there."

"Oh, yeah, that was Tommy's. His aunt told me I could take anything I wanted. Tommy used to love that radio."

"How 'bout we listen for a little bit?"

"Absolutely! But we have to keep it on low. Boardinghouse rules."

An Elvis song played from the radio. It was something slow, warbling, and beautiful. It was too poignant; Elaine switched the station. On came Chubby Checker with his hopping, catchy beat. Lisa got up and twirled her skirt, but Elaine stayed put on the bed, legs crossed. Lisa grabbed her by the hand and pulled her up to dance, with quick little steps, in the still, humid air of the night.

"Did you ever try the calypso?" Lisa asked. "It's like this: one, two . . . shuffle, then a slight twirl." She demonstrated. "It used to be on *American Bandstand* all the time!"

"I don't know, dear. I think it's another American phenomenon I let fall by the wayside." Elaine allowed herself to laugh, which felt good— and she let herself keep going.

It was almost time for curfew, but the two of them laughed hysterically, only intermittently muting themselves as they twirled around and around.

"You know what's so crazy?" Lisa asked breathlessly.

"What'd you say?" Elaine shot glances at the door. The landlady hadn't knocked yet.

"That night with Madeline, you know, like I said—well—I was driving there to see her and all. And Billy was going out with a few friends that night. Anyway, I was on the way to see Madeline, but there was all this traffic, so I couldn't get through, and then I spotted Billy's car—he must have been in the neighborhood, and I tried following him for fun, but he moved too quick and I lost him. I never told him I saw him. I don't want him to think that I follow him around like a crazy woman!"

"Well, I'm sure you didn't set out to follow him."

Lisa sat down and gulped. "No. But I'm wondering, if he was in that neighborhood, do you think it's possible he could have seen Madeline a few minutes before she died? He could have driven right past her. Maybe he was one of the last people to see her. I mean, I would never want to ask him about it—it just seems so silly."

"Why does that seem silly?"

"Like I said—I don't want to seem strange," Lisa admitted. It was near nine-thirty, and Elaine fiddled with her watch, trying to send a subtle hint, which Lisa picked up. "I'd better go—I don't want to get you in trouble. It was nice to spend some time with you, though. Hopefully I can go to one of the events you're organizing one of those days."

"Whatever you can make."

She left, and the room was vacant once again.

Elaine collapsed on the bed, holding her stomach, which was still empty.

49

Lisa

August 1962

"Can you please pass the meat loaf?"

Lisa had been unable to avoid this dinner invitation to Billy's house. Although she was exhausted from her lunch shift, she gave herself a quick brushup and drove the ten minutes to his apartment.

Billy was sitting with his father on the sofa, yelling at the television as the Mets missed some plays. "Come on, come on, come on!" Father and son punched the air as though they were the ones up to bat.

"It's so good to see you, dear." Billy's mother had set the table flawlessly, as usual, napkins folded crisp at the corners.

The game was ending—the Mets had lost.

Billy and his father sulked to the table. His mother served up rectangles of meat loaf and scooped up mashed potatoes.

"Extra gravy, Ma."

Lisa eyed Billy as he held out his plate for a soupy pour. His eyes were bloodshot and his chin looked red. His stubble was uneven, like he had stayed up too late and shaved. And his father was shoveling meat loaf into his mouth in animal proportions and slurping down great sloshes of wine from a goblet. Lisa turned away.

His mother smiled beatifically and passed Lisa a platter of green beans. "Billy tells me you two are going to look at halls this weekend?"

"Well, yes. I've been to most of the halls for my friends' weddings, but it would be nice to see them again in the light of day."

Billy's father lit a cigarette. "One of my buddies owns the one on Flatbush Avenue. I'm sure he could set you up with a fine deal." Smoke wafted up into Lisa's mouth from across the table.

"Oh well, maybe," she said softly.

"That sure is nice of you, Pops. We'll take a look at it." Billy smiled at his father, eager to please.

The television was still on in the background, in the living room. The post-game commentary had concluded, and the nightly news was starting: "What really happened with Marilyn Monroe? Coming up next."

It had been all over the news since the morning.

Marilyn was gone too.

Lisa had tried to channel her in the mirror at least a thousand times, raising her lip just so, making her eyes coquettish, pretty.

Now she was dead, like Madeline.

Billy's father got up from his empty dinner plate to hover over the television as the newscaster used words like *barbiturates* and *overdose*.

"She was a foxy babe," he muttered.

Billy's father's mistress had to have been *foxy* too, with her blonde hair and her plump lips next to his, over the city of Paris.

Lisa's heart thumped hard in her chest. There was no way that she could tell Billy about his father and that woman on the plane. His father would deny it anyway. But her throat seized up watching Billy's mother, trying so hard to be a family woman at the kitchen table when her own husband didn't care.

Billy's mother wiped her mouth with a napkin and got up, throwing away her half-eaten plate of food. "What a shame this all was. She was still so young, with so many years ahead." She changed the subject. "I made a peach pie, if anyone wants a piece. Lisa, dear?"

"I'm still working on the meat loaf. But thank you."

Their forks clinked against their plates as the news broadcast continued. Billy was usually more talkative, but he was quiet. Droopy.

Worn out from work, maybe.

Or maybe she was looking at him differently.

☙

Billy walked her down to her car after dinner.

It was a dark, humid night, and he leaned her up against the car and stuck his tongue far into her mouth and for too long. But she didn't pull back. He had his arm around her after that, and a group of teenage girls sauntered past, turning their heads to stare at him. He was wearing a nice shirt, something more expensive than Lisa could ever afford. Some of the girls giggled, like they thought he was cute, and Billy puffed out his chest and set his shoulders back.

"I'm going to go to a party with my friends tomorrow night," Lisa told him. It was a good moment to let him know she wasn't desperate for him.

"Which friends?"

"The Starlite crew. My friend Elaine has been getting some of them together. It's a get-together at one of the girls' apartments."

"Sure, babe. Go ahead and get all of your single-girl stuff in now." His face was ugly again as he spit on the sidewalk.

"You don't mind, do you?"

"Nah—I'm just joking." He smiled, and then his face relaxed, gorgeous once more, with his dimples.

Billy's arm was tight around her again.

Her future husband.

"Billy, you know what? I keep meaning to ask. That night that Madeline was killed, and you were out with your friends—well, you know, I was on my way to see Madeline that night. I think I saw your car in the neighborhood. Was that you? I was thinking maybe there was a chance you could have seen her, just walking down the sidewalk or something. Maybe you could have even been one of the last people to see her before that guy hit her. Did you see her, Billy? I can't even imagine seeing someone in their final moments."

Billy shrugged and turned away from her, coughing and spitting on the sidewalk. "There's no way I could remember back that far, babe."

He guffawed, proud of himself, and turned to face her with a grin. "Hey, you saw me that night? Were you following me? I must be irresistible, huh?"

"Far from it." Her face was turning red.

He came around and grabbed Lisa's waist. "Just kidding again. My oh my! You're a little uptight tonight, aren't ya?"

Then he gave her a smack on the rear, like it was a big joke. His dull, large hands made a loud clap, as though taking ownership of a round slab of meat.

"I'm going home, Billy."

She moved past him, opened her car door, and got into the driver's seat.

He chuckled to himself like a hyena. Then he lit a cigarette, still laughing, gazing into the distance.

"Tell your mother thank you for dinner," she said primly, then drove away.

⤙

She kept her engagement ring off the next day as she served tables at the luncheonette. A male customer gave her butt a pat after she set down his bowl of soup, bare-knuckled. She gave him a look of dismay and cleared his table later to find an extra-large tip.

Back at her apartment, she covered up the ring, wrapping a dirty nightgown around it, shoving it under her dresser. This girls' night would be good for her.

⤙

Lisa hadn't been to Brooklyn Heights since the day Madeline died.

Harriet's apartment was in Brooklyn Heights, not too far from the Starlite Dress Shop.

It was hot that evening, and she drove with the windows cracked. The sign was still up at the Starlite, although the windows were dark.

She folded in her bottom lip and parked her car on Livingston Street, stepping out with some caution.

The neighborhood was quiet. All shoppers in the local stores had gone home for the evening.

Lisa peered inside the Starlite.

It was empty, as far as the eye could see. Shadows in a vacant space. A great and gloomy contrast to the hum of energy the first time she'd stepped in—so bright she could barely cross the threshold.

Now it stood as a nothing.

Lisa stared through the window, as though Madeline would come out and greet her. It had been three months since Madeline passed.

A fire engine screamed past her on the street. She jumped, and her hand brushed up against some grit in the window frame. It was a thick, grayish dust that stuck to the edge of her palm, like soot. She blew it from her hand; specks floated into the crevices of the sidewalk. Other specks adhered to her arm, which was coated in sweat.

There were no signs of an incinerator in the building—no openings for a chimney. Lisa leaned in closer to the window. There was a black spot on the glass, above the patch of ash.

It was like a vandal had tried to torch the building.

It was growing darker, and the street was desolate.

Lisa was alone.

She left to go to the party.

50

Elaine

Elaine was in the back of Harriet's apartment with a few other women. They were making watercolor paintings, splashing colors on yellow paper to the sounds of the radio. They had the windows wide open, with electric fans at full blast. They projected their voices over the noise, which lent some excitement to the gathering as they painted away in the warm indoor winds of the evening.

Harriet came around with a platter of little buns, and Elaine ate with gusto. She was making up for lost time, eating. She gripped her bun in one hand and held her paintbrush in the other.

Everyone was talking about who they were dating.

"I actually went on a date last night," Elaine admitted, blushing.

She had been a little more open lately. Maybe it was that expensive psychoanalyst, though she had been to only a few sessions.

"Spill the details!" The ladies sat on their heels, watercolor brushes in hand.

"Well—" She faltered as they stared, ready to latch on to every word. "He's very nice. David is his name. He's a reporter at the *Chronicle*. Very intelligent."

"If he's so nice, then why wasn't he taken yet?"

"He was married, actually. His wife died a few years back."

"Oh."

The room fell quiet with a fragile silence. The women returned to making art—soft, watery applications of paint on the creamy white paper.

"His wife died in childbirth," she told them. "He has a daughter—his mother watches her while he's at work."

"How sad."

She and David had dived deep on their first date. She had refused to go out with him at first, but he'd kept asking her—and he really did seem funny and friendly, with a lightness that Tommy had never had. On a whim she had finally agreed to go out with him, and they'd enjoyed a very pleasant evening at a restaurant. They had dined slowly and chatted, allowing time to swirl around them as they talked about their lives.

Elaine was surprised to find herself talking about Tommy, but David didn't flinch; he even spoke about his own late wife.

They talked about everything: hobbies, the cinema, the *Chronicle*.

It was all very normal. A functional conversation. He seemed to understand Elaine on another level, in the way of those who had felt grief in their own times.

"Do you think you'll see him again?"

"I think so." She painted a pink heart on her paper absentmindedly. Catherine noticed and teased her, spilling a little of her red wine and smudging it on the borders. Elaine surprised herself by laughing.

From inside, the door to Harriet's apartment kept opening and shutting as more women entered.

Lisa arrived, and she entered the painting room shortly thereafter. She looked fair and even more dainty than usual in a pretty pink outfit.

She glanced around Harriet's apartment with hesitation, raising her heels to avoid stepping on pieces of art.

"Hullo! How are you?" Elaine put her hand on Lisa's arm to put her at ease. "We're having a little art time! Care to join?"

Lisa accepted some paper and brushes without paying much attention to the materials. She sat next to Elaine and made little jabs at her paper with a brush.

After some time, she darted her eyes about and whispered to Elaine, "I went by the Starlite before I came here."

Elaine gulped. "You did? I can barely bear to look over there."

"There were ash marks on the window, traces of something. I don't know what."

"Someone had a smoke outside?"

"More like fire had been on the window."

"Vandals of Brooklyn."

"Why would anyone want to mess with that empty place? She's dead!"

Elaine shuddered. "It could be an ugly reminder for some people. The empty shell of a place that belonged to Madeline. And she got all that attention after she died."

"What are you saying? Who do you think could have done something like that?"

"Who knows? Maybe Fred Abbott?"

Lisa paused her brushstrokes and swallowed. "You think Fred went there and did that himself?"

"I'm sure he wouldn't step foot near that place." Elaine was still painting. She made a big black *X* to cross out the images. As if it wasn't enough to have it all gone, someone was trying to mar the shell of the Starlite.

The other ladies weren't hearing any of it as they argued about Marilyn Monroe, debating the cause of her death, shaking their paintbrushes in frustration.

"I don't think Marilyn could have done that to herself. It had to be someone else, someone who was jealous of her."

"How do you know what she was thinking?"

"She wasn't the melancholy type. People who would do such a thing are usually the melancholy type."

Elaine slid herself into the debate. "You never can know what's going on inside someone's head."

Outsiders had mostly seen Tommy as suave, lively, and intelligent. And that *was* how he was—before the fourth drink.

"*Of course* you don't know what someone's thinking, but Marilyn was different," Gloria argued.

Elaine looked over for Lisa's response—but Lisa had left the room, abandoning her smudged artwork.

Nothing was ever in full color. Even if they tried to pretend.

51

Lisa

Friendly women tried to feed Lisa snacks and drinks as she escaped the painting room. They even shoved cocktail napkins into her hands to make her stay. But suddenly she couldn't grip anything, and she couldn't be among people.

It was the Starlite. The shell of it, topped by those burned bits.

The fuzzy wool over her eyes had started to separate.

Strands had begun to unfurl as the pieces of ash showered down on her hands.

People were out there who wanted to destroy things.

Like relationships. Billy might have destroyed the two of them.

So much of her had been wrapped up in him.

Yet his hand had moved without hesitation to slap her bottom. Like he was the cowboy and she was a steer.

He'd never even asked how she was doing.

She opened the door to leave the apartment. Harriet stood with a tray of pigs-in-a-blanket, laughing as she tried to balance it. Lisa claimed that she had to go, and then she gave Harriet a hug, though they never had talked much.

Billy would hate her if she left him.

He would tell his friends that she was a prude, and then he would move on to another girl who would linger on his dimples.

Maybe one of those teenage girls who had ogled him outside his apartment.

❧

In bed, Lisa couldn't sleep. The night was sticky, and her father was up late, watching the television on a high volume.

A beam of a streetlight caught the edge of a large bag in front of her closet. The bag was packed with all her wedding magazines and the wedding lists. Her wedding shoes were at the top. The satin heels dug into the silky lingerie she had purchased for the honeymoon.

Girls didn't break engagements.

She had been a stewardess. She had left the glamour of the uniform, the travel. Any extra flesh stayed tucked under her blazer; the passengers had never seen the rows of scales in the weigh-in room. Jane had hidden her crueler admonitions and saved them for hisses in Lisa's ears.

But Lisa had seen the plume of smoke in the bay. She couldn't pretend anymore.

She couldn't with Billy either.

It could all end quickly.

Billy's poor, cheated-upon mother would answer the phone, and then she would have to get him on the line so Lisa could break up the engagement. It wouldn't work.

She would go down to the bridge site instead.

She would meet him after his shift ended and ask him to join her for a walk. In the thick air of the evening, she would tell him that things were over. She would leave before she could see his anger.

The tavern would be close enough for him to blow off some steam and get a drink with his friends. He could talk about Lisa—the bitch. He could foam up a storm, then drink it down. Then he wouldn't come back.

For one more time, she would play the part of what he wanted her to be. This time, she would become the boring prude.

She threw a pair of wrinkled slacks onto the dresser for the next day.

She would soon become a nothing and vanish from his life.

∽

At the construction site, she looked small.

Insignificant near the towering beams.

The metal frames rose above her head. Liquid concrete was spinning in trucks and being poured into massive blocks in front of her, and she was a nothing.

All around was dirt, muck, and the strong scent of heavy work.

Billy worked in the distance, a piece of metal hoisted over his shoulder. He didn't see her.

She called out his name and approached.

He coughed and spat, startled a little.

"Hi," she said. Her hand was behind her back, without the ring. "Sorry for interrupting."

"No, babe. I'm just about done. Rough day."

"What happened?"

"Wait a second." He pulled her aside, behind a temporary trailer, spitting into the muck, and whispered, "Mack got the can today."

"Why?"

"I guess he snuck some crap off the site."

"Like what?"

"I don't know. Stuff around the site. Every guy sometimes takes things for a little side project—he wasn't doing anything unusual."

"What did he take?"

"Scrap metal, tools, whatever. There's plenty of stuff floating around that nobody's using."

"So, taxpayers are paying for people to steal stuff for their side projects?"

"It's not a big deal." He lowered his voice. "Listen, let's get out of here. I told Mack I'd meet him at the bar after my shift."

"Why do you want to see him?"

Billy didn't answer. He threw his piece of metal in a pile of other metal.

She followed him helplessly, like a puppy. He gave a hand signal to the other guys that he was leaving.

The air around him was charged. He didn't look at her as she tailed behind him. He walked at full speed down blocks and blocks, pausing only occasionally to smoke a cigarette in the hot evening air, without a word.

They arrived at the bar. It was packed. Mack and some other guys clustered together at a side table, throwing drinks down their throats and slamming empty glasses on the table in bursts of hyena laughter.

Mack's eyes were red and veiny, and he gesticulated his points in quick, chaotic motions.

Billy ordered another round of beer. Lisa squeezed herself on a stool to the side of the table. It was dark outside. If she left the bar, she would be catcalled in this neighborhood. She would be safe next to Billy, at least.

"Then the mobster said to the policeman, I bet you did!" Mack grew louder, his jokes more screechy.

Billy and the others laughed their heads off, and one of the guys tossed a pack of cards out from his pocket. Suddenly coins flew across the table, and even Mack emptied his pockets. Lisa did a double take; Mack had been fired only a few hours prior.

Billy won the card game. "Burgers on me!"

They left the bar, so Lisa had to follow them. The guys formed a loose huddle on the sidewalk, which was almost abandoned at this hour of the night. They were drunk in plain sight, with few people around.

They moved block by block, and Billy put his arm around Lisa's waist. His breath was sour and she gagged a little, quietly. They were near his car.

"I don't think you should drive. You had a lot."

"*I don't think you should drive. You had a lot.*" Billy mimicked her, and the guys laughed.

Tears smarted in Lisa's eyes, and she walked away into the desolate neighborhood.

She would leave, no matter the darkness.

Billy chased after her and tapped her arm. "*Saw-wee.*" His baby voice.

He was extremely intoxicated, his eyes glassy. He said he was fine, but Lisa grabbed his keys from his hand. The guys teased him, but he got in the passenger seat, his lids half-closed.

She drove carefully to the burger joint. The four other guys were crammed into the back seat, and Billy twisted the radio dials. Their howls heightened some difficulty with parallel parking in a tight spot, but soon she did it, and then she shut off the engine.

The guys sprinted into the burger place to grab a booth. Their food came out quickly. The bill arrived quickly too. They didn't notice the hand signal the manager had given their waitress.

Lisa slunk down in her seat as they grew louder and louder.

Billy said he had to piss; he left Lisa at the table with the four of them. They crumpled their grease-stained burger wrappers into little balls, blowing them across the table at each other.

"So, Mack, do you think you'd like to still work in construction?" Lisa spoke, disconnected, as everyone in the burger joint stared at their booth.

"I'm just gonna work for Billy's pops, like I been doin'."

"You're working for him already?"

"A little campaign work for Mr. Abbott, you know? Helping out Billy's pops." A wrapper flicked against Mack's dirty shirt.

"Campaign work?"

Mack laughed and pitched the wrapper across the table. He didn't answer Lisa; instead, he screeched at a guy hoarding the wrappers.

Billy emerged from the bathroom; he threw money on the table, ready to go. "Hey, let's split this joint!"

They piled out of the restaurant, and Lisa jumped back into the driver's seat before he could do it. The guys crowded in as before, slapping each another and singing off-key.

It was almost midnight.

She asked the guys where they lived, but they didn't answer, distracted. She repeated her question. One lived in Greenpoint, one was out in Williamsburg, and the other lived in Bay Ridge, a few streets down from Billy.

As she drove, Lisa kept the windows wide open. It was still warm in the car, with fumes of beer and body odor.

She kept her eyes open. It would all be done soon.

One more big haul, and their relationship would be over.

She headed north, past industrial yards and housing complexes—skirting past Greenwood, Red Hook, Carroll Gardens. The guys were a little more subdued; their speech was slowed and slurred. But after someone made a comment about the Dodgers, they all started to yell at each other, and Lisa made a wrong turn down a side street.

She ended up in Brooklyn Heights, not too far from Livingston Street.

They were near the empty shell of the Starlite.

"Could you believe what happened with that dame? She must have just flipped!"

Lisa's throat started to react; at first it was a tickle. Then it became an unbearable cough.

"You gotta be a little less crazy next time, Mack."

"She must have just wanted to get out of there, pronto!"

"Well, could you blame her?"

"And all over the papers, too."

"Cool it, gentlemen." Billy cleared his drunken throat and hissed.

They became strangely quiet, and Lisa could barely speak above her own coughs. She managed to summon her words.

"What are you guys talking about?" She scanned the streets for a turnoff point to Greenpoint or Williamsburg. She was lost.

"It's none of your concern what we're talking about." Billy spoke in a deep voice. He didn't sound drunk anymore, and Lisa shook, barely able to turn the steering wheel with two hands.

She closed her eyes for a split second at a stop sign.

"What was her name again? Marilyn?" Mack asked. They were all smoking little stumps. A thick cloud of smoke wafted up to the front seat, suffocating her, and her coughing fit returned.

Lisa looked for a place to pull over; she flicked the turn signal. "Do you mean Madeline?" Billy raised the volume on the radio dial, covering her voice.

"You've heard of her? You know, it's not like we killed the dame. We just scared her a little, on Freddy's orders. It's a shame that dame had to go and die, to keep her mouth shut."

It was black as night as Lisa turned off her headlights.

∽

"What happened to you?" They were in the parking lot of an abandoned warehouse. Billy stood over her, yelling. "You almost ran us off the road! Good thing I got the wheel, or we'd be smashed! *You* must have been the one who drank too much! I should've just drove!"

"I guess so," she said.

52

Elaine

October 1962

The president had informed the nation that there were missiles in Cuba.

Elaine and the other fact-checkers worked into the evening, making phone calls to see if the missiles could reach New York.

Elaine was the first one to speak to a ballistics expert, who said yes.

At nine PM, she was back in her boardinghouse room, flipping through a book, small in a small room, which could easily be wiped out. Her life was tenuous and tiny again, like when she had been evacuated from London as a child, not knowing if the bombs would hit.

David was staying at the *Chronicle* until the morning hours as the staff argued over which stories to publish and which usual sections to do away with.

Radioactive smoke could consume them all. Just when she had David.

He was a different sort of man. Warm, caring, and intelligent. There wasn't an arrogant bone in his body. She had met his family. He lived with his parents so that his mother could watch his daughter. His mother was interesting and elegant, a sculptor of some kind.

It had been a different sort of experience to visit David's house. A good one.

But it too could go up in a giant puff, then fade to ash.

53

Lisa

It was Lisa's fourth week at the boardinghouse.

At home, she couldn't escape, with her mother always asking about the wedding and Billy. She had moved out without explaining too much. She'd said she was growing up; she had to learn to be on her own before she married. She'd left some money on the table for their groceries.

She hadn't told anybody about Mack—about what he'd said that night. Nobody would believe her. And she didn't have any proof.

They could try to silence her next—if she talked.

Her mouth would stay closed.

She would be silent.

She kept playing along as Billy's girl. But she was getting a little distance, going back to the boardinghouse every night.

It was a plain boardinghouse, and strict. But it was clean and safe.

It was nice to be near a friend. Elaine was right upstairs, and sometimes they chatted well into the evening over cups of weak tea. Sometimes Lisa could forget, for a few moments, in this new place—before it all came back to her.

She struggled to keep her own small room clean. She vomited almost every day, within five minutes of walking through the door.

When she saw Billy, she put on her diamond and she wore her nice clothes. She was quiet, mainly, but he didn't seem to notice. Sometimes she would erupt in shakes. She kept the spasms hidden underneath tables and extra layers of clothing. She would hold her pocketbook close to her chest and push it in to create a heavy, dampening pressure. Sometimes Mack would join them. Her tongue would swell and her words would come out thickly.

Billy never said anything about Mack's confession, but his chiseled face grew more rounded, cheeks puffy and red. The whites of his eyes were cast in pink whenever she saw him.

Sometimes she threw up morning and evening.

Tonight she shampooed her hair in the sink, trying to get out the filth and grease of the luncheonette and her own sickness. She set it in waves, trying to get the curls just right, though eventually she gave up and made herself horizontal, on her pillow, so she could lie on the hard rollers and apply pressure to her damp hair.

Someone knocked at her door as she was securing loose strands in the front with bobby pins.

She got up from the bed; she could use some company.

"I hope I'm not interrupting." Elaine was polite as usual, though incongruously disarrayed in an old nightgown, her hair out of place.

"You're not interrupting."

The two of them sat on Lisa's bed, cross-legged in their nightgowns, like two girls at a slumber party.

Elaine spoke slowly and cleared her throat in her delicate way. "You heard about all of this business with the missiles pointed at the United States. Cuba has got them square and centered."

"My God, are you serious!"

"They might even reach New York."

"New York?" Lisa pulled a curler from her hair, and a number of hairs came out along with it.

Her eyes widened and her neck jolted; she was small, one of a number of targets.

She might dissolve, along with everything else, along with her secret. She would perish without even taking in all the punishment, all the loathing, from everyone. Or she would absorb it all and take it with her to the beyond; she would fester quickly in their pile of hate.

They could turn their hatred onto her, at the end.

Elaine talked more about the missiles and the political crisis; it was life-and-death for everyone in the country now.

Lisa's life was tiny.

She ripped out more curlers, fast and hard, exposing a small spot of scalp. Billy saw her as someone else. Elaine didn't know her reality. She herself was hidden from her truth.

Nobody would believe her.

Someone would have to catch Mack and the others in an act of malfeasance. Have a cop see the evidence. Otherwise it would be her word against his.

Obvious who would win.

Lisa's body shook uncontrollably, and she pulled her nightgown tight around her legs as she spoke through gritted teeth. "I'm terrified," she admitted.

"Me too," Elaine agreed, though they were talking about different things.

Elaine was quiet, bolt upright on the bed. She told Lisa that she had been evacuated from London as a child. Now the missiles were pointed at her again, on the other side of the world.

Lisa turned the radio on, to the news station. They were talking about the missiles, about duck and cover—about what to do if something happened.

The two of them listened, wide-eyed, until Elaine shut it off.

"Nothing we can do now, right?"

"Right."

The secret was crawling its way up Lisa's throat, like an itchy insect. She coughed and laid her head down.

"What do you think the end would be like?" she asked, from her pillow.

"Who knows? We won't remember it," Elaine said. It was gallows humor. The scratchy pestilence in Lisa's throat rose further upward. "You know, I used to work at that radio station you just had on. I actually met Tommy there."

"Oh." It was yet another mistake she had made, flipping to just the station that would remind Elaine of Tommy.

Elaine paused. "I was wondering, thinking—"

"Yeah?"

"What do you think Madeline would have done about all this?"

Lisa was short. "Done about what? She couldn't stop a missile."

"I don't mean that. Do you think she would have gathered us together? Like a going-away party, just in case?"

"For herself, or us?"

"Either one."

"Yeah." She pressed her face down and hid her eyes.

Elaine was twisted to face the wall. She got up to go to Lisa's dresser and silently moved the radio antennae, in a hard swallow, a sick choke.

"I miss her."

Lisa was a mass of heat and chills. She raised herself.

"Me too."

"I can't still believe she's gone."

"She was a beautiful person." Lisa stared, without blinking.

The election was coming up very soon. Fred Abbott was in the lead. He would probably get reelected.

Madeline's truth would be hidden, as Fred Abbott would get to continue as if nothing ever happened.

"She was like a glimmering light, snuffed out." Elaine's lip trembled.

Lisa's eyes closed in a rapid blink.

Her trance was condensing and reaching a critical mass.

They could do something to her too.

After all, she knew.

She rose to her feet.

"Hey, Elaine, I was wondering—about your job? About what it's like . . . ?"

"Bloody hell—it's crazy at the newspaper right now."

"What I mean to say is, well—how does it work with reporters? I mean, do you have certain people who are like investigative reporters?"

"We have a few investigative types. I'm not particularly involved with their day-to-day. Why do you ask, love?"

"I have a situation." Lisa was on her feet now, hand on her head.

About to vomit for the third time that day.

"Oh?"

"Someone I know—" Lisa paused, as her tongue wouldn't form sentences. "Well, there's a situation—"

Elaine looked at her strangely. Lisa's hair stuck up at odd angles, and she was stammering. Elaine glanced out the window, as if at any moment the bomb would explode. With one eye focused outside, she raised her lip, prompting Lisa to speak. "Yes, do go on."

"My fiancé, you know. Billy? Well—"

"What's going on, dear? Are you about to break off the engagement? I keep seeing you without that ring."

"It's not that. Well, I guess it is, but—" She paused. None of it would make sense. "I need someone to tag along with me, a reporter. Do you know anyone like that?"

She was doing it; they would come after her next.

It was inevitable. She was doomed—by an attack from an outside force, or an attack of someone she knew. She would report on the truth to the press and be made to run. Another woman made to run. Another casualty in the headlines.

"You want someone to tag along with you? I don't quite get your meaning, dear."

"It's just—well, you know Billy—well, you never met him, but . . ."

"Yes?"

Things could go up in smoke. The itchy insect had crawled to the tip of her tongue.

Finally it flattened itself out, rolling into a smooth truth, shedding its skin. Then it released at once, converting to a metamorphic fluid, and the words flew from her mouth.

"Well, Billy's friend—Mack—is working for Billy's father, on the campaign for Fred Abbott, and—" She coughed out bits of spit. "Well, a few months ago, Mack was talking about that night with Madeline . . ." Her limbs were frozen, but she went on. "Well, that night with Madeline . . . Mack was trying to scare her. He admitted he was at her window with fire, and she ran out onto the street."

Her nightmares were constant. Madeline—arising, coming to the window of the Starlite. Seeing a man with fire by her window, she runs to escape. She rushes toward the street and is slammed.

Stilled, ended, severed.

Dead.

Lisa sobbed. Her tears covered her body, Elaine, and the bed.

Elaine was pale and still. Her color faded quickly, even more, until she was the whitest she had ever been. She was withdrawing from Lisa, moving away from her as though she were tainted.

As if she were evil.

As if Lisa could have done that to Madeline herself.

"You knew about this?" Elaine backed away from Lisa as though faced with a loaded gun. "For how long . . . did you know?"

Lisa breathed heavily, sweat pouring from her face. "I don't know . . . I guess it's been nine weeks . . . or ten . . . or a little more . . . I don't know!"

"You've known for *a couple of months*?" Elaine's eyes grew wide in horror.

"Oh, God, Elaine! I did!" Her skin throbbed, as if she could jump out of it, escape, and watch it all from outside herself. She screamed into her blanket, shoving her face into the bed, and then she punched her fists into it hard. Her fit grew wilder, fiercer, until she had thrashed off all the covers. She thrashed with heavy force, in blows of her full strength.

Her hair hung in front of her face, and Elaine sat out of view.

Slowly she exhausted her reserves. The thrashing came to a halt. She sat down, breathless, gasping for air.

Elaine was quiet, watching.

Then she gulped, and her thin frame inched toward Lisa.

With a small movement, Elaine touched Lisa's contorted arm. "So . . . tell me . . . are you still with him?"

"I've been pretending to be with him. One of his friends admitted it a couple months ago. I don't want him to think I'm going to report them. They might retaliate."

Lisa bawled and shook, and her face was aflame and swollen. She had been pretending for nearly three months now. Pretending while he kissed her good-night, pretending to be stupid. At the movies, she would snake her hand away from his grasp, slowly, so he would barely notice. She would spend time with his friends and made faint smiles at their antics, as if she were just the ditzy girl he was going to marry.

She was tainted with him; she was also trapped.

Elaine whispered, patting her back. "Was Billy trying to scare out Madeline too? Or was it only Mack?"

"I don't know. I saw his car in that neighborhood that day. I don't know what happened, but I think Mack was the one in Madeline's window. But obviously Billy knew all about it. And his own father is scum—he set up Mack to do it! And Billy's father is cheating on his mother too. I saw him on a plane when I was a stewardess. I've been hiding it all, Elaine! All of it!" She cried, more and more and more.

In the distance, missiles were pointed at them.

"Do you still love him?"

"I don't!" This was loud, and the boardinghouse walls were thin. "I want to make it public. I want everyone to know what happened. But I don't want to be a target. I don't want to be the snitch. How can I? I don't know what would happen." Her nose and throat were compressed; she struggled to breathe.

"Is that why you were asking me about an investigative reporter?"

"Yeah." She took sharp inhalations.

"What are you looking for, exactly?"

"I don't know—someone who could follow them, stay with them, make them speak. Make it come out of them and publish it. The election is in two weeks. It has to be quick. It has to come out. Fred can't win. He can't think that he's won—that he's silenced her."

Finally she stopped crying, slumping down, chills racking her body.

Elaine patted her back again, her hands unsteady.

Then she spoke, shakily. "There is one reporter I've become a bit friendly with. She's actually one of the only female reporters. She's shrewd, and she knows how to blend in. She's a smart one, I think."

A woman.

Yes.

They would never suspect that a woman might be a reporter.

"Can she come to a Halloween party in Bay Ridge?"

"I'll have to ask her. We'll see what we can arrange."

It would be a new chapter in Lisa's life.

She would be bringing in other people.

She would do something too. She had been saving up some of her tip money from the luncheonette in a little jar. She would empty the jar and use the money to buy tons of alcohol—drinks to make Mack and the boys nice and drunk.

They wouldn't turn down free drinks.

⁓

A few days later, she met Billy outside his apartment.

The Brooklyn air was unseasonably warm, with clouds.

Clouds could hide the missiles until the final seconds.

Lisa wasn't in costume—she was just wearing all black.

"Pleased to meet you. I'm Samantha."

Billy wasn't there yet, but the reporter was right on time. She wore a glittery white eye mask with an even lovelier white gown, which shimmered with gold thread. A Halloween angel.

Lisa hadn't stopped shaking in days.

She looked up at the clouds. News reports remained frantic about Cuba as her own insides quaked.

"Thank you so much for coming." They shook hands.

Samantha's hand was warm, unlike Lisa's own hand, which was cold and clammy.

Samantha whispered, beneath her breath, "Tell me who I'm supposed to be listening for tonight. Elaine said his name is Mack?"

"Yes—Mack. He should be hanging out near Billy—my . . . fiancé. Or . . . my ex. He'll be my ex." Lisa twisted the sharp edge of her diamond toward her pinkie.

"And what am I to ask Mack exactly?"

"Just wait until he's good and drunk. Ask him what he does for a living, or something like that. Ask him to tell you stories about his *job*."

"You think he'll actually admit to something?"

"I don't know. But you have to try. Please." Another retch of hopelessness almost fell from her mouth, onto the sidewalk.

After all, Mack wouldn't have reason to talk about Madeline that night.

She was wasting this woman's time.

A real *Chronicle* reporter, and Lisa was wasting her time.

Billy emerged from his apartment. He was dressed like a bum for Halloween, grease around his eyes, holes in his clothing. The tight-fitting shirt under his jacket accentuated the muscles in his chest. He loved to show off his body. His face was getting fat with alcohol, but he was still lifting weights.

"Pleased to meet you." His eyes did a quick sweep over the reporter's body. Samantha had a shapely figure and luminous skin.

As they all drove to his friend's apartment, he asked her all sorts of questions.

"So where do you live, Samantha?"

"Over in Queens."

"Oh? I have a buddy who lives in Queens. Whereabouts?"

"Astoria." Samantha was convincing—nice and quick with her answers—yet Lisa trembled.

"And you work at the luncheonette with Lisa?"

"Monday through Thursday, and sometimes on a Saturday afternoon if they need me."

He had the radio off, for a change, as he gazed at Samantha in the rearview mirror.

Lisa's head spun, dizzy. She inhaled.

Madeline was hovering out there somewhere, beyond the clouds, beyond what they could see.

The skies were growing dark, and she tracked a cloud as they drove. At any moment, it could all turn blindingly bright.

Then there would be an unnatural darkness, followed by a flash. She rolled the window down a crack to get some fresh air, and a cold breeze blew into the car.

"Close it, babe." Billy talked like he owned her.

"Sure, I'll close the window." She raised her lips in a smile.

But before she rolled up the window, she pulled off her engagement ring and dangled it through the opening, out of his field of vision.

No.

It would be greedily grabbed up by someone who spotted it on the street.

Instead, she would sell the ring, and give her parents some money.

⌒

At the party, most people wore masks. They hid behind strips of black or gray cloth, huddled together, drinking and laughing in the dingy apartment.

Samantha had positioned herself next to Mack, who appeared to be enjoying her attentions. He smirked and rambled and chugged shot after shot of the liquor Lisa had dumped on the table nearby.

The party was not as rowdy as these things usually were, with the threat of missiles in the forefront. Billy and a friend played a slow game of table tennis nearby, and Lisa watched Mack from the corner of her eye. He had turned hyperactive again, louder after his umpteenth round of beverages.

Lisa was too far away to discern what he was saying.

She went over to get herself some water, pouring a glass from the tap, and Billy's friend Ted sidled up to her. He slurred his words and pointed to her bare finger.

"So, you and Billy, are . . . ?"

"Oh, we're still engaged, Ted. I just had to take it off for a moment to wash my hands."

"I see." Ted switched his attention, pointing across the room to the table at which Samantha and Mack were sitting. "Say, over there, that friend you came in with. Who's she?"

"Oh, I work with her at the luncheonette."

"She looks just like someone my brother used to date. Wild chick, I think. I think she became a reporter for that newspaper or something. The *Chronicle*?"

"Oh yeah? Well, I don't know. Unless she's secretly working two jobs!" Lisa's panic bled slightly to her cheeks.

Ted was still fascinated with Samantha; he started walking over to her and Mack, but Lisa ran behind him, grabbing his sleeve.

"Oops!" Lisa pretended to trip, grabbing on to his arm, and Ted laughed.

Billy looked up from his table tennis game. It was loud in the apartment. He seemed to be trying to tell her something from across the room, but she ignored him as she raced to prevent Ted from joining Samantha and Mack.

Through the crowds, Ted got there first. He started to talk to Samantha in front of Mack, shaking her hand.

"Hey!" Lisa flew right up next to them, quick as could be.

Ted had already begun. "Samantha! Good to see you. Gorgeous as always! How are you doing? How's it going at the *Chronicle*?"

Samantha was a professional; she looked up without a flinch, poised underneath her gorgeous white eye mask. "I'm sorry, but I don't know who you are."

"I'm Ted Jones. You dated my brother a couple years back, right? I remember you had just gotten this job at the *Chronicle*, like a new hot-shot reporter. One of the only dames on the team, right?"

Samantha smiled, unflappable, with smooth lips. "I'm sorry; I'm not sure what you're talking about."

Mack, who had been floppy and drunk in his chair, turned with a sudden hard stare, like he was sobering. His lips tightened; his eyes were stone-cold. "Hey, so you work for the *Chronicle*? You said you were a waitress."

"What do you mean, the *Chronicle*? Is that the newspaper?" Samantha smiled innocently and ran her fingers through her long, silky hair.

Mack's lips were a straight line. He reached into his pocket. His eyes were yellowed with drink.

He brought something out, under the table. Samantha's eyes grew round and terrified, and Lisa darted her eyes to Mack's lap.

"So, *Samantha*—what sort of crap have you been giving me with all your questions about my *job*?"

His lips barely moved. Lisa kept her eyes on the thing near his knee, barely visible.

Samantha jumped back.

It was the edge of a sharp point, about to pierce into her leg.

Lisa skirted behind Mack. She pretended to trip, pushing her arms down with a quick shove, falling over his back, falling over him onto the floor, and he was pushed down.

Onto the blade.

There was a sickening grunt, a gush of blood, his skin losing color, and everyone was silent.

Billy was gaping at her, like he was seeing a ghost.

Mack was bent over, with soft, gurgled whispers coming from his mouth.

Everyone fell quiet, staring at Lisa.

⌒

The ambulance was loud as it squealed and screeched down the street. Someone gave Mack some rags, trying to stop the bleeding.

Everybody was in a ruckus, trying to figure things out, to understand what they had just seen, and Billy was watching—looking at her, then backing away. Samantha had disappeared—slipped out the door.

Lisa headed out the door to the sidewalk.

She waited for the police.

Her face slackened; the cuffs would be hard, entrapping her wrists.

Mack had been the one with the weapon.

A tall bus rounded the corner, an express bus to Brooklyn Heights. The bus would connect to the train to Manhattan.

The flicker of a police siren came down the street.

Without another glance at the police cruiser, Lisa headed to the bus stop. She would leave, and she would ride the bus dressed in black, for Madeline.

～

At the boardinghouse, Lisa knocked on Elaine's door.

Elaine opened it immediately.

"Samantha just rang. Oh my God." She grabbed Lisa's arms and pulled her into her room. "Do any of them know where you live?"

"I never brought any of them here."

"Okay. Okay." She looked around, as if someone could be in the room with them. "You should be safe for the night. And everything will be on the front page in the morning."

"The front page?"

"Absolutely, darling. I've already begun calling the girls from the Starlite for a little celebration tomorrow night. I'll bring us some complimentary copies of the newspaper."

Lisa held her head. Her hair was damp against her forehead. "Am I going to be in the paper?"

Elaine smiled. "I'm not sure why you would be in the paper, darling. It sounds like Mack fell on his own knife, did he not?"

Lisa hadn't seen Billy when she escaped the apartment. He could be looking for her.

～

Lisa stared out her boardinghouse window all night. Someone had a light on in an apartment across the street, and she gazed at it like an insect, dazed.

Dawn broke, and she opened her crusty eyes.

She threw a coat over her nightgown and ran down to the corner of the street, where a man was selling the early edition of the *Chronicle*. She got her fresh copy for ten cents.

The article had no byline—just a headline.

BROOKLYN COUNCILMAN CONNECTED
TO DEATH OF EX-WIFE

The Chronicle's *own reporter was at a Bay Ridge Halloween gathering last night when a local, unnamed 25-year-old man confessed to having been hired by Brooklyn councilman Fred Abbott.*

"Fred's campaign manager pays me to do some work he doesn't want to do."

When questioned further, the man admitted to throwing fire in the window of [Abbott's ex] Madeline's store immediately before she ran out into the street and was killed by a car.

Upon learning that a Chronicle *reporter was present at the function, the unnamed man drew a knife on our reporter, but injured himself on his own blade. He is currently in police custody at a Brooklyn hospital.*

Both Fred Abbott and his campaign manager deny any connection with the unnamed man; however, sources reveal that Abbott's campaign manager's son is a good friend of the suspect.

The Chronicle *will have more details as they become available.*

54

Elaine

Elaine woke to hear choked-up inhalations from behind her door. Gasping sounds.

She rose from her hard little bed and tiptoed to the front of her room, listening.

A girl was crying, taking deep breaths, as though she was trying in vain to stop tears.

Elaine cracked the door a tad to find Lisa. She was curled up in a messy, bawling ball, knees inside her nightgown, hair in knots.

"I'm sorry to bother you." Lisa looked up at her pathetically.

"Hush." Elaine pulled her into the room and gently closed the door.

Sitting upright on the hardwood floors, Lisa laid her wet cheek on the seat cushion. "I had the dream again," she choked out. "The dream where I'm too late to save her."

Elaine stroked Lisa's mussed-up hair and allowed her to cry for a long time, until all her tears were dried up.

After some time, Lisa stood, unsteady in bare feet. "I'm sorry to bother you again." She gazed at the floor. "You probably wish that I never moved into this boardinghouse."

"Not at all, dear."

Elaine rubbed her back. The fabric of her flannel nightgown had adhered to Lisa's skin, sticky with the sweat of the unsettled.

Elaine glanced down at her own forearm, where there was a scar from several months ago; she had thrashed in the night, and her skin had split wide open on the corner of the bedside table. She couldn't sleep that night, with the echoes of Tommy's voice.

Now she slept better, if not perfectly.

None of it was her fault.

"What do you think Madeline would say to you if she could talk to you right now?" she asked Lisa. "It's a question my psychotherapist asked me—think about the person who died, and what would they say to you right now . . ."

"I don't know." Lisa started to mist again, but then she seemed to think about it and smoothed down her nightgown. "I guess she might tell me to get dressed," she chortled.

"That's brilliant, darling."

Elaine scrounged about in her little closet and found a crisp beige number, something woolen and tailored. Madeline had made it for her many moons ago. It was still in perfect condition. "There, now, try this one."

She handed the garment to Lisa, still on its hanger.

Lisa headed to the washroom, and after a flurry of faucet sounds, she emerged, her cheeks rosy and scrubbed. She looked ready to face the cold streets of New York—and the world.

"Fabulous, darling! Remember, you are brave," Elaine said.

And she smiled.

It was as though Madeline were here with them, to celebrate.

Madeline would be busy in the corner of the room, setting up a little table with a phonograph, then removing a record album from its sleeve. She would set the needle down and Elaine would tell her to hush— these boardinghouse walls were too thin—but Madeline would laugh and unlock the narrow little door, bounding up and down the halls, inviting every woman she encountered to an impromptu get-together in the tiny room.

Epilogue

November 1963

Elaine arrived at the luncheonette where Lisa worked. It was six o'clock in the evening, and the restaurant was closed for the day.

They would have the whole space that night for free, and they wouldn't even have to pay; they would only have to finish the dishes from the last shift.

The place would be theirs for three golden hours.

Lisa had brought her portable record player and a stack of records, and Elaine had carried in a stack of books.

"Tell me what to do first," Elaine said to Lisa, and together they scrubbed the teetering piles of dishes. It was a massive amount to clean, but the two of them made quick work of it, singing songs and telling stories.

Elaine talked about her work. "You wouldn't believe what they did at the *Chronicle*. You know about that proposed amendment to the Constitution here, the Equal Rights Amendment? There's been more agitation about it lately, and the *Chronicle* doesn't want to seem behind the times. So instead of giving the female fact-checkers a raise, they just promoted the only two male fact-checkers, and so now they can't be accused of unfair pay."

"That's ludicrous."

"You're telling me. Samantha really wants out, you know. She's been there for five whole years without any talk of a raise."

"What does David think?"

"Oh, I didn't tell you? He quit last week."

"Oh yeah?"

"He got a job at a different newspaper."

"Why is that?"

"He doesn't like the way they're treating me and the other women."

Lisa whistled. "Wow, sounds like you got yourself a catch there!" Then Lisa changed the subject—she had been off the dating scene since Billy. "Hey, did you bring that Beatles album with you?"

"Of course, dearie!"

At last they finished the stack of dishes. They dried their hands and applied fresh coats of lipstick, using the tin tiles of the kitchen wall as their mirror.

Afterward, they headed into the main area of the luncheonette and sat down at a large booth, flipping on the record player and bouncing in their seats to the rhythm. They laughed their heads off and did silly things, dancing with their shoulders and sliding across the floors in their stocking feet. Soon ladies started to knock at the glass door, coming in one by one, then streaming in all at once. They poured in with food and decorations—laughing and prancing through the door.

It all shone in their faces and their smiles, their energy and movement. Elaine did a reading of a new poem, and they turned the music back up; Lisa jumped up and down, the most energetic she had been in some time.

"I can't believe I'm dancing!"

"Well, why not?" Elaine said, and joined her, twirling all around.

It was a warm glow, almost like a light, radiating from within all of them. The feeling shimmered throughout the space, propelling them across the luncheonette floor in the wildest dance of their lives.

Elaine, breathless, paused between songs, sitting down with Lisa for a glass of water.

"Hey Lisa—" As Elaine gulped down the cool liquid, her voice assumed a different quality. "I wanted to bring this up before the night is through—I got a new article to fact-check today. It was about Madeline's ex, Fred Abbott. It sounds like he's being arraigned tonight, and I heard that others are next."

"Really?"

"I called the courthouse, and it's true." Elaine grinned; a pleased flush spread across her cheeks.

Lisa stared for a moment, wide-eyed; she seemed struck in disbelief.

Dizzy, she hunched down in her gingham waitress uniform; then she stood up, wearing one of the widest smiles of her life.

The night was beautiful.

More and more ladies streamed into the luncheonette, new friends and old.

Together they danced the night away, and Lisa's face grew more and more relaxed as the corners of her eyes lifted in unbridled delight.

She was free.

When the night started to simmer down, Elaine flickered the lights to get their attention. "Let's do a little poetry, ladies."

The women read their gorgeous pieces, full of light and hope. Elaine stood with her notebook, ready to say something—but then she paused. The words were so palpable that they could barely emerge from her throat.

But then someone shouted out, in the way of Madeline, "Read us a poem, darling."

So she started again: "I have something to share—I wrote it quickly, on my way here. It seems as though the words are flowing out of me again lately."

> *Don't let them tell you who are.*
> *Don't stop yourself, darling.*
> *I hope you shimmer, darling.*
> *Glimmer as you can.*

Their eyes all sparkled as they applauded, all aglow, like Madeline.

Even in fear, she had never let the shadows consume her; she had radiated outward in a million beams of light, as a reminder to allow their full selves to shine. They too would try to always give forth this resplendence, even in a world that would prefer otherwise.

Elaine's eyes were lively and gleaming as she took a bow.

Acknowledgments

First, to Jenny Chen at Alcove Press, thank you for your editorial wisdom. Your support and insights have been invaluable. I can't thank you enough for helping me to bring this book to life! To the rest of the team at Alcove, including Madeline Rathle and Melissa Rechter, thank you for your work "behind the scenes." To Rachel Keith, thank you for your attentive read.

Thank you to Cassie Hanjian, whose guidance was key to the development of this book. Thank you to Denise Gibbon and Aroop Sanakkayala—I appreciate your support with the business of publishing. Thank you to Stephanie DeLisi for research assistance—your valuable time is appreciated.

To my sister-in-law, mother-in-law, and father-in-law, Julie, Susan, and John—and to Paul and Aunt Dot—thank you so much for the encouragement during the years that it took to write this book! To my amazing husband, Rob—thank you for taking this book journey with me. I love taking every life journey with you! To my wonderful son— my sweet child—thank you for sharing in my happiness as my word count grew. (You can read this book when you're an adult.)

To my mom—one of Brooklyn's best. Your vibrancy and sense of humor always lighten up the room, even when you're on "speaker phone" thousands of miles away.

Finally, to the memory of my Grandma Phyllis. You were a fantastic writer; more importantly, you were an amazing human being. Thank you for your encouragement and for your joy. Your light will forever shine.

Readers Club Guide Questions

1. At the start of the story, Lisa is twenty-two years old. How much of her "blindness" about Billy would you attribute to her relative youth? What were some warning signals about him that she could have picked up on earlier? What are some reasons Lisa may have found it difficult to walk away from Billy despite the warning signs?

2. The Starlite is a welcoming enclave for women of all walks of life. In your own life, have you ever experienced a setting where barriers of class and life experience were temporarily demolished? If so, share your experience about what made it work. If not, what usually stands in the way? How was it different at the Starlite?

3. In different ways, both Elaine and Lisa run up against barriers that affect their involvement in the workplace. In which ways would you say that these barriers have changed for women since the early 1960s? Are there any "invisible" barriers that persist to this day?

4. Elaine hoped that she could help to reform Tommy from his hard-drinking ways, although she eventually learned that she was not able to save him from himself. Do you believe that it's ever possible for a partner to change the other's entrenched habit or addiction? What do you think a partner should do if the other person's addiction begins to spiral out of control? Can the relationship ever come out on top of the addiction?

5. When Madeline initially played the part of the "political wife," she was trying to preserve her own future. For wives of philandering (or otherwise corrupt) politicians, what choices do you think they have

to come out on top? Is it possible for the wife of a politician to seek retribution without facing significant consequences? Why or why not? What do you think is the best recourse for a politician's wife who has been betrayed?

6. The Starlite social club offers a host of activities for every interest. If you were going to organize your own social club, where would you like to host it? What activities might be available?

7. Elaine uses poetry as an expressive outlet for her complex feelings, but she finds herself temporarily unable to write after Tommy's passing. If you feel comfortable sharing, have you ever used writing of any kind as an expressive outlet? Or have you used another expressive outlet? Discuss the way(s) in which your outlet has helped you—and whether you have *always* been able to use it.

8. Throughout the story, Lisa evolves as an individual, growing less and less naïve. At what point do we see hints that Lisa is starting to "see the light"? Describe some of these moments—does she accept her new understandings immediately? What are some "blockades to enlightenment" that stand in her way?

9. Madeline knew how to make all newcomers to Starlite feel welcomed and comfortable. Is there anyone in your own life who has a knack for putting people at ease? What does that person do to make others feel accepted and honored?

10. The ladies of the Starlite find a way to honor the spirit of the Starlite, even after the unthinkable happens. Have you ever been involved in a powerful group or organization that needed to adapt or adjust its course in order to persist?